BLACK KNIGHT

A Black's Bandits Novel

LYNN RAYE HARRIS

The Hostile Operations Team® and Lynn Raye Harris® are
trademarks of H.O.T. Publishing, LLC.

Printed in the United States of America

First Printing, 2021

For rights inquires, visit www.LynnRayeHarris.com

Black Knight
Copyright © 2020 by Lynn Raye Harris
Cover Design Copyright © 2020 Croco Designs

ISBN: 978-1-941002-63-6

Chapter One

"WHAT THE HELL?"

Jared Fraser swore as he drove up the private drive to the mountain cabin where he intended to spend the next few days getting the heat, blood, and dust of the latest mission out of his head. He wanted solitude after the violence. Craved time to reset his brain.

But it looked as if someone was intent on interrupting his retreat before it began. A woman stood in the center of the driveway a few yards from the cabin. She blinked as his headlights hit her, lifting her arm to shield her eyes, but she didn't move away.

The truck jerked to a stop and Jared shoved the gearshift into park before popping open the door to stand on the running board. "I'm good, thanks," he called out. "I got the key from the management office in town. I don't need anything else."

He'd told the woman in the office that he didn't want to be bothered, but apparently listening wasn't big on her list of skills. She'd probably sent someone to make sure the bedding was turned down before he arrived, or to leave a welcome gift.

He didn't want either of those things.

The woman in the road lowered her arm a little, blinking at the light. Blood streamed down her temple and over her cheek. Jared swore and grabbed his Glock off the seat as he stepped onto the ground. He kept the gun at his side as he flipped the headlights off, letting the parking lights illuminate the area instead. It was more light than he wanted, but he needed to see her so he could assess her condition.

As he approached, her arm dropped and she frowned. She wore a light jacket, not at all what she needed for the dipping temperatures tonight.

Alarm buzzed in his brain. Something definitely wasn't right about this situation.

"Hey," he said softly, scanning their surroundings like he was back in the war zone. He'd learned to never underestimate a situation over the years. "Where's your car? Did you run off the road?"

It was possible since the ground was covered in six inches of snow. The roads were being cleared, but with the temps dropping, ice was a danger. Perhaps she'd hit an icy patch somewhere, though he hadn't come across any cars that had skidded off the road on the way up the mountain. She could have been coming from the opposite direction, though.

"I… I don't know," she said, her voice scratchy, as if she didn't know how to use it. She lifted a hand to her head, then looked at the blood staining her fingers. "I feel…."

She started to swoon and Jared tucked the weapon in its holster and caught her before she could fall. Her body was solid in his arms, but there wasn't much warmth. How long had she been outside? Too long if the way she shivered was any indication.

She made a sound of distress as Jared picked her up. He left his truck running and carried her the short distance to the cabin. He'd put the keys in his pocket at the management office. He fished them out as he stepped onto the porch and then fumbled with the lock. Once the door was open, he flicked on a light and carried the woman over to one of the couches that perched on either side of a big rock fireplace.

She moaned as he set her on it. She wasn't unconscious, but he wasn't sure if she'd stay that way. He did a quick check of her vitals and then probed her head wound. She flinched and gasped, but he was relieved to find there was nothing more than a deep scrape making her bleed. She also had a small lump near the wound, as if she'd knocked into something. There was another cut on her throat, right below her jaw. It was a clean cut, like she'd had an encounter with something sharp. Glass maybe. It wasn't deep, but blood trickled from the part of the wound that hadn't dried up yet.

"Does it hurt anywhere else?"

"I don't know," she said on a whisper. "I'm too cold."

"What about a headache?"

She shook her head slightly. "I don't think so. It only hurts in one spot, but not terribly."

He took the lack of excruciating pain as a good sign.

Cold wouldn't stop her from feeling broken bones, and it definitely wouldn't stop her from feeling a headache that was unlike any she'd ever had before. If there was a brain bleed, her head would pound from the pressure. Her eyes stayed closed, dark lashes fanning over wind-reddened cheeks. She had dirty blond hair scraped back in a ponytail that was coming undone, and two indents on the bridge of her nose where she'd worn glasses. He expected she'd lost them somewhere since they didn't appear to be at hand. Maybe that was the source of the cut on her throat.

Aside from the light jacket, she had on black yoga pants that exposed her ankles and tennis shoes that weren't any protection from the snow. She looked like she'd gone out for a jog in suburbia rather than for a snowy mountain hike.

If she'd run off the road, had she been alone? Or was someone else out there, perhaps unconscious?

Jared straightened and grabbed a blanket from a wicker basket by the couch, draping it over the woman. He needed to get his truck and gear, then clean her wound and build a fire. The woman's lashes fluttered. She gazed up at him with brown eyes that weren't having any trouble focusing. Another good sign.

He knelt and took out his phone, turning on the light. Then he shined it in her eyes. Though she gasped, her pupils instantly shrank. He held her chin and looked into both eyes, then shut the light off when he was satisfied.

"What did you do that for?" she asked.

"Checking for concussion. You don't appear to have

4

one, which is probably a miracle considering the shape you're in."

"I feel like I went three rounds with a prize fighter."

Jared's gut tightened. He knew what that looked like. What it felt like as a child watching his mother cry after she'd been punched and kicked for nothing more than serving the wrong brand of baked beans with his father's fucking hot dogs. Anger swirled deep inside. It was an old anger that he was used to, but he still hated it.

He had to consider that this woman could be the victim of domestic assault rather than a car accident. He'd experienced that kind of assault firsthand and he knew how irrational men like that were. How cruel. If her asshole boyfriend or husband was angry enough, he could have dumped her off in the snow just to teach her a lesson.

"Did someone leave you on the road?"

Her brow furrowed. "I don't remember." She blinked at him, frowning harder. "Maybe I'm dead."

He frowned. Maybe she was hurt worse than he thought. He'd have to take her back down the mountain, find the nearest hospital. It would be slow going in this weather, but it might be necessary. "You aren't dead."

"Oh." She waved a hand around as if that explained everything. "I'm glad. I just thought…"

"Thought what?"

"I could be dreaming," she muttered. "Though why would I dream up a man who looks like an angel and then make myself sick in the dream? Cruel and unusual punishment if you ask me."

Jared didn't know whether to laugh or be concerned. "You aren't dreaming either. You're very much alive and awake."

"Well, there's that."

She closed her eyes again and huddled under the blanket.

"Can you tell me what happened? Are you alone?"

"I-I don't know. I don't remember anything." The corners of her mouth were white.

It wasn't unusual to forget the details of trauma when it had just happened, but it wasn't helpful either. He'd have to go see if he could find a car. If someone else was out there, unconscious, he needed to get them to safety. He wasn't discounting the idea she could be abused, but a car accident was equally likely and he needed to verify.

"I'll be back in a few minutes," he told her. "Don't go anywhere."

"Nowhere to go," she said. She didn't open her eyes.

He went outside and got into his truck, reversing in the yard and then backtracking to the road. He drove two miles farther up the road from the cabin. The snow was coming down heavier now, but there was no sign of an accident. No cars on the side of the road, no busted guardrails, no skid marks in the snow. There'd been none on his way up the mountain either, which meant there was no evidence in either direction.

He needed to find out who she was and get the truth out of her. In his experience, abuse victims often didn't want to name their abusers out of fear something worse would happen. His mother would never go to the police over his father. She'd also never gone to his Air Force commander. Jared had been too young to realize that was something she could have done, or he might have done it for her. It probably would have gotten her a worse beating though. And him. His dad's fists were most often for his mother, but he'd hit Jared too.

Jared returned to the cabin with a hard knot in his gut. He pulled up beneath the carport next to the house, retrieved his duffel and grocery bags from the backseat, then went inside. The woman was where he'd left her. Her eyes opened as he walked in, her gaze seeking his.

"I was beginning to wonder." The relief in her expression was evident.

"I told you I'd be back," he said gently.

"I know, but I thought maybe you'd changed your mind."

"Nope." He put the grocery bags on the counter and tossed his big duffel onto the floor beside it. "I drove up the road a bit. I didn't see a car or any sign of an accident."

"Oh." Blood streaked the side of her face and throat in scarlet, contrasting vibrantly with the Snow White paleness of her features. Her cheeks were no longer red and she shivered under the blanket.

Logs had been laid in the fireplace by whomever had prepped the cabin for the next visitor. Jared grabbed the lighter from the mantel and touched it to the firestarter beneath the grate. The paper and kindling crackled to life. Once the fire was going, he retrieved the medicine kit from his duffel and got out the antiseptic and gauze along with the clotting agent. He put them on the coffee table and sat down beside the woman.

She watched him curiously as he dripped some antiseptic onto the gauze. He was glad to see she was alert and interested in what he was doing. She didn't ask him any questions, which he found slightly odd. Some people didn't, though. Some people observed first.

"This is going to sting," he said as he turned to her.

She looked at him with those big brown eyes. Her pupils weren't dilated, which was good. She took a deep breath. "Okay."

He touched the antiseptic to the scrape on her head. She flinched. "Ouch!"

"Sorry."

Her eyes opened again. This time they were filled with tears. His heart twisted at the look on her face. He was used to tending wounds, but they were usually combat wounds. Warriors didn't look at him in wide-eyed panic, nor did they look as lost as this woman did. He'd wanted medical training because of the way he'd grown up, the times he'd had to watch his mother try and fix up her scrapes and bruises and couldn't help. He'd tended a lot of combat wounds over the years, a lot of physical trauma, but there was something about a woman with injuries consistent with domestic violence that got to him more than he cared to admit.

If someone had done this to her, he wanted to find the asshole and give him a taste of his own medicine. Not that he knew she'd been abused, but *something* had happened to her. And it wasn't a car accident, or at least not that he could see. So what was it?

He had to consider the possibility she was here on purpose. Sent by someone with a grudge against him and the organization he worked for. He didn't think it the most likely reason she'd been alone and injured outside his cabin, but he'd have to be on his guard just in case it was a setup.

"Can you tell me how you got here?" he asked as he gently cleaned her wound.

"I—I don't know. I don't know where I am. What happened to me?"

"You're in Shenandoah National Park. Closest town is Hall Green."

He chose this place because it was remote. Not too near the city, not so far he couldn't get back within a few hours, though that was on a normal day when the snow wasn't piling up outside. Jared dabbed at her scrape until he was satisfied, then moved on to the cut on her throat. When that was finished, he swiped a wet wipe over the blood until it was gone.

She kept her eyes downcast while he worked. "Do you think I was in an accident?"

"I don't know."

Before he'd gone looking for a car, he would have thought that's precisely what'd happened. And maybe it was. Maybe she'd managed to walk farther in the snow than he'd thought she could. He'd prefer that option over the one that seemed most likely to him. The one that made him want to kill any miserable motherfucker who'd dared to hurt her.

He prepared to apply a clotting agent to her

wounds. "This is going to sting again, but it should stop the bleeding."

She nodded and clamped her jaw tight while he applied the powder. Her jaw worked but she didn't make a sound. He'd fully expected her to cuss him out this time but she didn't. He finished by taping small bandages over the wounds and sat back. "How many fingers am I holding up?"

"Three."

"Do you know what today is?"

She pursed her lips. "Um, Thursday?"

"Yes. Who's the president?"

"President Campbell. I think."

He smiled to reassure her. "Right so far. I'm Jared, by the way."

He stuck his hand out like they were being properly introduced. He wanted her to know she could trust him. If she *had* been abused by someone, she might tell him about it if she felt confident he wasn't a threat. He intended to make sure she knew he was safe.

She gave his hand a quick squeeze and then tucked both hers beneath the blanket again as he moved away from her, giving her space. She drew it up to her chin as she stared at the fire. She appeared to be concentrating, the line between her brows growing more pronounced as she frowned. She was pretty in a girl-next-door kind of way, with creamy skin, long lashes, and a full lower lip that she seemed to be chewing on.

"Why don't you tell me your name and we'll try to figure out what happened," Jared prodded gently. If he could get her talking, maybe she'd spill the truth about how she'd ended up hurt and alone in the snow.

Knowing who she was would be a start. He could call the police, but he preferred to use his own connections. It'd get done faster and they'd dig deeper than a local police force might. Someone at Black Defense International could run a background check on her. Find out everything about her, including what kind of car she drove and whether or not she had a man in her life. If she did, then they'd check the dude out too. And if he was the type who had priors for domestic abuse, or if there'd been calls about domestic situations between him and this woman, then Jared would get a couple of the guys to pay the man a visit. After that, he'd do everything he could to make sure she got a new life and stayed safe from retaliation.

Not that every woman wanted a new life. That thought twisted inside him, but he'd seen it before. Battered women were often mentally abused as well, and too many of them went back to their abuser because he had such a tight control over their emotional state.

Jared prayed that wasn't the case with her, but he wouldn't know it until he got more out of her.

She kept staring into the fire. Her lip quivered and a tear spilled down her cheek. He didn't want her to cry, but he refrained from gathering her in his arms and comforting her. If she was going to tell him anything, he couldn't interfere before she found the strength.

Liquid brown eyes met his. "I-I don't know my name. I can't remember."

Chapter Two

HER HEAD THROBBED WHERE HE'D CLEANED HER CUT and her body felt like she'd run headlong into every tree in the forest. In other words, she ached.

None of that compared to searching her brain for answers and finding none. How could she know the day of the week and the president, but not her name? Her heart hammered in her chest as she huddled beneath the blanket, shivering.

It didn't make any sense.

The man—Jared—frowned down at her. He was a little blurry from a distance, but he was really, *really* pretty up close. Blue eyes, dark hair, and a scruff of a beard that would probably feel sinfully sensual scraping along a woman's thighs.

Not her thighs because she was too sore, too cold, and too confused to care. Maybe she didn't even like men.

She thought about that. No, she definitely did. She was much too interested in how handsome this guy was not to like men. He was pleasing to the eye, but he was also calm and in control. She liked that. She knew she needed to be careful, but at the same time she felt like a man who'd done everything he'd just done to help her wasn't intent on hurting her.

"Can you check your pockets for ID?" he asked.

She liked his voice. It was gravelly and smooth at the same time. Not too deep, but not forgettable either. She'd started to worry when he'd been gone for so long, but looking for her car made sense. Except he hadn't seen a car. How had she gotten here?

Beneath the blanket, she slid her hands down to her pants. They were stretchy and soft and had no pockets. The jacket she wore was thin, but it did have pockets. There was a key inside one. She pulled it out and held it up.

"This is all I have." There were no markings, nothing to indicate what the key went to. A house or an apartment, maybe. But where?

She breathed in and tried not to cry. She felt like she wasn't the sort of person who cried a lot but right now she couldn't quite help the urge.

The feel of something metal tickled her collarbone as her chest expanded. It took her a second to realize it was the chain of a necklace. She fished it out from under her shirt. There was a small gold rectangle attached to either side of the chain.

Jared leaned closer and she caught the scent of wood smoke and outdoors. "Libby," he said.

"What?"

His brows twitched down for a second. "That's the name on the bar. It says Libby."

She turned it around in her brain. It sounded right when he said it. In fact, she wasn't certain if she'd been answering his use of the name or asking him what he'd said. "My name is Libby. I guess."

"It's better than *hey you,*" he said with a smile she knew was meant to reassure her.

Her belly flipped. Why did he have to be so darn pretty?

Was she pretty? She didn't have the faintest idea, but she felt as if a man who looked like this one was probably out of her league. He was tall, with broad shoulders and the kind of form that said he worked out regularly. Strikingly handsome and fit. She wasn't fit. She could tell by the way her belly folded over the top of her pants as she sat beneath the blanket.

"I guess so," she said. "Libby. Seems rather old-fashioned, doesn't it?"

"Could be short for something."

"Like what?"

He shrugged. "I don't know, but we can look it up. See if anything resonates with you."

She bit the inside of her lip. "What if I never remember?"

"I think you will. Trauma can have weird consequences, but it's not necessarily permanent. It'll probably come back to you soon enough."

She hoped he was right.

"Are you hungry?"

She thought about it. Her stomach took the opportunity to growl. "I think so."

He went over and stoked the fire, adding a log to the top. The flames leapt and sparked and the warmth reached out to where she sat and made the chill in the air a little less noticeable. It didn't hurt that Jared was bending over to tend the fire, giving her a nice view of his butt in faded jeans.

He straightened and turned, and Libby dropped her gaze to the blanket, hoping he hadn't caught her staring. Really, what did she think she was up to anyway? She didn't know who she was or where she was from or how she got here. Not to mention she hurt all over.

And what if she was married? What if her husband was looking for her? She felt around her ring finger with her thumb. No ring.

Okay, so what if she had a fiancé instead of a husband? He probably wouldn't appreciate knowing she'd been ogling a stranger's backside.

Libby hugged herself beneath the blanket and tried not to wince as she shifted her hip to ease the pressure on one side. She was a mess in more ways than one.

Jared took something out of the small medical kit he'd been using. "Here. Take these."

She looked at his palm. "What is it?"

"Tylenol."

She took the pills from him, her fingertips burning where they touched his skin. "What if I'm allergic?"

"I've got an EpiPen."

She tilted her head. There was a dull ache in her temples and an even sharper one beneath the bandage. "Are you a doctor?"

"No. A medic."

"A medic. Like an EMT?"

"Like that, yeah."

Lucky her. If she had to have an accident and get lost in a forest, this was the guy she wanted to meet. Score one for Team Libby.

"Should we call the police?" she asked. She didn't know where she was, no matter what he told her, or who she was. It was possible the police could figure that out in no time at all. Someone had to know the answer.

"I can," he said. "But we're quite a distance from town and the snow's coming down harder now. It's a small town and a small force. They might have their hands full with the weather right now. If they can get here tonight, it'll probably take a couple of hours at minimum."

She didn't like the sound of that.

"I know it's a lot to ask you to trust me," he continued. "But I have the medical training to take care of you for the night. Physically, you've been banged up a little, but you're not critically injured. Once it's daylight, it should be safe to get down the mountain and take you to the police station. In the meantime, I'll have a buddy of mine check the police scanner for any accidents in the area. In case you weren't alone."

Everything he said made sense. She turned her gaze to the huge picture windows on either side of the fireplace. It was awfully dark out there and she couldn't see anything through the windows except blackness—and a white blanket on the ground close to the windows. Daylight would come soon enough, and he'd been nothing but helpful since the moment he'd walked up to her in the snow. In fact, he'd saved her. That much she knew. If she'd stayed outside much longer, she'd have frozen to death.

"I guess it's better to wait here, then. And thank you for checking the police scanner."

"If anyone was with you, we'll find that out. I'll get a bottle of water so you can take the pills, then I'll fix something to eat."

He went over to the kitchen and she heard him rustling with the grocery bags he'd carried in. A few moments later, he returned with the water.

She took the bottle and downed the Tylenol, then sat staring at the flames as they leapt and danced. Her body throbbed with aches and pains. It was like she'd fallen off a horse or something. A horse? Did she even know how to ride one?

She thought about climbing into the saddle, picking up the reins, clucking to get the horse to move. She couldn't see herself in her mind's eye since she didn't know what she looked like, but she could see the view from the horse's back—so maybe she did know how to ride. Not that she planned to find out anytime soon.

Stop the fantasyland, Libby.

Fantasyland? Where had that come from? It sounded like something she'd heard before, but she didn't know where. She could hear an exasperated female voice saying those words to her.

Jared was back in a few minutes with a paper plate that contained a sandwich. "Turkey and cheese," he said.

"Thank you."

She didn't hesitate to take the sandwich. Why should she? If he intended to poison her, he'd have done it when he'd given her the pills. Or maybe he had a syringe in that bag of his and he'd have already injected her with something when he was tending to her injuries.

No, he wasn't trying to poison her. She took a bite and nearly moaned. Maybe she was a turkey sandwich aficionado and this was a damned fine one. Or maybe she was just really hungry.

Jared returned with his own sandwich. He sat on the couch opposite and picked up the remote to turn on the television. "Maybe there'll be something on the news about an accident. Or a missing person. We might solve this mystery in a matter of minutes, and then I'll call the police and let them know you're here. I texted a friend to check the scanner in the meantime."

She hoped there was something, but she also worried that she hadn't been alone and whoever had been with her was hurt or dead. It was a terrifying thought and not one she wanted confirmed through an announcement on the television. But what choice did she have when she didn't remember anything?

The television flickered to life. Jared went through the channels until he found a local news program. They ate in silence as the anchors talked about various happenings in the area. Nothing was familiar to her. She kept hoping something would spark a memory and she would suddenly remember everything about herself, but it didn't happen.

Her stomach twisted at the thought of remembering,

as if it was too terrible to know how she'd gotten here. She felt vaguely uneasy as she tried to force her mind in that direction. Why? Was someone out there, waiting for her to return? Had she abandoned someone who was counting on her?

When she stopped trying to remember, when she glanced at Jared and took in how calm and capable he was, she breathed a bit easier. She had to stop imagining the worst. He hadn't seen an accident, hadn't found a car or anyone else stumbling through the snow. She could just as easily have been alone out there.

But why?

Jared got up and fetched a bag of potato chips—the wavy ones—that he opened and held out to her. She took a small handful and put them on the paper plate. "Thank you."

She was surprisingly hungry and her stomach was tolerating the food quite well. Her unease didn't translate to queasiness, thankfully.

He sat down again. "You feeling any warmer?"

She thought about it. Though she still huddled beneath the blanket, with only one free arm to eat, there was a growing warmth emanating from her core. Her feet were still cold, but she wasn't shivering anymore. "Yes."

"Any new aches or pains to tell me about? Worsening headache?"

"I don't think so. It feels like I fell from a height, like maybe off a horse, though I doubt I was horseback riding in this outfit."

He studied her. An odd heat bloomed in her belly. It wasn't pain, though.

"No, not too likely." He popped a chip in his mouth, clearly unaffected by whatever was affecting her. "Nothing on the news, which isn't a bad thing." His phone dinged and he picked it up, studying the screen for a moment. "And no accidents in the local area on the scanner."

"That's good," she said. "Right?"

"It is. Means no one else is hurt or lost. So we'll stick to the plan and take you to town in the morning."

Libby's throat tightened at the thought of leaving this place. *Why?* "Okay," she said quietly. "I'm sorry to be a bother."

"You aren't a bother."

His voice was a little gruff and she wasn't sure she believed him. "Are you expecting company?"

She said it in a bright voice and then immediately regretted it. *Sounded a lot like prying, Libby.*

His blue eyes lasered in on her. "No."

"Oh, good. I would hate to ruin your plans if you were expecting a girlfriend or something."

Libby groaned mentally. *What the hell?* She didn't know who she was yet, but one thing was becoming clear about her—she didn't know when to shut up.

"I came up here for a few days alone. No one's coming to visit." He said it with finality, but she was no longer surprised that her mouth didn't want to accept he was done talking.

"Do you do that often? Come to the mountains to be alone?"

"Not often enough."

"What do you do here by yourself?"

His eyes glittered. Might be amusement. Might be irritation. Probably irritation, she decided. Yet she had a need to talk. Like talking kept fear and uncertainty at bay.

"I sit in silence and read books. I don't talk to anyone for days. It's perfect."

"I like to read." She blinked as those words popped out. "I think I do anyway. It feels like I do."

"I'll loan you a book."

"That would be nice. Thank you."

He studied her. "You're very polite. And very chatty."

Her skin flushed a little at those words. "You can't learn anything about people if you don't talk to them."

"True. But there aren't many people I care to know anything about."

"But if you don't talk to them, how do you know?"

"I don't. But I also don't care."

Libby could only stare at him. What a grump. But a gorgeous grump, no doubt about it.

He got to his feet and motioned at her plate. "You done?"

"Um, yeah."

He took it and went into the kitchen. She heard him moving around but she didn't know what he was doing. Thankfully, she was finally warming up and her belly wasn't turning itself inside out anymore. Her eyelids drooped a little, but she forced them open again. She was worried about not knowing who she was, but deep down she was certain it would come to her very soon. Maybe after a nap. Or in the morning.

"Hey."

She dragged her eyes open and met his gaze. She wasn't alarmed by his presence. He didn't make her uneasy. She wasn't sure why not, but she was glad of it. He might be a grump, but he didn't make her feel unsafe. He stood a few feet away, not looming over her, not hovering. Just waiting to speak when he was sure she was listening. She wriggled her way into a straighter position and fixed her gaze on him. "Yes?"

"You can stay on the couch if you want, but this is a two-bedroom cabin. Both have their own bathrooms." He held out a book. "Take this with you if you like. Guaranteed to put you to sleep in no time."

She accepted the book. The title was a little blurry but she could still read it. She noted that things were blurry far away and slightly blurry up close. Maybe she needed glasses. "A biography of Lyndon Johnson?"

He shrugged. "I like variety."

Libby pushed herself to her feet, wincing as she did so. "Oh shit," she breathed as everything ached.

The corners of his mouth turned down, his expression growing hard. "Maybe you should take a hot bath. I'll give you a muscle relaxer to help you sleep."

"I think I'm going to need it." Maybe she shouldn't so readily accept drugs from a man she didn't know, but she didn't have much choice if she wanted any relief. Not to mention he clearly had medical training, and nothing he'd done thus far had set off any alarm bells.

"Here, let me help."

He held out his hand and she took it. He tugged her upright with a gentleness that was surprising considering his size. She tried not to moan. When she was standing, wobbling in place, he wrapped an arm around her and steadied her against his solid form. She didn't even care that she melted into his side.

"This okay?"

"Yes," she breathed, her heart hammering at his proximity.

Nothing demonstrated so forcefully to her that she was at his mercy like leaning against him because she couldn't stand unassisted. A current of fear slipped through her as she considered the facts. She was utterly alone in a cabin with a stranger, she didn't know her name beyond the unhelpful and old-fashioned Libby, and she had no way to protect herself or call for help if he turned on her.

He could have killed you a dozen times by now if that's what he wanted. Stop being an idiot.

"We'll go slowly," he said, clearly unaware of her chaotic thoughts. He supported her as they walked toward the bedroom, and though he had an arm firmly anchored around her waist, his hand didn't stray. That was something, wasn't it? Would a murderer be so careful with her? Would he feed her, care for her, give her a book, and help her to bed?

He threw open a door and flipped on a light. The room was small but cozy and the bed was piled high with a fluffy comforter and pillows. A huge window fronted the room. She wondered what the view would be when it was light.

Jared walked her over to the bed and she sank down on it. Her heart beat surprisingly hard for that short trip, but she wasn't sure whether it was the physical exertion or his nearness.

"Do you want me to run a bath for you?"

"As much as I think I'd love it, I don't think I can get in and out by myself. So no. Thank you." Accepting his help while she was naked and vulnerable was definitely going too far for comfort.

He went over and drew the curtains without argument. "I'll get that muscle relaxer for you. Get beneath the covers and I'll bring some more water."

Libby toed off her tennis shoes but didn't remove her socks. She also didn't remove any clothing, including the jacket. She just climbed into the bed and pulled the covers up. The bed was chilly, but it would soon warm up with all the blankets.

Jared returned with the pill and water. He also brought the book and set it on the bedside table. He switched on the lamp for her. She gazed up at him.

"I hope you're not a serial killer." She said it jokingly, but a little part of her actually meant it. Serial killers could be charming, after all.

He shook his head, frowning down at her. "Not a serial killer, Libby. My job is to help people, not hurt them."

It really seemed to be true. Her heart believed it anyway. "Do you think I'll remember what happened when I wake up?"

"I don't honestly know. But I hope so."

Chapter Three

JARED LEFT THE DOOR TO THE BEDROOM OPEN A CRACK, in case Libby called out in the night. His room was directly across from hers but he wasn't bedding down just yet. He picked up his phone and placed a call. Ian Black answered on the second ring.

"You tired of the solitude already?"

Jared could hear the grin in his boss's voice. "Haven't had any yet."

"Uh-oh."

"Yeah." Jared frowned at the door to Libby's room. "I found a woman."

"Oh boy, here it comes."

"No, I mean I literally found her as I was driving toward the cabin. She was on foot, dressed in tennis shoes and what looks like workout clothes. She was bleeding from a cut on the head and throat. She's fine, though bruised and sore. She doesn't know what happened and she can't remember her name, but she's wearing a necklace with the name Libby on it. No phone, no ID, no jewelry other than the necklace. I put her in the spare room."

"I'd wondered why you asked Dax for any accident info in the area. I assume you did recon."

The boss always got to the heart of the matter. "No car accident that I could see within two miles either direction but I needed to make sure there wasn't one in the area in case she hadn't been alone. I didn't drive any farther because of the snow, but honest to god I don't know how she could have walked farther anyway. No reports on the news of any accidents or missing persons. Domestic violence is a possibility too. Maybe she got in a fight with her boyfriend, or husband, and he kicked her out of the car."

"Could be. Could also be a trafficking attempt gone wrong."

"That too." There were too many possibilities, and all of them sucked.

"Guess I'd better see if we have any missing Libbys in the region. Description?"

"Five-five, dark blond mid-shoulder-length hair, pulled back in a ponytail, brown eyes. Appears to wear glasses, but didn't have them on her. Average build."

He said average, and she was, but when he'd held her against his side as he walked her to the bedroom, he'd been very aware of the dip of her waist beneath his hand and the thin slice of cleavage revealed beneath her jacket. Besides the antiseptic, he'd also smelled the flowery scent of her shampoo.

"Got it. I'll see what's out there, if anything." He could hear Ian tapping his pen. "Do you think there could be something deeper at work here? The closer we get to the inner circles of the Gemini Syndicate, the more likely they are to figure out who we are and where to find us."

Jared blew out a breath. "I thought of that. But why not pop me where I stood instead of going through an elaborate ruse? It seems like a lot of trouble to go to— and for what?"

"Maybe they're looking for an inside track. Get close to you, get information."

Jared sighed. "Yeah, that's possible. I don't think I believe it, though. She seems genuinely confused, not purposely so. I can't explain it, but I've got no alarms ringing inside."

Anything was possible in this job. His instincts hadn't been wrong yet, but there was always a first time. Since leaving the Air Force and joining Ian Black's team, he'd learned a lot about the shadowy world of covert ops— and about the kind of people who inhabited it.

Nothing was beyond them and not all of them were good. Not all of them had the best interests of national security and global stability at heart. Some of them were only concerned with wealth and power. It didn't matter if entire populations teetered on the brink of catastrophic poverty and disease. It only mattered that they could fund their elaborate lifestyles and prepare for the next war they were certain was coming.

A war where they'd hole up in bomb proof bunkers and wait it out. Survival of the fittest, they believed, though what they thought they would emerge to find was beyond him. Why not spend your money trying to fix problems rather than exacerbate them? Because if there was some sort of cataclysmic global event, you weren't emerging in a year and going to Fiji for a five-star vacation. Who'd be left to wait on you if you did?

"That's a good sign. I'll get back to you when I find something," Ian said.

"Thanks, boss."

"Keep an eye out for trouble in the meantime."

"I will." Because it was second nature to him. Because it could mean the difference between life and death. His instincts hadn't failed him yet, but that didn't mean he was home free. Shit went wrong. He knew that better than most.

The other end of the line went dead. Jared clicked the television on again, leaving it on mute, and picked up a thick tome about national security. He took the Glock from its hidden holster beneath his waistband and set it on the table beside him before opening the book.

After a few minutes, he lifted his head. He'd been reading the same sentence over and over because he couldn't seem to stop thinking about Libby and how he'd found her.

His gut told him she was *in* trouble, not trouble. He'd be careful, just in case his gut was wrong, but what he really wanted to do was go into her room and hold her close again. Tell her she was safe with him. Tell her that he wouldn't let anyone hurt her.

And then he wanted to kiss her softly and promise everything would be all right.

Jared eyed her door. Then he shook his head to clear it and went back to reading. Or tried to, anyway.

LIBBY WOKE SLOWLY. Her head throbbed, though not from a headache, and her body hurt whenever she moved. She was stiff and sore and she groaned when she tried to push herself upright in bed. But she persevered, levering herself up on one elbow.

The curtains were closed, but it was clearly daylight out. It wasn't bright, but there was a large square of light behind the curtains. Last night, everything had been black. There was a sliver of light coming from the door too, which was slightly open.

Libby blinked and tried to process what had happened. She remembered a man—Jared—and she remembered a fire and food. She remembered standing in the snow, the headlights of a car coming at her. She had an impression of riding in a vehicle at some point, but when she tried to seize on it, the memory slipped away.

Memory.

She tried to will herself to remember her name, but nothing came. Nothing but cold fear. She reached for the necklace and clutched the thin bar. *Libby.*

Jared had said they could see what Libby was short for, but they'd never done so. She would ask him today, fear be damned.

Her belly squeezed at a different thought. What if he was gone? What if he'd left and she was alone? She didn't have a phone, or a way to call for help.

"Stop," she whispered.

She didn't know that he would leave her. He'd

helped her, and he'd said he wasn't a serial killer. Not that a serial killer would admit he was one, but Jared had helped her to bed and given her a book. He hadn't done anything inappropriate. Not only that, but she was still alive.

By degrees, Libby got herself upright. Movement was painful but not impossible. Somehow, she got out of bed and hobbled her way into the bathroom. Her face in the mirror was a surprise. She hadn't looked last night, but now she studied herself in the glass. She was young, in her twenties probably, and she had dark blond hair. She'd seen her hair color because her hair was long, but to see it framing her face was a surprise. Her skin was clear, her eyes were brown, and her nose was thin. She wasn't wearing makeup, though she felt like it was something she typically did. Not that she knew for sure.

She was pretty, but not beautiful. Certainly not beautiful enough for a man like Jared.

Oh well.

She looked longingly at the tub but decided a shower would be better. The shower was walk-in, and that's what she needed right now. There were thick, fluffy towels, a white fluffy robe, toiletries, and even a pair of slippers. She didn't stop to wonder how any of that was possible. She just turned on the shower and thanked her lucky stars it was.

After a long, hot shower where she thoroughly soaped, washed, and rinsed everything, she stepped out of the tub with muscles that didn't scream quite so much as before. She had some bruises, but so long as she didn't touch them they weren't too bad. The bruises on her arm looked a little like fingerprints. That made her frown. She also had a bigger bruise on her hip and side, like she'd knocked into something. She pulled on the robe, gnawing her lip when she thought about underwear. But she couldn't put dirty panties back on. If her luck held, there was a washer and dryer in this cabin. She could wash her clothes before putting them on again. By then, maybe she'd remember something else about herself.

Like where she lived. Because if she didn't, then what? Jared wasn't going to keep taking care of her like she didn't have a life somewhere else. He would take her to the police station and leave her so they could figure it out and he could go back to his vacation.

She tamped down on the bubble of panic rising in her belly. What did it matter if he helped her or the police did? She shouldn't care—and yet she did. She felt safe here, especially now that she'd spent an entire night in the same house with him and nothing bad had happened. Maybe it wasn't a high standard, but it was something.

Still alive. Check.

Unmolested. Check.

Libby shoved her feet in the slippers, belted the robe tight, and balled up her clothing. When she opened the bathroom door, the scent of bacon slammed into her nostrils and her belly growled.

She clutched her dirty clothes and went out into the living room. A fire blazed in the hearth. The floor to ceiling windows on either side of it revealed a snowy landscape that made it seem like they were alone in the world. The living room was vaulted to allow for those huge windows that captured the view. It was spectacular, if a little fuzzy, and somehow lonely as well.

When Jared said he liked to be alone, he wasn't kidding.

Movement in the kitchen drew her eye. He was standing at the stove, dressed in a plaid flannel shirt and faded jeans. He moved something in the pan and Libby went a little closer, clutching her balled up clothes, her heart suddenly in her throat.

He turned to get something and his eyes met hers. One corner of his mouth lifted in a grin. Hers went dry.

Flipping hell, he was fine. And so out of her league…

"Morning," he said with that gravelly voice.

"Morning," she croaked. *Sexy, Libby. Very sexy.*

"I hope you like eggs and bacon and grits."

"With butter?"

"Is there anything else?" he asked, one eyebrow arching.

"I think some people put sugar on them."

He made a face. "Yeah, I've heard that before. Disgusting. Sit," he said, indicating one of the seats at the bar.

She held up her clothes. "Is there a washer?"

"Yep. Behind those doors." He nodded to a set of double doors in the kitchen. "Drop 'em on the floor and I'll put them in for you after breakfast."

"Okay." Part of her thought she should protest that she could do it herself, but she also rather liked the idea of letting him do it. She thought maybe she didn't get a lot of that at home, wherever home was. Libby climbed onto the bar seat, tucking the robe between her legs so it didn't fall open to reveal all her secrets, and eyed the plate of food with a watering mouth.

He put a couple of slices of bacon, some scrambled eggs, and a dollop of buttery grits on the plate. Then he added a slice of generously buttered toast and slid the whole thing toward her. "Go ahead," he said as he fixed his own plate.

Libby dug into the eggs, nearly moaning at the buttery goodness. The bacon was equally delicious.

Jared eyed her with amusement as he ate a slice of bacon off his plate. Instead of coming around the bar to join her, he stood opposite. "Your appetite is good. How do you feel?"

"I took a hot shower. I think between that and the muscle relaxer, it helped. I'm stiff though, and there are some bruises on my right side and arm. I feel like running a marathon is out of the question."

"Probably. Did you start the book?"

She blinked before she remembered. "No, I fell asleep right away. I think I need glasses though. The words are a little fuzzy."

"What about outside?" he asked, pointing at the window.

She glanced at the landscape. "It's fuzzier the farther it gets. I can tell there are woods and snow. That's about it."

"There are probably some readers around here, but I don't think we can do anything about the distance just yet."

"It's not bad. But I feel like I probably couldn't drive without glasses."

"Good thing you don't have to drive anywhere."

"Suppose so." She crunched a bite of bacon. Apprehension was a low-level hum in her belly. "I still don't know my name or what happened to me."

He didn't seem surprised. "It happens sometimes. It'll come back to you."

"How can you be sure?"

He shrugged. "I've seen it before."

"Because you're an EMT?"

His gaze was steady, blue eyes piercing. "No, because I'm a combat medic. Trauma does things to help the brain cope."

Libby processed this information. "A combat medic. I'm not sure I know what that means. I mean I *do* know what combat is, and what a medic is—but how do those two things get together?"

He poured more coffee in her mug. She hadn't realized she'd finished it. "Thank you," she murmured.

He smiled as he put the pot down again. "So polite. A combat medic is someone who provides medical assistance on the battlefield."

"Oh." It still wasn't all that clear to her. "Is there much need for that?"

"More than you think. The US is always engaged in a skirmish somewhere, and warriors get hurt. That's where I come in, though I'm also a warrior."

Her head was reeling. *Combat medics?* "I see. And sometimes in these… *skirmishes*… people forget who they are?"

"It's happened. They remember eventually. Never saw one yet who didn't."

Libby concentrated. "It's all a blank. Well, most of it. I think I was in a car, but I don't know if I was driving or not. Did you look up names for me?"

He picked up his phone and swiped. "Libby can be short for Elizabeth, Isabel, Liberty, Lydia, or even sometimes Olivia. It can also be a name on its own. Any of that ring a bell?"

"I think…" Her brain hurt with how hard she was thinking about it, but one name resonated with her. Was she right or just latching on because it was different from the others? "Liberty seems familiar."

"Liberty. Okay." He typed and she heard the swoosh of a text message.

"You're texting someone about me?" If only she'd had a phone on her, the mystery of who she was would be solved. Why didn't she have one? Didn't everybody?

He set his phone on the counter. "My boss. He knows how to get things done. If there's a missing Liberty somewhere, he'll find out."

"How can he do that?"

He shrugged. "Finding people is part of what he does."

She wanted to ask questions, but she sensed he wouldn't answer them. Besides, if his boss could find the answer, that's all she really needed. "I could be wrong. I keep thinking it's familiar, but what if it's just unusual?"

"It is that. I don't think I've met any Libertys before."

Libby chewed her bacon. "It could also just be Libby

since that's what's on the necklace. Maybe I always wished it was something cool like Liberty, but it's plain old Libby."

Jared finished the food on his plate and turned to the sink to wash it. When he finished, he picked up her clothes and opened the folding doors to reveal a washer and dryer. Before she could protest, he unfurled the ball. Her panties and sports bra fell out and her cheeks heated when he calmly tossed them into the washer. Then he checked the labels on her shirt, jacket, and yoga pants before dropping them in too and adding soap.

"What?" he asked when he turned back to her.

"You read the labels." *And touched my underwear.*

"You don't read the labels before tossing your clothes in the wash? That's a good way to ruin them."

"I don't know what I do, remember?" She said it defensively but he only grinned.

"You knew the day of the week and the president. I'm guessing you know if you read labels or not."

Okay, so maybe he was right. "I think I do. I'm surprised you do."

"Because I'm a man, right? I was an only child and my mom worked a lot after my dad left us. I learned to do laundry the right way." He nodded at her plate. "You done or you want more?"

"I'm done. Thank you. I can get it," she added when he took her plate and put it in the sink.

"You're still recovering and you're sore. I've got it."

She thanked him again but he waved her off. "You can do dishes tomorrow."

Her heart thumped. "Tomorrow? I thought you were taking me to the police station today."

He jerked his head toward the window. "Can't. We're snowed in, I'm afraid. We aren't going anywhere for a couple of days."

Chapter Four

LIBBY WAS A TALKER. JARED HAD THOUGHT MAYBE LAST night was simply nerves and disorientation from her accident, but she showed no signs of stopping today. She kept up a running commentary on the snow coming down outside, her own state of mind as she tried on and discarded several scenarios for how she'd come to be on the road to the cabin last night—none of which involved a violent boyfriend, he noted—and the books he'd laid out on the coffee table. He'd brought five physical books, two of which were on the table, and he had more on his phone because you couldn't carry a whole library in your duffel bag.

He'd wanted her to be comfortable with him, and she clearly was. He was glad of that, even if he wasn't used to the constant chatter.

Jared finished her laundry and she hobbled to the bedroom to dress. He didn't like that she was still in pain, but at least she was improving. When she finally returned, she had on the jacket too.

"Are you cold?"

"Not right now, I'm not."

He went into his room and retrieved a quilted flannel shirt anyway. "You can wear this instead of the jacket if you like. It'll be warmer and cover more."

She seemed to hesitate a second. "Okay, thanks."

She discarded the jacket and slipped into his shirt, shoving the sleeves up and sighing. "Oh, this is warm. The best. Really, I love flannel. I mean I think I do." She tilted her head. "What if everything I think I love is really something I hate? What if I'm completely wrong about everything?"

Her mouth was off to the races again. He had half a mind to shut it with his own. The fact it was a colossally bad idea was all that stopped him. It would shut her up, sure. But it would entangle him in something he didn't need. Her either if someone was out there looking for her.

And if she was a Gemini agent running a con, it was an especially bad idea. For the life of him, he couldn't figure out what that con might be, which made the whole thing unlikely. On the other hand, it wasn't impossible and he wasn't letting down his guard entirely.

"You might be wrong," he said. "I wouldn't worry about it too much."

"Easy for you to say. You know who you are. What you like." She turned and looked out the window, folding her arms over her chest. "We're really stuck here, aren't we?"

"For the time being."

"I wish I had clothes. I'll be washing my panties in the sink every night."

She bit off the last word as if suddenly embarrassed. He'd noticed that she'd had red cheeks when he'd dropped her laundry in the wash. Like she'd been mortified that he'd handled her underwear.

He'd done it without thinking, but he'd definitely noticed once he had his hand on the scrap of lace and cotton. Her sports bra was nothing sexy but her panties had a lacy behind that made him think of her ass cheeks and how they'd show. In fact, the only fabric was the scrap that covered the front. The rest was see-through, and that had his imagination working overtime.

It was still working, damn him.

Been a while since he'd had any pussy. A couple of months at least. Not from lack of availability. He'd had plenty of opportunities. He just hadn't taken them. It happened that way sometimes. He got caught up in work and surviving and he let it go. He didn't want to play the game, flirt and pursue and talk and drink and pursue some more until they finally got naked together.

He wasn't pursuing Libby, but he'd been thinking about her ass in lace all morning. She had a generous ass. Plump and shapely, with the kind of cheeks a man could hold onto while he fucked her from behind. He wanted to grab handfuls while he sank into her.

Jared shifted to give his growing cock relief from the press of his jeans. "I've got some sweatshirts you can borrow. Can't help with the underwear though."

She turned and frowned. Her hair was loose, long and thick as it brushed over her shoulders. It was dark blond, but there were hints of caramel in it. Probably from the salon.

"I guess the storm could be over tomorrow and I'll be on the way home. I shouldn't complain."

"Complain all you like."

She strolled over and sat on the couch opposite the one he was on, pulling her legs beneath her and wrapping her arms around her knees. She seemed small and vulnerable when she did that. "I hate not knowing. It makes me feel like I have no control."

Jared picked up the remote. He knew what it was like not to have any control over your life. It sucked. "Let's look at the noon news. Maybe there's something about a missing person."

He doubted it since Ian hadn't called, but it would give Libby something to hope for. The broadcast blared to life and Jared closed his book. He wasn't getting anywhere with Libby constantly chattering at him anyway.

They watched the news, but there was no mention of a missing woman or an accident. He left the television on afterward though it was a soap opera. If it kept her distracted, then good.

But the program kept freezing, finally blanking out entirely.

"What happened?" she asked.

"It's the weather. It's interfering with the satellite."

She looked worriedly at the windows. "What if we're stuck here for days?"

"We've got food and shelter. We'll be good."

Though he wasn't going to get any quiet time with

her around, that's for sure. He was glad she wasn't so traumatized she didn't speak though. He'd lived through the aftermath of his dad's rages and he remembered his mom sitting in a chair, staring at nothing. Then she got up and got back to cleaning house or making dinner, not speaking a word for hours. He'd wanted to fix everything for her, but he was too small back then to make a difference.

Libby picked up the book he'd given her with a sigh. She'd found a pair of reading glasses in the bedside table in her room and she put them on. "Guess there's nothing to do but read then."

"Guess so."

Jared opened his book, though he kept glancing at her over the top of it. She frowned at the pages, turning them steadily and muttering to herself from time to time. He wanted to laugh, but didn't. Worse, he wanted to ask her what the problem was. Which meant they'd be talking again and he wouldn't get any of that quiet he craved.

He looked at the page he was supposed to be reading and forced himself to concentrate. He'd barely gotten through two pages when his ears picked up the dull buzz of a motor in the distance. He strained to listen.

Correction, two motors. Snowmobiles, probably.

Shit, what he wouldn't give for one of those right about now. The motors echoed in the woods like two chainsaws, coming closer as the minutes ticked by. Libby finally noticed.

"Someone's out there," she said.

"I'm aware."

"I…" She swallowed. Her face was a little pale.

His senses went on high alert. "What?"

"I-I don't know."

Jared got to his feet and retrieved his jacket. "Stay inside. Don't show your face no matter what happens, you got that?"

She hunched on the couch, legs beneath her, looking as if she were trying to make herself even smaller. "What's going to happen? It's probably teenagers having fun or something."

"Nothing's going to happen. Just stay inside and don't make a sound. It might be the rental company coming to check on me," he added, though he didn't think anything of the sort. "If they know I've got a guest, they'll charge me more."

Libby made a face. "Oh my god, you're a cheapskate."

"That's right. So keep it zipped."

Jared closed the door behind him as he stepped outside, the weight of the Glock in the hidden holster at his waist reassuring. He didn't discount the fact that Libby could still be conning him, but her fear had seemed real enough. If she was on the up and up, then her gut could be telling her something her brain hadn't yet admitted.

She feared being found.

Jared went out to the woodpile and gathered some logs. There were plenty inside, but it was the excuse he needed. The snowmobiles were nearly upon him when they finally came over the rise. Two men with hunting rifles slung over their shoulders. They slowed when they saw him.

"Nice day to have a snowmobile," Jared said when they were within earshot. "Whatcha hunting?"

They came to a stop, engines idling. Both men were dressed in hunter camouflage. One had a beard and knit cap and the other wore a gaiter on the lower half of his face. He thought that one of these men could be Libby's abusive boyfriend, assuming that was how she'd gotten hurt, but that didn't mean he planned to admit she was here. Until he got to the bottom of what'd happened to her, he wasn't handing her over to anyone.

"Wild boar," one of the men said. "You see any?"

"Nope, sure haven't. Saw a small herd of deer earlier. They went east, into those woods."

"This your place?" the one with the gaiter asked. A little too curiously, Jared thought.

"Rented it for the week."

"You alone?" bearded guy asked casually. He had piggish eyes in a broad face and he stared at Jared like he was looking for trouble. Jared didn't like him on sight, but that wasn't a good enough reason to shoot him. Yet.

He thought about saying he was with his girlfriend, but something about these two pinged his trouble meter. Didn't mean anything, but the fact he'd found Libby bleeding and hurt last night, and these men were here today asking if he was alone—well, he hadn't lived through as many missions as he had by being oblivious to the undercurrents. A boyfriend would at least pretend to be frantic to find her. An abductor not so much.

"Yep. My fucking wife ran off with my best friend so

I'm up here alone rather than ending up on the news for double murder, you know?"

Gaiter-man nodded. "Yeah. That's rough, dude."

"Thanks." Jared tossed a couple of logs into a pile. "Just gonna drink and watch movies today. Not sure about tomorrow. Maybe in a week I won't want to kill them."

After a short conversation about fickle women and the weather, the men rode away. They didn't mention Libby at all, but that didn't mean he thought they were legit. Even if they weren't looking for her, they weren't harmless hunters out for a bit of sport. Jared kept gathering logs until he was certain the engines had faded in the distance. He listened in case one cut out and one kept going, but there were two engines the entire time. Which meant they weren't doubling back.

At least not yet.

He'd given them no reason not to believe him, but that didn't mean he trusted they were gone for good.

Chapter Five

"Who were they?" Libby asked when Jared returned.

He closed the door behind him and locked it. "Hunters."

He went around to all the windows and closed the curtains, including over the large picture window where she'd been staring out at the snow. The windows were two stories, however, and light still came in from the top ones. But the serene view was gone and that made her anxiety spike.

"Why did you close the blinds if they were hunters?"

He fixed her with a look. "Why did you get scared when you heard the snowmobiles?"

"I don't know. I just—I don't know how I got here, and that bothers me."

"It's more than that, Libby. You don't know how you got here, but you know deep down that something isn't right about the situation."

Her mouth was dry. Her heart pounded. Was he

right? She feared he was. When she'd heard those engines, her adrenaline spiked. She'd wanted to run and hide, but she'd convinced herself she was being silly. Why would she need to hide from anyone?

I don't know why. But I do.

Libby shivered. "If you're right, why am I not scared of you?"

"I helped you when you needed it. You can trust me and you know it."

"I don't know anything about you. Not really."

He flopped into his chair and shifted his book from the arm to the side table. "You know I'm a combat medic. You know I like to read, that I know how to do laundry, and I make a mean breakfast. I also make lunch and dinner, by the way. What else do you need?"

"You forgot cheapskate," she said primly.

He laughed. "That's right."

"How old are you?"

"Thirty-two."

"Where are you from?"

"Everywhere and nowhere."

"What does that mean?"

"It means I don't claim any place in particular. My dad was in the Air Force and I was born in Germany, but we moved a lot." He shrugged. "That's the fate of most military brats, really. From everywhere and nowhere."

Libby considered that. If things were normal, she'd be telling him about herself. She'd looked in the mirror and she knew she wasn't old. But she didn't know her age. She also knew she was passably pretty, but nothing spectacular. She was shapely but not thin, with a big butt and reasonably sized boobs. Probably a B-cup. She didn't know for sure because all she had was a sports bra and that didn't have a cup size.

All she knew about herself was what she could see. The rest was frustratingly blank.

She circled back to her original question. "Why did you close the blinds?"

"Because I told those guys I was alone. I don't want them getting a glimpse of you through a window."

"You think they're looking for me?"

He seemed to consider it. "I don't know. Probably not, but we can't be too careful."

"Why didn't you just tell them I was your girlfriend or something?" Surely that would have been easier even if it wasn't true.

"What if they asked to see you? Or forced their way in here because I had a female companion and they're looking for a missing female? If they're looking for you, but didn't tell me that up front, then they don't have your best interests at heart. A relative or friend would have led with that because they're frantic to find you."

Her heart thumped. "I didn't think of it that way. I'm kind of amazed you did."

"Goes with the job."

"Combat medics are a suspicious lot then?" She was trying to inject a bit of humor, mostly for herself, but he didn't take the bait.

"No. Combat operatives are."

She didn't like the sound of that. "Is there a war going on?"

"There's always a war somewhere."

Libby sighed. "You're just full of sunshine, aren't you?"

"You asked. I'm keeping it real. Human beings are pathologically motivated to fight about things. Sometimes it turns violent."

He sounded almost angry when he said that. Libby nodded toward the books on the table. "Maybe you need to read something besides books about the NSA and CIA. Something funny or happy."

He picked one up and looked at the cover. "This is interesting. Not reading it won't change reality."

"No, but it might make you happier."

"I doubt that." He kicked back and opened the tome. "Might as well get some reading done. It's going to be a long day without satellite."

Libby stared morosely. "Do you have anything else besides this book on Lyndon Johnson?"

It wasn't that she didn't like to learn things, but the book wasn't exactly entertaining.

Jared got up and disappeared into his bedroom. When he came back, he held out a book.

Libby read the title. "*War and Peace*. I'm sensing a theme here."

"You asked for something different. It's the only novel I've got. Take it or leave it."

Libby took it. She spent two hours reading about the French invasion of Russia during the Napoleonic wars. It wasn't a bad story, but it wasn't uplifting either. Naturally. She glanced at Jared. He turned pages regularly, but he hadn't said a word. His phone pinged occasionally. He picked it up, glanced at the screen, then set it down again. A couple of times he tapped out a reply.

The last time it pinged, he stood and went over to the window. "Snow's coming down harder. The weather app says it won't stop until tomorrow." He shrugged into his coat. "I'm going to get more wood and check the generator just in case we lose power."

"You think we will?"

The lights flickered as if to illustrate the point. "I think it's possible," he said, looking up at the ceiling. "Best to be prepared."

She set the book aside. "What can I do?"

"You could fix lunch if you feel up to it."

She was a bit stiff and her muscles ached, but sitting didn't help anything. "I think moving around would be good for me. Not that I know if I can cook, but what the hell? We'll either have something yummy or I'll set the place on fire."

Jared fixed her with those piercing blue eyes. "Try not to hurt yourself—and try not to start a fire."

"Of course I'll *try*."

"Libby."

She rolled her eyes. He was so serious all the time. "I'm kidding, Jared. I think I can manage not to start a fire. Really."

He hesitated a moment. When he walked out the door, he was muttering under his breath.

Chapter Six

"That smells good."

Jared took off his jacket and hung it on the peg by the door. He'd been outside for about half an hour, gathering wood to bring to the front porch and making sure the generator was operational. There was gasoline in the shed and a full tank, so he wasn't worried about losing power. The generator was small, but it would run the lights and refrigerator. The heat would have to be shut down, but that's why they had a fireplace.

"Apparently, I know how to cook." Libby smiled. It was a big smile, full of happiness.

He was glad that something so routine made her happy. "What are we having?"

"Potato soup with cheese and some of that leftover bacon. Oh, and garlic toast."

He was impressed. "How did you fix the soup?"

"I peeled and boiled potatoes. When they were soft, I drained them and added some milk, then mashed them up a little bit in the pot with more milk and butter and some flour. I also added some dried herbs. We don't have any green onions, unfortunately. But I'll sprinkle cheese on the top along with crumbled bacon."

"Sounds really good." Especially after spending time outside in the cold.

"Is everything okay?" she asked as she dipped a spoon into the soup to taste it.

"We've got plenty of wood and the generator is operational. It's not automatic, so if the power goes out I'll have to start it. But there's extra gas so we should be good."

"The power flickered again, but not for long. Maybe it'll be okay."

If they were in town, it would be. But up on the mountain he wasn't so sure. That's why there was a generator. "Maybe so. When can we eat?"

"Five minutes. I just need to pop the toast into the oven."

He went around the island to help her. While moving around was good for loosening the muscles, he didn't want her to overdo it. She moved slowly enough that he reached the baking sheet before she did. "I got it. You get the soup."

"Thank you."

He waited for the broiler to turn the toast brown, then removed the baking sheet and put the toast on a saucer she'd set out. She was ladling soup into bowls. She'd managed to set out placemats and napkins at the bar. It was oddly domestic, and not something he was used to these days. He didn't set out placemats or napkins at home, and he never invited anyone over for a meal. Not yet anyway. He'd only been in the house for a few months now, but once summer arrived, he might do a cook out.

He set the saucer with the garlic bread between the mats and waited so he could place the bowls for her. Her arms weren't long enough to reach across the island like his were.

She sprinkled cheese on top and followed that up with the bacon she'd crumbled. "I think this is gonna be good."

He grabbed the bowls. "You go sit and I'll take care of this."

She did as he told her, hobbling around the island to pull out a bar stool and climb onto it. When they were seated, he dipped his spoon in and took a bite. "Guess you *can* cook."

Libby looked ridiculously pleased with herself. He liked the way her eyes lit up at the compliment. Her skin wasn't the pale mask of last night, but warm and glowing with life. The bandages were small where they covered her cuts and the bruising on her face was minimal. He'd been relieved to see that this morning. Whatever had happened, nobody'd punched her there. That didn't mean she hadn't been abused though. His dad had gotten good at hiding the evidence whenever he'd hit Jared or his mother. He'd slap faces and punch stomachs, or he'd pinch flesh hard enough to bruise.

Still, Libby didn't strike him as someone who'd been regularly beaten up. Even without her memory, she didn't behave the way he would expect her to if she had been. She didn't flinch or jump or look at him with wary eyes. The one time she'd been wary was when the snow-mobiles were approaching. Since they'd gone, she was back to being mostly cheerful.

"I don't know what made me decide potato soup was the thing to do, but I knew all the steps. I never doubted myself."

"Good thing. Soup is perfect on a cold day."

"I thought it sounded better than a sandwich. Not that your sandwich last night wasn't perfect because it was," she added.

"It was a sandwich, Libby. You don't have to worry I'm gonna be offended if you say your soup is better. It *is* better."

She swirled her spoon before taking another bite. "You said you were born in Germany. May I ask where?"

"Landstuhl. It's the big American hospital near Ramstein Air Base."

"I've heard of that. I don't think I've ever been to Germany. I mean I guess I don't really know, but I feel like it's somewhere I'd like to see if I haven't already."

"I don't remember living there. We moved back to the US when I was two. But I've been a few times as an adult. I like it."

"I guess you never learned German then, huh?"

"Not true. I took it in high school, and I went TDY there a few times when I was in the Air Force."

Libby blinked. "You were in the Air Force?"

Jared sighed inwardly. He didn't usually like talking about himself, because it tended to reopen old wounds, but it wasn't easy to have a conversation with a woman who knew nothing about her own life. "Yeah, I was. It's where I learned to be a combat medic."

"But you aren't in the Air Force now?"

"No. I work for an international agency that specializes in protective services." That was the official version. The unofficial version was that Ian Black's organization worked to protect far more than individual clients. They were crusaders for justice and peace in a chaotic and unpredictable world.

She looked confused. "Protective services? Like bodyguards?"

"Precisely."

"And you work as a combat medic?"

"That's right."

"That doesn't really sound right, you know." Her eyes sparkled with mischief. "Do you work for the CIA? Are you a spy?"

"Do you really think you should be asking me these questions?"

"I don't know. Maybe not. I don't think I've ever met anyone like you before."

"But you don't really know."

She made a face. "I guess I don't. I'm sorry to ask so many questions."

"It's not like you've got answers to mine."

"No, not really." Her brows drew together. "I've been trying to remember things. I see a woman sometimes. She's older, with hair like mine, and she's always telling me to behave myself. She seems exasperated with me a lot of the time."

"Who do you think it is?"

"I think it's my mother."

"Could be. Can you remember anything else?"

She concentrated. "A tractor. A man in overalls. Chickens and pigs and fields filled with tall green plants that sway in the breeze."

"What kind of plants?"

"Corn maybe. Or soybeans, though I don't think those get tall. I'm not sure. It's a farm, though. Definitely a farm. I see myself going into a henhouse to gather eggs and coming out with a basketful. It's like an Easter egg hunt, only the eggs are found in boxes filled with straw. They're warm too." She put a palm to her forehead, then dropped it and shook her head. "I *wish* I could remember."

Jared put his hand on hers and squeezed. Her skin was warm and soft. He had an urge to trace his fingers up her wrist to her elbow, but he didn't do it. He pulled back instead. "You will, Libby."

Her breathing seemed a little off, or maybe he was imagining it.

"I don't know how you can be so sure."

"I just am."

They finished the soup and Jared washed the dishes. He made Libby sit down. She didn't go to the living room, however. She stayed and watched him, keeping up a running conversation the whole time.

Damn but she liked to talk. He had to admit it was a pretty amazing feat considering she didn't know much about her life yet. She was relegated to the past few hours, her vague memories of a farm, and *War and Peace*. None of that slowed her much. She hadn't gotten far in the book, but she had plenty to say about it.

He actually kind of enjoyed it, once he let himself just listen and didn't try to say much in response. He was accustomed to measuring his words, thinking about what he said. But Libby just said whatever was on her mind. And she really *was* a cheerful person. Her thoughts weren't focused on the negative. He envied her for that. He wasn't a negative person, but it was his job to consider all the bad things that could happen. If he didn't, he wouldn't be prepared.

"What do you think?" she finally asked.

Those words jerked him out of his stupor. "About what?"

"The book. Tolstoy."

"I haven't read it yet."

Her eyes bugged. "Oh my god, you gave me a book you haven't read? What if it sucks?"

"Does it?"

"It might. I'm not sure yet."

Jared wanted to laugh, but he didn't. "So keep reading and let me know if it sucks. If so, I'll avoid it."

He wouldn't because he had a thing about reading the classics. His mom had been a literature major in college before she'd dropped out and married his dad. She'd always talked about the classics like they were the holy grail, though when he'd been growing up she'd mostly read historical romance novels because she said they were happy books. God knew she'd needed happy books. These days he read the classics for her since she'd missed out on so many.

She'd had to work two—sometimes three—jobs to make ends meet once his dad left them. She'd rarely gotten to read then. She'd never complained, though. Three jobs were preferable to a man with a temper who knocked you around.

"Ha, I don't think so, mister," Libby said. "I'm going to tell you it's fabulous no matter what now."

He shook out the towel he'd been drying dishes with and hung it on the dishwasher handle. He pressed his palms to the countertop, leaning toward her. "You would, huh?"

He didn't know if she licked her lower lip on purpose or what but the sight of her pink tongue did things to his groin. *What the fuck?*

"I would. Will. It's the greatest piece of literature I've ever read," she intoned snootily.

Then she laughed and Jared laughed with her. Damn, he was liking this girl.

She made a face.

"What?"

"I feel cooped up with the curtains closed."

"So do I, but it's better this way." His phone pinged with a text. He glanced at it.

Ian: *Found 8 Libertys in the metro area, none in the vicinity of your cabin. Tracing them now. How's it going? She remember anything else?*

"Gotta answer this," Jared said, holding up his phone.

"I'll go read. Unless you think the satellite is back."

"You can try but I doubt it."

She wandered over to one of the couches and curled

58

her legs beneath her before trying the TV. Nothing but a black screen. She dropped the remote and picked up the book with a long-suffering sigh. He stifled another laugh.

"Drama queen," he teased.

"I thought you had to reply to your text?" She managed to say the words with a haughty look, but he didn't take her seriously. She was still being silly, making him want to laugh more than he had in a long time.

"Doing it now." He typed out a reply. *Nothing of importance. Thinks she grew up on a farm. Possibly a corn or soybean farm, though they had livestock too.*

That was pretty basic stuff to describe the woman in front of him. Nothing about how funny she was, or how she managed to brighten the room with her sunny disposition. Damn, he was going soft if he was thinking about sunny dispositions.

Ian: *Everything helps. How's the weather up there?*

Jared: *Sucks. Satellite's out. We have wood and a generator with plenty of gas. Plenty of food. Expect to lose phone service if it keeps up.*

Ian: *Sorry about that. Reports say it's going to keep coming down, especially in the mountains. Expecting two feet when it's all said and done. There's a chance the storm will move out before it gets that bad, but they don't really know yet.*

Jared closed his eyes. *Great,* he typed.

Ian: *Snowmobiles come back?*

Jared had told Ian about the two men and his feeling they weren't hunters. They weren't necessarily looking for Libby. Could be drug dealers. Cooking meth in hidden places like these woods was nothing new. They'd be suspicious of strangers they encountered, and they'd want to know what kind of plans those strangers had as well. Jared might be in a rental cabin, but that didn't mean there wasn't anyone around these parts who wouldn't want him getting too nosy.

No. Nothing. Maybe they found what they were after.

Ian: *Maybe. I'm afraid you're on your own until this shit stops. Could be one day or several.*

Ordinarily, he wouldn't care. Being alone in the woods for a few days had been the plan, after all. But now he wasn't alone. He was with a woman he knew next to nothing about. A woman who probably couldn't keep her mouth shut if you paid her. Or not for long anyway.

There was a way to shut that mouth—put something in it.

Except that was totally off the table because, again, he knew nothing about her. She was cute and funny, but what if she went into psycho stalker mode like Glenn Close in *Fatal Attraction* if he kissed her?

Ian: *Keep in touch. I'll text you when we narrow the Liber-tys. Ping me once an hour so I know if you still have signal. If you disappear, I'll have Dax get to work on the cell towers.*

Jared: *Roger that. Thanks, boss.*

Ian: *I always take care of my own.*

Much appreciated, Jared replied.

That was the reason he would work at Black Defense International until he either retired or died. BDI was his family. The only family he had left these days. The only family he needed—even if he sometimes wished for more.

Chapter Seven

"Here, put these socks on."

Libby looked up from the book—she'd been reading the same paragraph for the past twenty minutes because she kept dozing off—to find Jared standing over her, holding out a pair of long socks.

"Okay. Why?" She took the socks and dropped the book to the cushion.

"Your ankles are exposed."

Libby arched a brow. "Are you suffering from some kind of Victorian prudery? Do my ankles disturb you?"

He snorted a laugh. "Not in the least. But it's cold and I thought you might want to cover up that bit of skin between your yoga pants and your running socks."

It's true that her ankles were feeling a little cold. Her pants ended right above the ankle, and her socks were meant not to show over the top of her shoe—which meant that she had a good three inches of skin exposed. She'd had them curled beneath her on the couch, but every time she walked around the cabin, there was a cool breeze on her skin.

She tugged on his big crew socks, uncaring that the heel was somewhere around her achilles tendon, or that they didn't look particularly fashionable with her yoga pants. Did she care about fashion? She didn't know, but she suspected she cared about warmth a lot more.

"Thank you," she said.

"You're welcome."

"You wouldn't have women's jeans and a parka hidden anywhere, would you?"

"Nope. Sorry."

Libby stretched until she regretted it. "Yowch, that's sore."

Jared retrieved two Tylenol from his medical kit. "Take these."

"No more muscle relaxers?"

"I'll give you one of those at bedtime."

"Fine." Libby swallowed the Tylenol with water and leaned back on the couch. "Did your boss have any information about me?"

Jared sat opposite her and kicked his feet up on the coffee table. "There are eight women named Liberty in the DC metro area. None have been reported missing yet. He's tracking it down."

"You think I came from DC?"

"He doesn't think you came from around here. No Libertys. Unless you're mistaken on the name, in which case you could be from anywhere."

Libby frowned. "Maybe I am mistaken. Why doesn't

my necklace say Liberty? Maybe I'm just plain old Libby. Named after a grandma or something."

"Could be. But we'll go with what we've got right now. If that doesn't turn up anything, we'll think of another tactic."

"Sounds methodical."

"It is. You don't get anything done by applying a scattershot approach."

She kind of felt like her life was lived through a scattershot approach, though she didn't know for sure. "Do you think we're going to be stuck out here for long?"

"A day or two, maybe. It's remote, but the main road's necessary to the local economy. There are usually a few Bubbas with plows on their vehicles. Between them and the transportation department, I think they'll get it cleared up as soon as the snow stops falling. But we've got enough food and fuel. We'll be fine."

"Are you always so confident?"

"Yeah, pretty much. That's a good thing, by the way. When I'm worried, you can worry. Relax."

She blew out a breath. She felt like maybe she was a worrier by nature, but there was definitely something about a strong man who oozed confidence. "I'll try."

Libby looked up at the top windows. All she could see was snow coming down in big fat flakes. It was getting darker now that the afternoon was wearing thin, but the snow fooled you into thinking it was lighter outside than it was.

"Seems like a lot of snow," she said.

Jared stood and went over to slip one of the curtains

to the side so he could peer out. "It's steady. Nothing to fear."

When he turned around again, the lights flickered. A second later, they blinked out.

It was a lot darker in the room with the lights out and the curtains closed. Libby shivered. She wasn't cold, but she didn't like how it felt to be without power with the snow coming down steadily. Hadn't she seen documentaries where people froze to death in weather like this? Not to mention she'd been out in it dressed in clothes that wouldn't keep a mouse warm for long.

Jared grabbed his coat from the hook by the door. "I'll start the generator."

"Can I do anything to help?"

Not that she felt like she could do much with the way her body ached, but if he needed help, she wanted to offer. She could at least try.

"Stay here. That's all you need to do. I'll be back in a few minutes."

When he closed the door, Libby grabbed a folded blanket and pulled it up to her chin. She didn't like the hard knot in her belly, or the way dread tried to close around her throat and choke the breath from her.

———

JARED GOT THE GENERATOR GOING, brought in more wood, and stoked the fire. Libby sat silent, staring at the flames as if transfixed.

He could tell she was worried. He didn't know why,

but he figured it was a gut deep thing she couldn't control. Somewhere in her past, she'd been stranded and afraid. Or maybe it was as recent as last night when she'd been out in the snow alone and injured. He hadn't completely ruled out an abusive boyfriend, even if she didn't seem afraid of him whenever he was near. Just because his mother had always been nervous around men after his dad left didn't mean another woman would react the same.

The lamps burned brightly and the darkness had been chased into the corners, but she seemed pensive. If he knew her better, he'd sit beside her and put his arm around her, offer some human warmth to chase away the chill inside. He knew how welcome that could be when everything seemed dark and frightening. But he didn't know her, and he didn't want to make a wrong move. She trusted him, but it was a tentative trust. If he made her afraid of him, it would make the next couple of days more difficult than they were already going to be.

Jared dragged a hand over his head. For a man who'd wanted peace and quiet, he was getting anything but. He was going to need a retreat from his retreat the way this was going. And yet there was something about Libby's chatter that he missed when she wasn't doing it.

"You okay?"

She turned her head. She had the blanket beneath her chin and she smiled weakly. "Fine. You?"

"Perfectly. But I'm not the one who looks worried about something."

Her brow furrowed. "I think I don't like how isolated we are. And that we have no power. When the lights were on, I could pretend everything was normal."

"We have lights, heat, and food. It'll be fine."

"But what if the generator stops working? Or what if it runs out of gas? Then what?"

"Even without lights, we have a cord of firewood and a gas stove. We can stay warm and eat."

She nibbled her lip. He watched, feeling oddly fascinated by the sight. There was a flicker of interest deep inside, no matter how much he might want to deny it. He didn't know what it was about this woman, but he was drawn in by her gestures, her laughter, her chatter—and even her silence.

"I guess we'd have to be stranded for a month or so to really be in trouble, right?"

"At least. And we won't be, Libby. Look at this like a snow day from work. It's bad right now and the snow trucks can't keep up, so it's best to stay home. But in a day or two, the main arteries are clear and people are heading back to work and school. I've been in far worse situations, believe me."

She looked interested. "Really? Like what?"

He leaned back in his chair and watched the flame. He'd been in worse situations, yes. But which ones could he actually tell her about without scaring the piss out of her?

"I had to go to Alaska for a mission once," he began. "We were after a guy who'd done some bad things, and he was heading into the wilderness. He was a survivalist and he had a two day head start."

"What kind of bad things?"

"Not important to the story." And not something he could talk about either. National security shit to do with satellites and top secret facilities. "What is important is that there were two of us in pursuit, and on the fifth day, when we'd left the last supply station behind two days before that, our snowmobiles stopped running."

"Both of them? At the same time?"

He nodded. "Yep. Rascal and I were in a bit of a bind. Our snowmobiles had been sabotaged, but it was so subtle as to not be apparent until they quit. Which they did in the middle of nowhere. We had a tent and enough food for two weeks, but no way out except on skis. And there was a blizzard coming."

Her eyes were big. "What did you do?"

"We radioed for help, but we had to dig in and build a shelter. The wind was brutal, and the cold was biting. We huddled in that shelter for two days with no external heat and only MREs. We were both pretty worried we weren't going to survive, but then it happened."

She was holding her breath. "What?"

"The storm broke, the sun came out, and we survived. We found our survivalist. He drove his snow-mobile off a cliff, probably due to low visibility, and broke a leg. He froze to death because he couldn't move."

Libby's eyes were huge now. "Oh my god, that's horrible."

Jared shrugged. He kind of wished he hadn't told her that last part. Too late now. "He was a horrible person, Libby. He caused deaths, even if he didn't pull the trigger himself. And he betrayed his country. He would have caused more death and destruction if he hadn't been stopped."

"It sounds like a *Mission Impossible* movie."

Jared laughed. "Sometimes it does."

"What's an MRE?"

"It's a prepackaged meal ready to eat used by the military. No microwave or heat source necessary."

She accepted that information and moved on. Typical Libby, he was coming to realize. "And your friend is named Rascal?"

"It's a call sign or code name, whatever you prefer to think of it as. A lot of guys in Special Ops have them instead of using their given names."

"Do you?"

He should have known she would ask. "I did."

She gave him a look. "And?"

He hadn't used the name in a long time, for many reasons, but he suddenly wanted to say it aloud again. He wanted to hear it for the first time in years. "It was Knight with a K. I don't use it anymore."

"Why not? It sounds pretty cool to me."

He didn't know what to say. The name felt good on his tongue, and yet he'd left it behind when he'd left the Air Force. "I just don't. It's part of my past, not my present."

"How did you get it?"

He went to poke the fire, wishing he'd never mentioned it. He should have known she wouldn't let it be. Libby was curious and she asked questions. Lots of questions. But there were too many feelings tangled up with that name, and he wasn't prepared to examine them right now. "It's not important," he said, a bit more sharply than he'd intended.

She was quiet for a long moment. He didn't turn to look at her. He heard the rustle of papers. "Okay, if you say so."

He turned. "Libby—"

"No, it's fine. I think I'm going to get back to the book now. I need to know what happens to these people."

She didn't speak again. He didn't either, mostly because he didn't know what to say. He poked the fire and called himself an asshole for telling her his call sign in the first place if he didn't intend to explain it. But it wasn't an easy thing to say aloud. He didn't like failing, and what'd happened to make him stop using the name represented the biggest failure of his military career.

He closed his eyes and said the words to himself, like he had so many times before. He was called Knight because he always swooped in like a knight in shining armor to save the people who needed him. It was his mission, his calling. But that day in the Hindu Kush, that last brutal mission where his PJ squad had been dropped in to help a SEAL team taking heavy fire, he hadn't saved anyone.

Instead, he'd almost lost his own life. The fighting had raged for hours, and nothing his squad did changed the balance. They were overwhelmed. In the end, there weren't many SEALs or PJs who'd made it out of that battle alive. It had been an extraordinary failure. Not solely his, of course. A top-down failure of leadership, intelligence, and strategy that cost too many lives.

He'd survived the battle, but he hadn't let anyone call him Knight since.

Chapter Eight

Libby lay on the couch and listened to the wind howling through the trees and over the roof. She had no idea what time it was, but it was late. When she'd started to fall asleep, Jared had told her to stay on the couch for the night. He'd had to turn off the heat pump because it drew too much power from the generator. They were limited to the fireplace, which was plenty warm.

She'd slept for a while, but something had awakened her a few moments ago. Her heart raced as she strained to hear sound, but all she heard was the wind. She pushed herself up slowly, her body protesting. Jared had given her another muscle relaxer, and that helped, but she still had aches and pains. There was a bruise on her right hip that went partway down her thigh. It was just beginning to purple, so it would look worse in a day or two. She'd asked Jared if he thought the bruises on her arm were fingerprints, but he'd only looked at her with a hard expression and said he wasn't sure.

She did feel better though. The cuts on her head

and neck didn't throb as much anymore. Jared had looked at them again and pronounced them free of infection. She had him to thank for that. She was grateful to him, but he confused her too. He was prickly and growly, but also kind when necessary. He was really good at soothing her fears.

Carefully, she stood. A movement by the window startled her and she let out a little gasp.

"It's just me," Jared said as he moved back into the light.

Her heart thumped again. "I know."

"You seem surprised. Do you need something?"

"I didn't see you there. I was going to the restroom."

He nodded, and she left him and went to do her business. When she returned, he was lying on the other couch, hand behind his head, watching the fresh logs he'd tossed onto the fire catch and flare bright.

Libby crawled beneath the covers and pulled them up to her chin. The couch wasn't especially comfortable, but it wasn't too bad. At least her entire body fit on it. Unlike Jared, whose legs hung over the side when he lay on his back.

"What time is it?" she asked.

"A little after three."

"Wow, I thought it was later."

"Nope. We've got a few hours until daylight."

"I thought I heard something when I woke up."

"Wolves. They're howling extra loud tonight. Or so it seems."

She had a vision of wolves—or maybe it was coyotes —under a full moon that hung over a field. There was a farmhouse, and two men with shotguns heading into the field because a cow was missing.

"Liberty, stay inside with your mother." The words echoed in her head, the man's voice firm and commanding. And maybe a little cold.

"Sounds like a memory."

She hadn't realized she'd spoken the words. Her face was hot with embarrassment. "I think it might be. Either that or I'm replaying a movie plot in my head."

It didn't feel like a movie. It felt real. She closed her eyes. If only she could remember *more*. Who was she? What was she doing in a snowy forest in thin clothing and running shoes? What the hell was going on?

Tears stung her eyes. She swiped them angrily. She felt so helpless and out of control.

"They called me Knight because I was a pararescueman, or PJ," Jared said, his voice deep and reassuring in the stillness. "That's the Air Force equivalent of a Navy SEAL—except we're who gets called when the SEALs are in trouble. We're combat medics and warriors, and we show up to save the day when it goes to shit. I was always a knight in shining armor until the day I wasn't."

Libby realized she was holding her breath. She let it out slowly. "I'm sorry."

"Don't be. It's part of the job. It was a bad situation, and a lot of men didn't make it out. I did. I haven't felt like anyone's savior since."

She didn't know what to say. She was always full of questions—she had them now—but none of them seemed appropriate. "You didn't have to tell me."

"Maybe not, but I was short with you earlier. I shouldn't have been."

"I talk a lot. Maybe I deserved it."

His blue eyes were piercing in the light from the fire. "No, I don't think you did. You might talk a lot, but so what? Some people talk and some don't. We're all different."

He made her glow inside. "You're a really nice guy, Jared. I hope you know that."

"I'm not always, but there's no reason not to be nice to you. It's not your fault you're here, and it's not your fault you can't remember."

"I keep hoping it'll all come flooding back. Just a single moment and boom, Libby knows who she is." She bit the inside of her lip. "I hope I like myself. What if I'm awful?"

"I doubt that very much. If you're awful, you don't stop being awful because you can't remember. And I haven't seen anything to make me think you're awful."

"I'm afraid," she admitted. "Afraid of remembering how I got here. It can't have been good."

"I understand—but remembering *is* good, Libby. You need to know who you are and where you came from so you know where you're going."

She heard the wisdom in his statement, yet she still feared the unknown. So many possibilities.

"I feel like I'm in limbo. I don't know who I am, who my friends and family are, or where I live. I don't know if anyone is looking for me, or if they even know I'm gone. I see you using your phone, and I feel like I should have one too—but I don't. It's lost, along with my memory. It's been more than twenty-four hours since you found me and I still don't know."

"You will. Trust me."

"What happens if I don't remember?"

"First, you will. At some point, you will. Second, your identity won't stay secret for long. We all have a digital presence, Libby. You have a job, a life. Even if you live alone and work from home, you have a digital footprint. It's not hard to find, and my guys are the best. They'll get the answers. Besides, there's always DNA testing if nothing else comes up. One way or the other, we'll know who you are in a matter of days."

She should be relieved that he had the answers. But she wasn't. Fear of the unknown sat heavy in her heart, filling her with dread. It was a long while before she slept again.

―――――

IT WAS GETTING LIGHTER outside when Jared's phone pinged. He'd lost signal hours ago so he knew a text meant the cell tower was back. Either through the work of the phone company or Dax. Jared didn't care which, he was just glad to have it.

The text was from Ian, shortly before midnight. *Liberty King. She's the only one not accounted for. 25, 5'5", dark blond hair, 140 pounds. Admin assistant at Ninja Solutions in Chantilly, VA. They're a tech firm working on military AI applications. Lives alone in apartment in Arlington. Not a Gemini assassin. Let me know when you get this.*

Jared typed back. *Got it. She still hasn't remembered who she is.*

Liberty King. She'd been right about the name. What the hell was an admin assistant from the DC metro area doing in the Shenandoahs dressed in running clothes? It wasn't necessarily anything sinister, but something didn't feel right.

A fight with a boyfriend was still a possibility, of course. Or maybe she'd been kidnapped by a predator when she'd gone out for a run. A predator she'd somehow escaped.

Ian's reply came back. *She hasn't been reported missing yet. Her car is at her apartment building. Her cell phone is dead, but last known location is near Culpeper.*

Jared: *So someone grabbed her. And hurt her in the process.*

Raped her? Possibly. The thought filled him with hot rage. Not that she'd mentioned any vaginal trauma symptoms, but she could be too embarrassed to discuss bleeding or pain with him. And there weren't always signs of trauma, though considering she had other bruises, it would have been more likely there'd be *something* going on.

Ian: *Don't have much on her yet, but it seems most likely scenario. Question is why.*

Jared: *I'd really like to know that too. Why and who.*

He'd kick some ass if he found whoever had done this to her. Make them wish they'd never laid eyes on Libby King. He hadn't been able to do that for his mother because he'd been too young, but he damn sure didn't have that problem these days.

Ian: *Keep pinging me. I think the tower is solid, but if we get more snow, could go out again.*

Jared: *Copy.*

Jared tossed the phone onto the cushion and got up to visit the restroom and make coffee. Once the coffee was brewing, he returned to stoke the fire and add a couple of logs. The living room was warm, but the bathroom had been pretty damn chilly. Libby was sound asleep. She lay on her side, her legs curled beneath her, her arms under her pillow. Her hair was dark gold where it spilled over the pillow. She had a bruise forming on her head where the bandage sat, but otherwise her face was unmarked.

Under different circumstances, he might want to ask her out, see how it went. It was true she talked a hell of a lot, but it wasn't as annoying as he'd anticipated. He was pretty sure she'd have never read *War and Peace* on her own, but she was reading it and talking about it now, even if she'd rather watch television. He liked a woman who adapted to the situation without complaint.

He hoped she'd wake up with the knowledge of who she was, but if she didn't, he would tell her what he knew. It might jiggle something free.

He'd seen this kind of amnesia before, always trauma related. It went away within hours, sometimes days, but it always went away. Except for the kind of amnesia that followed an accident or violent encounter where someone couldn't remember the events immediately preceding or the aftermath. He'd seen people lose days that way, often permanently.

He'd never seen anyone lose who they were, however.

Jared got his coat and went outside to check on the generator and replenish the wood on the front porch. They still had gas and the generator was humming along. The snow was thick on the ground, but it had stopped falling. The only flakes coming down now were those that blew off the trees. He trudged down the driveway until he reached the main road. It wasn't as bad as he'd anticipated, but it wasn't great either. Maybe the plows would come through sometime today.

Jared returned to the house and stomped the snow from his boots before going inside. The smell of coffee greeted him. Libby was sitting upright on the couch, blanket tucked around her, cup of coffee in hand. She smiled at him.

"Good morning," she said brightly.

"Morning."

He waited, hoping she'd tell him she'd remembered who she was—but she didn't. He poured a cup and went over to sit on the opposite couch. The fire blazed.

"What time is it?" she asked.

"A little after seven."

"Is it still snowing?"

"Nope. Looks like the storm moved out after all. Nothing more predicted for the next few days."

"We'll be able to leave soon, right?"

"It'd be best if we wait until they clear the main road." His four-wheel drive would do it, but it'd be a harrowing trip.

"Right. Of course." She lowered her coffee to her

lap and sighed. "I still don't remember anything. It's frustrating."

"My boss texted." Her head snapped up, her eyes lighting with anticipation. "You were right. Your name *is* Liberty. Liberty King."

"Liberty King," she repeated. "It doesn't sound familiar at all. What else do you know?"

"You're an admin assistant at a tech firm in Chantilly called Ninja Solutions. You live in an apartment in Arlington."

"Okay, so I have a job. That's good. And I live in Arlington. Do I live alone?"

"Yes."

"Not married then. And probably not in a serious relationship because wouldn't we live together? Of course we would."

"Unless you have personal reasons, like religious beliefs, that prohibit it. Though I think you're right since a serious boyfriend would have noticed you were gone."

She frowned. "No one's reported me missing then. What else did you find out? Do you know how I got here?"

He didn't want to scare her, but at the same time he needed her to know that whatever had happened to her, it was probably serious. "No, not really. Your car is still at your apartment building. But your phone's last known location was Culpeper. It's likely, though not one-hundred percent certain, that someone brought you here against your will."

Her eyes were wide. "Why would anyone do that?"

"I don't know why specifically, but there are certainly

reasons why pretty young women are forced into vehicles and taken to remote places."

The color drained from her face. "I don't remember any of it, but what if someone—?"

His gut twisted. "I can't lie and tell you that you weren't sexually assaulted, but there could have been physical signs you'd have noticed if someone raped you."

He listed the symptoms she might have if someone had forced his way into her body. It made him sick to have to say it, but he had no choice.

She shook her head and some of the color returned to her cheeks. "No, none of that. There's nothing going on down there that shouldn't be going on."

"You're sure?"

"I'm sure. I admit the idea scared me, but there's nothing that makes me think I've had sex with anyone recently. Hell, I don't even know if I've *ever* had sex." Her cheeks grew rosier at that statement. "Well, okay then. I'm Liberty King. Libby King."

He recognized that she was embarrassed and trying to move on, so he didn't stop her. He thought if she'd had any of the symptoms he'd mentioned, she would have swallowed her embarrassment and let him know so he could treat her. At least he hoped so anyway.

Her gaze was bright. "I wish we could leave right now. I want to see where I live. I want to go through my things, change my clothes, find my phone. I must have contacts—friends, family, people who could tell me more about myself."

"I'm sure you do. When we can get out of here, I'll take you home."

Her expression clouded for an instant. "You're the only person I know right now. Please don't drop me off and leave me if I still haven't remembered."

"I won't, Libby."

"Do you promise?"

"I promise." How could he leave her? Until he knew how she'd gotten up here, he couldn't drop her off at home like nothing was amiss. He wouldn't leave her until he was certain she was safe and comfortable.

"How do you feel today?" he asked.

"Still sore, but not as bad as yesterday."

"Let me look at your head."

She was still as he peeled off the bandage and inspected the area. It was scabbing over nicely. He moved on to her neck. Same deal there.

"Will there be a scar?"

"Shouldn't be."

"Thanks again for all your help, Jared. If you hadn't found me, I'd have frozen to death out there."

"You didn't, though. You're safe. We'll get you home and back to your life in no time."

"I hope so. I want to remember. I hope I like where I live and work. What if I don't?" She looked genuinely concerned.

"Then you make changes."

"You make it sound so easy. Maybe it is. Maybe I've been stuck in a rut and this is just what I needed to get me out of it." She was back to sounding cheerful again.

He admired how she could take lemons and make lemonade. His mom would have liked her.

That thought stopped him in his tracks. Why was he thinking about what his mom's impression of her would be?

Probably because she was gone, and because Libby was the first woman he'd ever met that he thought his mom might find interesting. He'd had girlfriends as a teenager, but that wasn't the same thing. His mom had been gone before he'd become an adult, so he'd never know what she thought about any woman he dated.

In the distance, the baying of a dog echoed through the trees, slicing into his thoughts like a hot knife.

Libby jumped at the sound. "Is that a wolf?"

Jared listened, his blood chilling. "No."

She looked relieved. He was anything but. He recognized that sound. It was the sound of a dog tracking a scent.

Could be any scent. Could be a hunting dog going after prey.

But every instinct he had told him this dog was hunting a person.

Chapter Nine

"WHAT'S WRONG, JARED?"

He was utterly still, a look of concentration on his face. "I need you to get your shoes on. Put on the socks I gave you first. Put your jacket on, too."

Libby's heart raced as fear spiked. It was bad enough to know she'd probably been abducted and brought here against her will, but watching Jared now, that fear multiplied tenfold. He'd said he was a warrior, but that hadn't meant anything to her.

Until now.

He strode into the bedroom he'd claimed for his own, returning with a sweatshirt he threw at her. "Put this on over the jacket."

He dropped a bag on the floor and unzipped it. A moment later he was yanking guns from the interior, shoving bullets into the weapons, and dropping them beside him like his own mini-arsenal. The sheer number of weapons stunned her. She wasn't scared of them, though. Perhaps she really had grown up on a farm.

In the distance, the braying dog was joined by another one. And was that a snowmobile?

She didn't know what was going on, but she hesitated only a second before she did as Jared told her, fear a hard knot in her belly. She dragged the sweatshirt over her head, clawed it down until it draped over her hips. That was when she noticed Jared removing a big rifle from a case.

It was wicked looking, with a long scope and a tripod that he could unfold to prop it up. The barrel had a lot of holes in it. He glanced at her, his expression grim.

"What's going on?" she whispered, her throat too tight to speak properly. She couldn't get past the idea someone had forcibly brought her here, and it colored everything. She told herself that whatever he was doing didn't necessarily have anything to do with her, but deep down she knew it did.

"I don't know, but I mean to find out." He inserted a long metal piece filled with bullets into the rifle until it snapped into place with an audible click. Then he slung it around his body until it was across his back before bending to pick up the other weapons. Somehow he put several of them on his person. "Do you know how to shoot?"

Libby swallowed. "I-I don't know."

He took one of the weapons, dropped something from inside the handle, and held it up. "This is a magazine. It has bullets in it." He dropped it into his pocket. "Now pull the top of the gun back toward you. Like this," he said. He pulled and released a couple of times, then aimed at a kitchen cabinet before pulling the trigger. The gun clicked.

"Your turn." He handed it to her. It was difficult to pull at first because the top of the gun was tight, but he showed her how to hold it so she could put more muscle behind it. When she had that trick down, she repeated the motions he'd shown her.

Jared nodded. "You just cleared the weapon and dry-fired it. Now you put this magazine in and pull back the slide when you want to fire. Release it and you've loaded the chamber. Then point and squeeze the trigger. Preferably without closing your eyes."

He handed her the loaded magazine and she pushed it into the grip with shaking hands until it clicked.

"Don't pull the slide yet. This is a Glock-19. There's no safety on it so I don't want you standing around with a bullet in the chamber. Never point a gun at anything you don't intend to kill, even when it's empty. And don't shoot unless you have no other choice. Once you've fired it, the next bullet will go into the chamber—so be careful. It's loaded and ready at that point. Only shoot if you have to."

She felt like her eyes were huge. "What does that mean exactly?"

"It means that if anything happens and we're separated, you use that on anyone who tries to hurt you. And keep using it until they stop coming for you. The magazine is a double-stack, so you've got fifteen bullets in there. Don't try to save them."

The dogs and snowmobiles were growing louder.

She was cold, but sweat popped up between her breasts anyway. "Who would want to hurt me?"

"Maybe no one. But I prefer to be prepared."

Libby sucked in a breath. "I'm scared." Maybe she shouldn't admit it, but it was too huge a thing to ignore. She didn't know who she was, other than a name and occupation, but she was pretty sure she didn't encounter dangerous situations very often. She wasn't a warrior.

Jared wrapped an arm around her and tugged her against his side. It was unexpected, but welcome. When he dropped a kiss on her forehead, she couldn't help the shiver of delight that tripped down her spine.

Stupid time to be pleased, Libby.

"I know," he said softly. "But this is what I do. It's like winning the lottery, Libby. You happened upon the right guy at the right time. There's a lot in this world I can't do, but this is something I'm trained for and highly skilled at. No one's getting to you without going through me. And that's not an easy thing to do, I promise you."

———

THE DOGS and snowmobiles were getting closer. The dogs brayed, following the scent they'd been given. Jared had grabbed a small pair of binoculars and stood with them to the glass, sweeping across the view as he waited for a sighting of the men heading toward the cabin.

He hoped there weren't too many of them. He could fight them off, but the more there were, the more difficult it would be. And it would draw attention to their location because the fight wasn't going to be quiet. He didn't want to use any explosive devices, but he would if necessary.

He gave one longing look at his truck and shook his head. It was four-wheel drive and he'd make it out of the driveway given enough time—but they didn't have that kind of time. Plus, if he got to the road and it was impassable, they'd be sitting ducks.

The safer option was staying in the cabin, no matter how much he hated that idea. He'd texted Ian to let him know there was a potential problem, but it hadn't gone out. Jared looked at his phone and hit the screen to try again. Not that Ian could do anything to help, but at least he'd know they were in trouble.

"I can't believe you go on a solitary retreat with a whole arsenal of weapons," Libby said from behind him.

He glanced back at her. She sat on the floor because he'd told her to. She'd lain the gun on the floor beside her. She was currently staring at the weapons placed side by side in the center of the floor. The ones he hadn't managed to put in holsters on his body.

"It's part of the job."

"But the whole idea of a retreat is not to be working. Right?"

Jared arched an eyebrow. "And suppose I took my retreats with no weapons. Where would we be now?"

She frowned. "We'd be fucked."

He didn't anticipate the primal reaction snaking its way through him at that word on her lips. But he liked it.

"Yeah, fucked," he repeated. "And not the good kind."

She blinked rapidly and glanced away. Her cheeks flushed. It was a mystery to him how she could be so damned talkative and yet blush at any hint of innuendo. Though it was also a good thing after the talk they'd had just a few minutes ago.

"Sorry," he said. "Now's not the time for jokes."

She jerked her gaze back to him. "Oh, I think it's definitely the time for jokes."

"Yeah, but sex makes you uncomfortable, so I was out of line."

Her jaw dropped. "What makes you think that?"

He turned back to the window. Nothing visible yet, but they would appear any moment now. "Because you blushed. Just like yesterday when I saw your panties before I put them in the wash."

Any sign of discomfort or unease, and he wouldn't be teasing her. But there wasn't—plus it kept her from dwelling on what was happening right now.

"It was obvious, huh?"

"It was," he murmured, scanning the forest.

"To be fair, we don't know each other and you were handling my underwear. It was a bit disconcerting."

"Clearly."

A dog's head appeared, and then another. Labrador retrievers. Black. Two men on snowmobiles appeared behind them. A third brought up the rear. Same two men from yesterday plus one. *Shit.*

"I want you to lie flat on your stomach on the floor. Beside the couch," Jared said, not turning around.

"Cosy up to it as close as you can get. And don't move, no matter what. The only way you move is if I tell you to, got it?"

"I—yes."

Jared slid the AR-15 from his shoulders and propped it beside the door. Then he grabbed the beer he'd set on the floor and slipped out the door as the dogs and men headed straight for the cabin. He was pretty sure they weren't going to shoot him on sight, but he didn't stray from the door just in case. He'd left it open slightly so he could reach the rifle. Now he stood with the beer and pretended to be interested in what was going on.

The dogs approached, barking incessantly. The man on the third snowmobile called to them and they turned and loped back to him. The other two men came closer, sliding to a halt and looking at Jared triumphantly.

"Hey, man," Jared said, slurring his words a little. "Y'all find them hogs?"

The bearded man's eyes stayed narrow but the other one scratched his chin. "Seems like it, buddy."

The dogs were with the third guy now, but they were still restless. Probably hunting dogs rather than trackers —the kind that searched for deer blood—but they'd done the job.

"Thought you said you was alone," Beard said.

"I am."

Beard shook his head and slid his hand around to the rifle across his back.

Aw, damn. So much for bluffing his way out of this. Jared whipped his Sig Sauer P320 with the laser site out of the holster and aimed a bead at the man's forehead.

"Wouldn't do that if I were you."

"Shit," the other guy swore. "There's a dot on your forehead, dude."

Jared wasted no time dropping the beer and drawing a Glock with the other hand. He pointed this one at the man who'd just spoken. The guy with the dogs blinked. Probably deciding whether or not to go for his gun. Jared hoped he didn't. But if he did, Jared would drop these two and go for him.

"No dot on this one, I'm afraid," Jared drawled, jerking his chin toward the Glock. "But the aim is just as deadly. Hands up, both of you."

They slowly obeyed.

"Man, I don't know who you are, but you have no clue who you're fucking with," Beard said in a nasty voice. "Just give us the girl and we'll go. We've got no quarrel with you."

"Got no girl here, like I said. It's just me. And I'd say you're the ones who have no idea who you're fucking with."

"You're lying. The dogs tracked her here."

"Those are hunting dogs, not bloodhounds. How do you fucking know they got it right?"

Obviously the dogs had, but giving them props for being good dogs wasn't in his best interest right now. It definitely wasn't in Libby's.

"They're right," the third man called out. "She came here. And she's inside that cabin now."

"Guess it's my word against theirs."

Dog Man started to ease his hand across his abdomen.

"You go for your gun, I'm dropping these two and then dropping you."

"Huh. You ain't that good." Beard this time.

"Oh yeah? Don't have to be though, do I? You've still got a one in three chance of making it out alive. But honestly, man, I don't like your fucking face. I'll make sure I hit you before these two."

"Look," the guy on the snowmobile beside Beard said. "Our quarrel isn't with you. This girl you're protecting—she stole some stuff and we want it back. That's all."

"Must be mighty important for you to go to all this trouble."

"It's important. And she's a thief."

"Let's say there is a girl inside," Jared replied. "How'd she get those cuts and bruises? You boys been beating up on a woman?"

"You just hand her over and don't worry about it," Beard said.

Jared's gut churned with fury. He knew enough about Libby now, both from her chattering and from what Ian had found out, to know she wasn't the criminal here. These fuckers were. He had no problem putting an end to people like that.

"Naw, man, not the way I'm feeling about it. Tell you what, you motherfuckers get moving in the direction you came and I won't shoot you. You show your faces around here again, and I definitely will. In case you're wondering if I can manage it, spent ten years in a special forces unit. Dropped more fucking tangos than I can remember. Adding you to the pile won't be a problem."

The guy beside Beard flared his nostrils. "You're making a mistake, man."

"Not the way I see it. Start backing up. Slowly."

The men stared at him with hard jaws as they lowered their hands to the bars. They put the snowmobiles in reverse. It was a slow process, but they kept reversing until they'd dropped out of sight over the hill. Jared holstered the handguns and reached inside for the AR. Sure enough, the sound of the snowmobiles split, one going right and one left. One idled where it was.

Stupid fuckers. They were planning to return. Hoping to surprise him with a three-pronged approach. These guys were soldiers of fortune, not the kind with real world experience. They might have done a stint in the military, but not the special forces. They were average—and average wasn't going to cut it with him.

"Are they gone?"

Libby's voice sounded from the other side of the door and Jared growled. "Get down, Libby. They're coming back."

"They said I stole something. I don't know what they're talking about but I don't want you to get hurt because of me. I'm sure I could convince them I don't have whatever it is they want. Because I don't. You know that."

He did know it, but it didn't matter. "They aren't the kind of men you convince, honey. If they get through me, they're going to hurt you. They aren't going to listen to anything you say."

"What are you going to do?"

"Lie on the floor like I told you, Libby. Don't get up no matter what you hear. Anybody comes through this door but me, you drop them."

The snowmobiles shifted into high gear almost at once.

"Go, Libby! Now!"

Chapter Ten

Jared heard her footsteps retreating as quickly as she could. He hoped she did what he told her, but he had no time to check. It wasn't easy to separate which snowmobile was coming from where, but he raised the gun to his shoulder and waited, sweeping the perimeter with the scope.

The first one topped the rise, the man lying low over the machine. He had a pistol in his hand. Jared squeezed the trigger. The bullet hit its target and the man slumped over the side, dropping into the snow. The snowmobile kept going until it came into contact with a tree.

The next two snowmobiles appeared, both men lying low like the first. They were coming at him from opposite directions, but that didn't matter. Jared aimed and fired, aimed and fired again, with the kind of precision that only came from long hours on a range in all kinds of conditions.

Both men dropped, same as the first. Both snowmobiles slid to a stop, which meant the riders had been using the kill switch cords attached to their jackets.

Jared stalked off the porch, gun still at his shoulder, and headed for the closest man. It was Dog Man, and he lay gasping in pain, blood streaming from a wound in his shoulder. The other two men weren't moving at all.

"Looks painful," Jared said.

"Fuck you."

"Hey, told you not to try it. You want me to put you out of your misery or leave you in case someone comes along?"

"Fuck off, asshole!"

Jared reached down and removed the weapon lying useless near the man's arm, ejected the magazine and threw it over the rise. He took a picture of the serial number on the gun, then threw that as well. He'd do the same with the other weapons when he got to them.

Jared grabbed the man's ID from his pocket, snapped a picture of it, and dropped it. He went to the next man. It was Beard, and he stared up at the trees with glassy eyes. Jared took care of the weapons, fished around for an ID, found it, and snapped a picture. He did the same with the last guy, also dead, then returned to Dog Man.

"What does she have, Robert? Or do you prefer Rob?" he asked as he squatted next to the injured man.

"Fuck off."

"I'm a medic. I can fix that for you. Wrap you up and leave you here with a fighting chance."

The guy's eyes widened for a hopeful second before narrowing again. "You're lying."

"Same as I was lying about dropping all three of you if you returned, right?"

"You lied about the girl."

Jared scratched his chin. "Yeah, I did, didn't I? Guess you got a fifty-fifty shot at me helping you then. Tell me what you want with the girl and I'll dress the wound."

He could see the guy considering it.

"You don't want your dogs to suffer, do you? I know you must have tied them up somewhere." As if on cue, one of the dogs barked. The other started too.

The guy looked worried. "Don't hurt them."

"Hey, what do you take me for? I don't hurt innocent animals. But I can't take them with me, so I'll have to let them go. I think they'll make it if I do, but who knows?"

He was definitely lying now. He wouldn't leave the dogs. He'd pile them in the truck and take them somewhere he could safely leave them if it came down to it.

"I don't know what she's got. I just know it's important. I was only here to track her down with the dogs."

"Uh-huh. And what were they going to do with her when they got what they wanted?"

The man's lids dropped over his eyes. Pain etched his features. Jared stood and put his foot on the guy's shoulder. Then he pressed. The man screamed.

"Better tell me, Robert."

"Dispose of her. That was the order," he gasped out.

"Who gave it?"

Robert didn't answer, so Jared started to apply pressure again. "I don't know! I don't! I'd tell you if I did, I swear." He was blubbering now. "Don't step on me again. Please don't."

Jared took his foot away. "Well, that's not much to go on, but it'll do. I'll get my medical kit."

When Jared walked up on the porch, he called out to Libby. "It's me, honey. Don't shoot."

"I won't."

He walked inside. She was at the window, peering out from the curtains, but when he entered, she flung herself at him. He caught her as she wrapped her arms around his neck and held on tight.

"Hey," he said. "It's okay."

She shuddered in his arms. "You could have been killed."

He chuckled. He liked the way she felt pressed up against him. Her body was soft in all the right places. Libby wasn't skinny. She had curves. Nice ones. And that ass he wanted to squeeze.

"Not really, but it's sweet of you to worry about me," he murmured as he nuzzled into her hair. It smelled clean, like pine and flowers, and it was silky against his face.

She pushed back and looked up at him, her eyes shining. "You sh-shot them. All of them."

"I told them I would. I'm sorry you had to witness it though."

"I didn't see you do it. But when I heard the first shot, I ran—well, hobbled—to the window."

He squeezed her for a second. "I told you to stay down."

She bit her lower lip. "I know. But I was worried."

Not about herself. About him.

"Dammit," he swore. And then he dropped his mouth to hers and did what he'd been wanting to do for hours.

She gasped, but didn't pull away. Her mouth opened beneath his and their tongues collided.

Jared stifled a groan at the sweet, silky feel of her. He swept his tongue into her mouth, tasting her. His dick went from zero to sixty in a millisecond. If they only had time…

If she'd let him, he'd strip her naked and lose himself in her body for a while. He'd make her come over and over, until she was limp and sated.

But they didn't have time. He'd taken care of the men who were searching for her, but if he knew anything about this kind of shit, there would be more of them. He wasn't waiting around for whoever they sent next. Gently, he broke the kiss. It wasn't easy with the way her arms wrapped around his neck, or the way she stretched up on tiptoe and arched her hips against his.

"No time, Libby," he said. "I need to patch that asshole up and we need to go."

"G-go? How?"

"We're gonna take my truck. If that doesn't work, we'll take the snowmobiles."

"I thought we were stuck here."

"So long as it was less dangerous to stay here than to brave the roads, we were. That's no longer the case." Once he got onto the road, if he took his time and drove carefully enough, they'd make it down the mountain. He just had to hope no one intercepted them along the way.

"Oh," she whispered.

He stepped away and went to retrieve his medical supplies. "Grab the food and put it into some bags, okay? We'll take everything we can in case we get stuck."

"Okay."

He left her to do what he'd asked while he returned to the man bleeding in the snow.

"All right, fucker," he said, dropping down beside the guy. "Let's see what we can do with you."

———

"WHAT'S GOING to happen to him?" Libby asked as she looked over at the man lying on the ground. His dogs sat on the porch, tongues out, looking perfectly content.

Jared glanced at her and then at the man. "He'll live. He's going to have to crawl into the cabin at some point, and that's going to be hell on his shoulder, but it's that or freeze."

"You left it unlocked?"

"I did."

Libby hugged herself. She was shivering, but it wasn't just the cold. She had enough clothes on. She suspected it was the aftereffects of that kiss for one thing. Maybe seeing dead bodies for another.

And knowing they'd been coming for her.

"You're a compassionate man."

He shoved the truck into gear and pressed the gas. The truck moved slowly, but it moved. He'd worked to clear the ground out to the road, using one of the snow-mobiles to drag a log he'd chained onto it. The track wasn't clear, but it was passable. "Sometimes."

She thought about that. "Why didn't you kill him?"

"I meant to. He had the good fortune to come to a dip in the ground when the bullet arrived, or it would have hit him in the heart instead of the shoulder."

Libby shivered again. Jared had been nothing but gentle with her, but seeing what he was capable of had stunned her a bit more than she'd thought it would. *He did it for you, Libby.*

Yes, he had—and she was grateful for it. But what had it cost him?

"You dressed his wound, fetched his dogs so they could stay with him, and left him with shelter. Why did you do that? You could have left him where he fell."

He glanced at her. "I could have, but he gave me some information I wanted. I thought it was a fair exchange. He's still in trouble. It could be awhile before anyone comes looking for him, and he doesn't have a cell phone to call out because I smashed it."

"Was the information about me?"

"Yes, but it wasn't much."

She processed that. "What do they think I stole?"

"He didn't know. He just knew they were supposed to get it from you."

"And then what?"

He gripped the steering wheel and didn't answer.

"Jared. I have a right to know."

"Are you sure you want to?"

She swallowed. "Yes."

"They weren't going to let you live, Libby."

Her heart throbbed as panic threatened. She pushed it down. "Maybe you should have killed him too." The moment she said it, she felt sick that she had.

"Pretty sure we won't see him again. I told him I won't miss the next time." He hesitated a moment. "He told me they didn't sexually assault you. In case you were still thinking about that. I don't think he was lying. They were more concerned with getting the information from you first. I think they would have though. Before they killed you."

She squeezed her hands in her lap. "Well, that's something then. Did he tell you what else they did?"

"Some of it, yes. I'd rather not tell you right now. I think it's important for you to remember on your own."

She wanted to argue with him, but what if he was right? He said he had experience with this kind of memory loss, and she believed that. He hadn't been wrong about anything yet. She needed to trust him, no matter how hard it was not to press for answers. She sucked in a breath. "What about the other two? What happens when the police find the bodies and that man tells them everything?"

"Nothing will happen. The people I work for will fix it."

She gaped at him. "How do you fix that, Jared? They're dead. And he's a witness!"

He turned his piercing gaze on her. "If they weren't dead, you would be. And he's not going to say anything. My people will take him into custody until this is over."

Libby closed her mouth and didn't say anything else.

There was nothing she could say. She didn't know what was going on or how to extricate herself from it. Jared was the only friend she had right now, and she was thankful he was on her side even if she didn't understand the world he lived in.

They reached the main road and turned onto it. The snow was still thick on the ground, but there were wheel ruts where a few intrepid souls had driven through. Libby stared at the forest covered in snow. Those men said she'd stolen something and they wanted it back. But what? Was she really a thief?

She didn't feel like a bad person, but maybe she was. Maybe she cheated and lied and stole and it'd finally caught up with her. Maybe she ran with criminals, and they'd turned on her. Maybe she was just as bad as they were. Under different circumstances, maybe she'd be lying in that snow beside them, the victim of a criminal enterprise gone wrong.

She thought about everything she knew. Nothing about herself, but lots of other stuff. She had impressions about herself though. At least she thought that's what they were.

A hot summer's day, a field of tall corn, running through the stalks like it was a maze. Being chased—and chasing—other children. The tall man with the deep voice who'd told her to stay inside the night the cow went missing. The woman with blond hair who seemed perpetually exasperated with her.

They had to be her parents, but she couldn't see their faces. It was more or less an impression of people that she had, not a picture. Jared said it would come back to her. She hoped he was right.

It took them over two hours to make it down the mountain. She wasn't entirely aware of it until she realized that the road had straightened. The roads were clearer here, the track slushy with the passage of many vehicles. For the first time, it occurred to her that she didn't know where they were headed.

"Are you taking me home?"

Panic and excitement filled her at the thought of going to a place where all her belongings were located. A place that would give a more complete picture of who she was. That was the excitement part. The panic part was not knowing, and not wanting to be left alone, especially when she didn't know who was looking for her or what they wanted.

"I don't think that's a good idea. Since those guys didn't get what they wanted from you, it's very likely someone will go looking for you there."

"Maybe what they wanted is at my apartment. We could get it first. If we knew what to look for."

He shook his head. "Nope, all the more reason for you not to be there."

"Where are we going then?"

"My house."

Her heart thumped. "Where do you live?"

"Maryland. Near Annapolis."

Libby looked down at her feet. His socks looked ridiculous with her yoga pants and running shoes, but at least her ankles were warm. "I need clothes. Can we at least stop at my place so I can get some things?"

"Too dangerous. Until we know who's after you and what they want, you can't be seen anywhere near your apartment."

"I can't keep wearing the same clothes." Tears pricked her eyes at the thought. She sucked them back. It wasn't really the clothing putting her emotions on edge. It was the situation. The feeling of having no control. She didn't know who she was, and she couldn't go home. She couldn't ground herself with her own things for just a few moments before leaving again.

"I know, honey. We'll swing by Walmart or Target and grab some things, okay?"

"How am I going to pay for anything? I don't have money or credit cards—or identification."

"I'll pay."

"Jared—"

"It's a loan," he cut in. "You can pay me back later."

She lay her head against the cold glass, letting the shock of it still her thoughts for a moment. "Thank you." Another thought occurred to her then. "I have a job. I need to go to it, don't I? If I don't show up, I could get fired. I can't imagine that would be a good thing."

"It's Saturday. We'll get it figured out once we're at my place and I can talk with my guys."

"Your guys," she repeated. "Who are *your guys* really, and how are they going to help me with my job?"

He shot her a look. "They're the same guys who found your name, address, and work, based on nothing more than a vague idea about your first name. Do you really think they've got nothing more to offer here?"

She closed her eyes. "You're right. I'm sorry to put

you to so much trouble. I ruined your vacation, and I'm still ruining it."

He reached over and gripped her hand where it lay on her leg. His skin was warm compared to hers. She felt like she might never thaw out again. That didn't stop the electric sizzle of attraction from dancing along her nerve endings though. She went back to that kiss, to the way he'd held her tight while he'd plundered her mouth. He'd been hard, and she'd been more than willing. She'd forgotten for a second where they were, or why he was kissing her. She'd just wanted *more*.

"You aren't ruining anything. This is what I do. I'm one of the good guys, Libby. In case you're wondering after what happened back there."

He put both hands on the wheel again, and she felt the absence of his touch in the way her skin seemed to ache without his to warm it.

"I know you are. For what it's worth, I think you should use that call sign again. You're definitely a knight in shining armor to me."

His jaw tightened. "Maybe someday."

Chapter Eleven

IT TOOK HOURS TO REACH HIS HOUSE, BUT EVERYTHING was as Jared had left it when he'd headed up to the mountains. It was dark when they arrived, but the two-story colonial looked picture perfect in the snow. The house was white, built in 1903, with a wrought iron fence and carriage lanterns. He'd gotten it for a song because it had needed so much work. Work he did between missions. Work that helped keep him sane, just like his solitary retreats kept him sane.

He drove beneath the carport and turned off the engine. Libby startled awake, blinking at her surroundings.

"We're here?"

"Yep. Let's get you inside and then I'll bring every-thing in."

"I can help."

He frowned at her. "No, you can't. You're still hurting."

And he knew why. Robert had been very forthcoming with the information when he'd realized Jared meant to save him, though his information was second-hand since he'd only joined the other two that morning. According to Robert, Beard, otherwise known as Joe, had been trying to shake Libby down for information about whatever it was she'd stolen. When she didn't tell him what he wanted to know, he'd thrown her against a wall and threatened to cut her tongue out.

She'd lost consciousness. Gaiter Guy—whose name was Luke—and Joe had started drinking, waiting for her to wake up again. When she did, Joe injected her with sodium thiopental in the belief it would make her talk. Jared had listened with a hard knot in his gut, glad he'd killed them both but wishing he'd made it hurt more.

The drugs didn't make her talk. Instead, she'd passed out again and the men kept drinking until they were too drunk to care. When they checked on her later that night, the window was open and she was gone. It was a second-story drop, which helped explained her injuries (those in addition to being thrown against a wall). She was damned lucky she hadn't broken anything.

Luke and Joe had searched for her with the snowmo-biles the next day. When they didn't find her, they'd called Robert—who was Luke's cousin—and asked him to bring his hunting dogs. They'd given him two grand when he arrived and promised him ten more when they got the girl back. That'd been good enough for him. He didn't know what they were trying to get from her and he didn't care. His cousin was former military, and Joe had been one of his buddies. They often accepted jobs from companies and individuals who needed private security or protection. Robert didn't know who'd hired them.

"I'm sore," Libby said. "But if I don't move, I'll get stiff."

"You can move once you're inside."

She folded her arms and huffed a sigh. So Libby. In pain but feisty. He reached behind him and picked up the Target bags, then handed them to her.

"You can carry your clothes. How's that?"

Her expression softened. "Oh, sure. Thanks again for buying everything."

"It's fine, Libby. You don't have to keep thanking me."

"I feel like I do," she said primly.

He didn't argue with her because he knew it wouldn't do any good. Instead, he got out of the truck and went around to open the door for her. They'd stopped at the first Target they'd found. Libby hadn't picked much. Underwear, socks, bras, a pair of jeans and a couple of shirts. He'd made her choose a couple more, plus a warm winter jacket, then had her try on boots until she found a pair she liked. When they'd gotten back in the truck, she'd fallen asleep and stayed that way for the rest of the ride.

He ushered her over to the side door and slid his key into the lock. When the door opened, he punched in his alarm code on the panel and flipped on the lights. Libby walked in behind him and stopped in the small mudroom, her gaze sliding over the washer and dryer before moving on to the coat hooks and boot tray on the other side.

"It's so neat."

He snorted. "You have a low opinion of a single man's ability to do laundry, cook, and keep a neat house. Wherever did you come by your old-fashioned notions, Libby King?"

She frowned. "I am *not* old-fashioned. At least I don't think so. But apparently the men of my acquaintance, whomever they may be, didn't live up to your example."

He snorted again and led her into the hall and toward the living room. Again, she halted in the door and gazed at everything. "Wow."

He laughed. "Don't get excited. My buddy Brett's engaged to an interior designer. She started a new business locally after moving here to be with him. One of the perks for me was getting expert advice and guidance at a significant discount. She picked everything out from discount stores and flea markets, then she styled it. I just paid for it."

Libby let her gaze wander over the tall ceilings, wood floors, and period details along with the soft furnishings and artwork. Tallie Grant had done a great job pulling together a look that said masculine but welcoming in this room. Jared wouldn't have cared either way if not for his mom. She'd loved older homes, and she'd always wanted to buy one and turn it into a space she loved. A home for them both, she'd said, even after he was grown and only came back to visit. Since she never got to do it, he did it for her.

He did a lot of things for her, but none of them were hard. He bought an old home and fixed it up, read the classics, and tried to be neat and tidy because she would have wanted him to do those things. He'd give anything to have her back again, to make her life easy and comfortable, but since it didn't work that way, he honored her memory in the best way he knew how.

"It's beautiful. I don't know why you'd want to go to a mountain cabin when you have this, but whatever."

He shrugged. "Sometimes I like silence outside my window. You don't get that here."

As if in response to his statement, a car went by, the tires sloshing in the wet road. Somewhere, a dog barked. Libby tensed, but when the dog didn't keep barking, she let out a breath.

"I see what you mean."

"If you go upstairs, the second door on the left is your room. I'll bring in the rest of the gear."

"Okay. Thank you."

"We have to share a bathroom, I'm afraid," he called after her as she started up. "Old house, old plumbing."

"We'll manage," she replied. "I promise not to hog the bathroom."

He found himself chuckling as he went outside to bring in guns, bags, and food. He liked Libby King. She made him laugh, and she puzzled him too. She talked a helluva lot. Asked a lot of questions. He'd describe her as bubbly at those times. She was super polite, and she had notions about men whether she knew it or not. But she also had her quiet (for her) spaces, the ones he couldn't quite figure out. Just when he thought he knew what kind of person she was, she surprised him with something else.

He'd texted with Ian while she'd been shopping. He hadn't been able to call, other than a quick call after he'd patched up Robert to let Ian know what was going on. Fortunately, the call had gone through, though it'd dropped off again before they were finished. It was enough, though. Ian would send a clean up crew. The evidence would be gone before anyone tried to check on the cabin. The bodies would disappear, and Robert would be taken into custody where he'd be questioned and threatened before being turned loose again. If he knew more than he'd admitted, Ian would get it out of him.

After Jared got all the gear inside, he listened for footsteps. When he heard the floors creaking overhead, he knew Libby was still upstairs. He threw himself into a chair and dialed Ian.

"You make it home?"

"Yeah. Just got here. Libby's upstairs for a few minutes. Got anything for me?"

"A little bit. Ninja Solutions is working on military AI applications. The rumor is their top secret project is an exoskeleton with an AI component. The suit is supposedly capable of taking over during a battlefield scenario. The soldier has to activate it, but then the advanced targeting and survival systems do the rest. It's real groundbreaking stuff if it's true. The US Army is very interested."

"Damn. What could possibly go wrong with an assault suit that has a mind of its own?"

Ian laughed. "Right? Nothing wrong with letting your armor take control."

"Does Ninja have any other sensitive projects?"

"Not to that level. I think the exoskeleton is our most likely target. Ninja Solutions works on other projects, but this is supposed to be their big break. Daniel Weir is the founder and CEO. He's some kind of math genius. MIT grad. Libby has worked there for about eight months. She's lived in the area for a couple of years now. Before getting the job at Ninja Solutions, she worked at a clothing store in Pentagon City Mall."

"That's quite a change, isn't it?"

"One of her regular clients works at Ninja Solutions and helped her get an entry-level job."

"Not much chance she's working on the top secret project then, is there?"

"I wouldn't think so. I certainly wouldn't bring an entry-level administrative assistant into a project like that, but there's always a remote possibility."

"Or their security is shit and she saw something she shouldn't." He just hoped she hadn't *taken* anything she shouldn't.

"Truth. It'd be nice if we could ask her questions. I'm taking it she hasn't remembered anything yet?"

"No. She probably hit her head during the confrontation. Not to mention the aftereffects of the sodium thiopental they gave her. Memory loss isn't a known side effect, but the brain can react in strange ways to protect itself. I think she'll remember, but I don't know when."

"We should probably get her over to Riverstone. Let Dr. Puckett's crew have a look at her."

"Agreed," he said, though he felt like he'd done everything for her that could be done. But he wasn't a psychologist. Riverstone was a private facility used by the special ops community, and the doctors were all top notch. They were also trustworthy.

"Tomorrow then. I'll set something up."

"Sounds good."

"Hang on a sec. Colt just walked in."

Colt was Colt Duchaine, one of Jared's teammates. They'd been on some hairy missions together in some pretty shitty places. But they'd always come through. Thank God.

Ian was back in a flash. "Got some news, but it's not good. Colt just heard from the clean up crew. There's no one at the cabin, Jared. No bodies, no snowmobiles, no dogs—and no injured man."

Chapter Twelve

LIBBY AWOKE THE NEXT MORNING FEELING MORE HUMAN than she had for the first time in days. Her aches and pains were a dull throb rather than a sharp stab, and she had clean clothes to put on. She didn't know what time it was since she still didn't have a cell phone, but when she stepped into the hallway she could smell bacon. That meant that Jared was downstairs and it wasn't past noon. Unless he'd slept late too.

After a quick shower and blow dry, she put on the jeans and boots he'd bought for her along with a pale pink sweater that had a hood. She left her hair down, checked her reflection one more time, and felt good about what she saw. Jared had told her last night she could remove the bandages. The scrape on her forehead was healing and the cut on her throat was a thin red line. There was a bruise beneath the scrape.

She wished she had makeup to cover it, but she hadn't thought to buy any. She'd been self-conscious just buying clothes when it was Jared's money she was spending. Makeup seemed like a frivolity. She didn't actually know that she wore any, but the desire for it seemed to mean she did.

She went down the stairs and into the kitchen. The house was older so it wasn't an open concept design, but the kitchen was surprisingly spacious. She hadn't gone in there last night, so seeing it this morning with the light streaming in the tall windows over the sink was her first glimpse.

"Oh my god, I'm in love."

Jared turned from the stove, arching an eyebrow at her. "Really? With me or with bacon?"

She spread her hands to encompass the kitchen. "With this room. It's gorgeous."

He let his gaze slide over the four walls and then back to her. "It's a kitchen, Libby."

"But it's so bright and pretty. You renovated it, didn't you?"

"There've been some updates, yeah."

She ran a hand over the white cabinets. They weren't new, but painted. There was a built-in glass-front pantry along one wall, and the ceiling was at least nine feet tall. He'd added an island, but it worked in the space. There was a farm sink and a gas stove with a copper range hood.

It was nothing like her apartment. Libby gasped as the thought took hold.

"What's wrong?"

She met Jared's concerned gaze, a little bubble of excitement welling inside. "I was just thinking that your kitchen is nothing like mine."

"That's good. Do you remember what it looks like? Can you describe it?"

She thought about it. "Builder grade cabinets, cheap countertops that are meant to look like stone but aren't, and an electric stove. The walls are soft grey. There's an island, too, but it's not as long as this one. Oh, and pendant lights over the island."

"Anything else?" he asked when her voice trailed off.

"No, I… Wait, yes. I have a queen-sized bed with a fabric headboard and lots of pillows. There's a television on the wall, and my bathroom has a soaker tub. I think I like pink."

He looked pointedly at her sweater. "You don't say."

She glanced down and laughed. "Oh yeah, I guess that's a clue. It's a tasteful pink, though. And so are the pink touches in my room. Not electric pink or anything." She sighed. "That's all I've got at the moment."

He set a plate with bacon and eggs and toast on the island and slid it toward her. "That's a good start. You'll remember everything when you're ready. Sooner rather than later, I imagine."

Libby took a seat at the island and dug into breakfast. The bacon was crispy and delicious. "You like bacon, don't you?"

"Doesn't everybody?"

"Yeah, but I think there's something about cholesterol we're supposed to watch out for." She waved a piece of bacon around and Jared shook his head. Then he ripped into his own slice, biting it ferociously. She laughed at the fierce look on his face.

"Actually, I don't eat bacon every day," he finally

said, grinning. "But the pack was open so I wanted to finish it."

She liked him. He made her comfortable, which she thought was amazing. Knowing nothing about who she was made it difficult to know who she could trust.

But she could trust him.

"Makes sense. When I can go home again, I'll pay you for everything. Even the bacon."

"I know you will. Though maybe you can cook something for me while you're here. I'll take that as payment for my bacon services."

She laughed. "Maybe all I know how to fix is potato soup. What if that's all I ever make for you? Will the deal hold?"

He grinned. "Guess we'll find out."

"Guess so," she said happily. She didn't know why she was happy considering she still had a giant gap in her memory—and considering that three men with dogs had been hunting her yesterday—but she was. At least in this moment.

"I need to take you to my office today."

She blinked. "Combat medics have offices? I thought you were kind of a nomad or something."

"Hardly. I work for a company called Black Defense International. BDI for short. We have a headquarters building, and there are offices. There's also a gun range and a bar, smarty pants."

"Oh, that sounds like a good idea. Have a beer, shoot some weapons. Do you throw axes too?"

He snorted. "You're cute, you know that?"

Warmth spread through her at the compliment. It

wasn't quite the same as being called beautiful or sexy or exciting, but she'd take it. When it came from a man who looked like this one, she'd definitely take it.

"Just calling it like I see it." She forked up some eggs. They were creamy and delicious, not scrambled for so long they were dry. Jared had skills when it came to breakfast, that's for sure. She wondered what other kind of skills he had.

"You're blushing, Libby. What's going through your head?"

"Am I? I have no idea why." She took a bite of toast. "It's probably a hot flash."

He laughed, then shook his head and turned away to put his plate in the sink. Libby rolled her eyes. *Really? A hot flash?*

"When you're ready," he said, turning back to her, "We'll head out."

Her heart thumped. "Do you know what those men wanted from me yet?"

"No, but we'll know more when we get to BDI. After you finish breakfast, get your jacket on and we'll head out."

Libby did as he said and fifteen minutes later they were in his truck, heading toward the mysterious BDI building. It was a surprise when Jared drove into an underground parking garage attached to an unremarkable building on a typical city street. She'd been expecting a military compound or something, but though there was security, it was all very subtle. A perimeter fence with a gate at the entrance to the parking lot, and a guard shack. After passing through the gate, Jared drove down the ramp and under the building.

"This is it?" she asked.

"What were you expecting? The CIA?"

Libby grumbled. "Maybe. This looks like an office building with minimal security."

"Trust me, it's not minimal. It's also not obvious because we don't like to draw attention. Besides, BDI is an international security firm." He grinned as if to say *Nothing to see here. Move along.*

They got out of the truck and headed toward the stairwell door. She noticed there was an elevator, but they bypassed that. Jared didn't knock or anything. He stood in front of the door and announced himself. A moment later, the door swung open. A tall man with dark hair and dark eyes grinned at them.

"Aloha, friends."

Jared turned to her and put a hand on her back. "Libby, this is Ian Black. He's the boss."

"Hi, Libby," Ian said, shaking her hand. "This guy been treating you right? Or has he been boring you with books?"

Libby laughed in surprise. "Um, he's treated me just fine. But there were some books," she added in a conspiratorial whisper.

Ian's bark of laughter was immediate. "I bet there were. Tomes of unusually large size, I imagine."

"Fuck off, boss," Jared said. He didn't sound upset though.

Ian looped an arm through Libby's and tugged her down a narrow hallway. She liked this guy. He was fun, and hot too. Not as hot as Jared, but still hot. Closer to forty than thirty, though maybe he was a little over forty. She was never sure of ages.

"Welcome to the Cove, Libby," he said, walking her through a door and into what could only be termed a bar. The lights were low, with pendants over a pool table, and mirrors along the back wall. There were tables, a long bar, and an arcade machine on one wall. A neon sign blinked over the bar. It said *Pirate's Cove*. To complete the picture, there was a pirate in one corner. He was tall, with a feathered hat and a patch over one eye. There was a parrot on his shoulder.

Libby blinked, but he didn't go away. The darn thing was so lifelike it took her a second to realize it was a statue. "I thought you said we were going to your office," she threw over her shoulder to Jared.

He shrugged. "This is part of the office. It's a big building."

"This might be the best part of all," Ian said, leading her over to the bar on one side of the room. "What will you have?"

"Um…"

"Whatever you want. We can do it."

"It's a little early for alcohol, isn't it?"

"It's five o'clock somewhere." Ian smiled.

"You can get a virgin drink," Jared said from behind her. "Or stick with the easy stuff like water."

The man behind the bar handed Ian a bottle of beer.

"So you got stuck tending, huh, Jace?" Jared said.

Jace grinned. "I was wrong about, er, something Ian and I were discussing. This is how he makes me pay up."

Ian leaned against the bar. "It could be you the next time, Jared. You never know."

"Not him," another man said from a table in the center of the room. "He reads too much to let you stump him."

"Hey, Colt. How's it going?" Jared replied.

"It's going."

"Libby?" Ian prompted. "Anything?"

She said the first thing that popped into her head. "How about a banana daiquiri? Virgin."

"Good one," Ian said. "You got that, Jace?"

"Yeah, I got it." The way he said it made Libby wonder if she should have picked something simpler. Too late now. Besides, Ian was grinning like she'd made his entire day. "Beer, Jared?" Jace asked.

"Sure."

"I'll bring the daiquiri," Jace said as he handed Jared a beer.

They headed for the table where Colt sat. Jace delivered the drink like he'd promised and Libby took a sip. It was delicious. She'd felt a little guilty asking for it, but now she was happy she had.

The door opened and three more men entered. Jace got them drinks and they all came over to the table.

"Libby, this is Tyler, Dax, and Brett," Jared said.

"Hi," Libby replied, wondering for a crazy second if she was still asleep and dreaming. These men could be Chippendale's strippers if they wanted to be, though she thought they weren't quite as polished looking as the actual strippers. Which meant they didn't appear as if their good looks came from tanning beds and high-priced salons.

They each shook her hand. She appreciated that they did it firmly, but not so hard they made her hand ache. She had an impression of past handshakes where it felt as if the man were crushing the bones of her hand together.

Jared scooted his chair closer to hers as the other three pulled up a chair to join them. She could feel his body heat, smell his scent, and she found it comforting. Not that these men made her uncomfortable, but she didn't know them.

Not to mention she was nervous about what they were going to say. What she was going to learn about herself and how much trouble she was in.

Because there was little doubt she was in trouble. The question was how much—and if she was one of the bad guys.

"We're all here," Ian said. "Let's get started."

Chapter Thirteen

LIBBY WAS UNCHARACTERISTICALLY QUIET. AFTER BDI, Jared had taken her over to Riverstone where Dr. Puckett had thoroughly checked her out. Physically, she was fine. She had bruises and muscle pain, but those were on the mend. Jared still hadn't told her the things Robert had said about what Joe had done to her, or how she'd escaped, but he'd told the doctor before she examined Libby.

He wasn't keeping it from her because he didn't think she needed to know. He kept it from her because it wasn't pleasant, and because she'd already dealt with enough information about herself today. She might remember it on her own, or it might be the specific trauma her mind was blocking. Either way, she'd remember when the time was right for *her*.

Still, she was processing a lot of information right now. They'd kept the meeting at BDI friendly, but Jared knew there was some serious shit going down in the background. Ian had been careful about what he revealed, but he'd given Libby the facts about herself.

Liberty Grace King, twenty-five, from Ohio.

Two older sisters—Glory and Charity—and an older brother named Lincoln. Definitely a theme there.

Parents were Carl and Abby, a farmer and a housewife, both deceased. They'd had Libby late in life after their other kids were grown. Abby had caught pneumonia and died when Libby was seventeen, and Carl had died last year from a heart attack.

Jared had reached for Libby's hand beneath the table when Ian delivered the news. She'd squeezed his hand gratefully. He'd ached for her. Though she'd lost her parents and processed their deaths in real time, hearing it when she didn't remember anything had to be like losing them all over again.

Libby lived alone in a one-bedroom apartment in Arlington. She'd worked at Ninja Solutions for eight months, and she was supposed to be taking a week's vacation at the moment. Dax Freed had called the company to ask if he could speak with her, and that's when he'd been told she was off for the next week.

Jared had looked at his teammates when Dax said that. He could see it in their eyes that none of them thought it was a coincidence. Whoever had taken her to the mountain had known she wasn't due back at work. Plenty of time to get what they wanted from her and dispose of her before she was officially missing.

Nobody said it, but they all believed someone at Ninja Solutions was involved in what had happened to Libby. Unfortunately, information was scarce on that count. If she had information about the exoskeleton project, known as Renaissance Iron Man, or RIM, in the company, it was probably in the form of something physical since the men who'd abducted her said she'd stolen something. Something they clearly hadn't retrieved.

Jace and Colt had breached her apartment to search for evidence, but someone had been there before they had, which only confirmed that whatever she had—or someone thought she had—was physical. A memory card, papers, photos. Something.

"Her apartment is trashed," Colt had whispered to Jared a little while later when they'd gone over to the bar to grab some fresh drinks. "They sliced into her mattress and cushions, punched holes in the walls, and upended every drawer in the place. They were searching for something all right. But what?"

That was the question they couldn't answer. Fortunately, everyone agreed that Libby couldn't go home yet and needed to stay with Jared for now. She'd protested feebly but accepted it in the end. When she'd asked if she could have a cell phone, Ian had told her it was better if she didn't for now. She hadn't argued because she was smart, but Jared knew she didn't like it.

The one thing they *had* procured for her, though, was a pair of glasses. Colt had found a pair in her bedroom and brought them with him. Ian fudged the part about where they'd gotten the glasses, telling Libby they'd had a pair made from her prescription on file with her doctor. It was the kind of thing Ian could do if he'd had to, but he hadn't needed to this time.

"You okay?" he asked her after they'd ridden in silence for twenty minutes.

Libby jerked as if she'd forgotten he was there. "Um, yes. Fine. Thanks." She looked cute in glasses. They were pink, of course. A dark translucent pink that complemented her skin and hair.

"You're awfully quiet."

She dropped her chin to her chest and studied her lap. "It's a lot to think about."

"I know, honey. I'm sorry."

"I know who I am, but I *don't* know who I am. My parents are dead. My siblings are at least twenty years older than I am. I live alone and don't have a pet. But those facts are all so basic. It makes me sound sad and lonely, but that doesn't feel right to me."

"Then it probably isn't."

She was vivacious and talkative. Someone like her would have friends. They hadn't told her about Kristin Martin, the woman who'd helped her get the job, but Jared expected she had more friends than Kristin. She was that kind of person. Hell, she'd charmed his teammates in the short time they'd been together. Even Ian, who was as chill as they came.

None had reported her missing, though, which was a little odd since he thought she was probably someone who texted her friends a lot. On the other hand, if she'd had a vacation scheduled, maybe no one expected to hear from her yet.

"Dr. Puckett said I'll remember when I'm ready. I'm ready *now*. Why won't my brain do what I want it to do?"

Frustration bordered on panic in her voice. Jared reached for her hand. It was cold. He lifted it to his mouth and pressed a kiss to the back of it. He didn't miss the little gasp she made, or the way her fingers just sort of melted into his.

"You can't force it, Libby. Trying will only upset you. Think of it like an orgasm. The harder you try, the more elusive it is."

He let her go and she put her hand in her lap, studying it. He could see the slight flush of pink staining her cheeks and it made him want to pull over and drag her into his arms. He wanted to kiss her again. And more.

He'd lain awake in bed last night, knowing she was in the next room, and wanting to go in there and slip between the sheets with her. He couldn't say why that was—except that he'd been thinking about it since he'd kissed her at the cabin. He'd wanted more. He still wanted more. The longer he was around Libby King and her chatty little tongue, the more he wanted to taste her. Own her mouth. Shut it up with his own for a while.

"That's all well and good, but I don't exactly recall who my last orgasm was with or how difficult it was to achieve."

His dick was hard in an instant. *Shit. Focus.* "Maybe I shouldn't have said that."

"I'm not offended, Jared."

"But you blushed. You always blush whenever there's any innuendo, which is why I should probably be more careful about what I say."

She regarded him curiously. "You know when I blush?"

"It's hard to miss. Your lips and cheeks are rosy. You drop your head and study your lap."

"It's true you make me blush," she said softly. "I don't know why. Maybe I'm a serious prude or something. Or I could be a virgin who's never seen a naked man, much less slept with one. Or maybe it's just you and the fact I find you unbearably attractive. The possibilities are endless."

Jared swore. Then he whipped the truck into the nearest parking lot and shoved it into park before turning to face her across the seat. She blinked at him with big eyes. Eyes that held secrets even she couldn't unlock. She was lost and alone, and he wanted to comfort her.

That's what he told himself when he leaned across the center console and wrapped a hand around the back of her neck. When he tugged her forward and slanted his mouth over hers. Her lips parted and he dipped his tongue inside, groaning at the heat and electricity flooding his system.

She was still for only a moment—and then she wrapped her arms around his neck and kissed him back with a ferocity that made the blood beat in his temples. He slid a hand over her jaw, down her throat, and over her breast, cupping it in his palm. He could feel the bud of her nipple beneath the fabric and he wanted to shove her shirt up and release her from the bra so he could lick and suck while she clutched him and gasped his name.

He broke the kiss and trailed his mouth down her

neck, intending to do just that, when someone rapped on the window. Jared reached for his weapon out of instinct, trying to shield Libby as he did so. He was a heartbeat away from drawing when he realized this wasn't an attack but a woman standing outside his door with a frown and crossed arms.

Libby had squeaked and turned her head away when the knock came, which left Jared to deal with the woman. He hit the button to roll the window partway down.

"Can I help you?" he asked.

"Yes. You can stop doing whatever it is you're doing and get the hell out of my parking lot before I call the cops."

The lady had one of those blonde hairdos that was all porcupine on the rear and smooth bangs on the front. He'd heard that referred to as 'I want to speak to the manager' hair. And this lady looked like, if there were a manager in this situation, she'd be asking for him —or her—so she could complain about Jared.

"We're going," he said, because it was no use to argue.

The lady huffed. "You should really do that stuff in the privacy of your own home. Do you want children to see you?"

Jared frowned. He thought about telling her to fuck off, but he could hear his mother in the back of his head telling him to be polite. And, truth be told, he was the one in the wrong for pulling into this parking lot—an insurance agency, it turned out—and kissing the living daylights out of Libby in public when what he really wanted to do was kiss her in private. *All* of her.

"No ma'am," he said dutifully. "We're leaving."

"See that you do."

Libby was making a sound over in her corner of the truck, but he didn't know if she was crying or cursing him. He pressed the button to roll up the window and put the truck in reverse. When the lady was firmly in the rearview, he glanced over at Libby. Her shoulders were shaking. Alarm flared.

"I'm sorry," he said, "I shouldn't have embarrassed you like that."

She turned toward him—and burst out laughing. "Oh my god, the way she dressed you down!" Libby said between giggles. "What will the children think?"

Jared laughed as relief rolled through him. He didn't know what had come over him when he'd kissed Libby like that, and he'd been worried he'd fucked the whole thing up by doing it. She was still vulnerable, and he wasn't the kind of guy to take advantage of that. Sure, he knew a lot about her, but those were only facts. He didn't know what kind of past she had. If she'd been in love, if she'd had a bad breakup, if she was guarding her heart—or protecting her virtue because it was a personal choice that reflected her values.

In short, he didn't know enough about her—and she didn't know enough about herself—to act on the attraction simmering between them.

But the fact she was laughing about it made him feel better. She wasn't offended or embarrassed, and that was a good thing. He wouldn't want to do that to her.

"She had a point, I guess. Not that we were sitting in a school parking lot or anything."

Libby was still giggling. "Oh, the horrors. To kiss in broad daylight like that."

"Probably a good thing Ms. Moral Police arrived when she did. I was well on my way to forgetting where we were."

"Why did you kiss me, Jared?"

She sounded as if she couldn't quite figure out why he would want to. Which was crazy. "Why wouldn't I?"

She shrugged. "I don't know. It's just that I've caused you a lot of trouble since you met me. Without me, you'd still be enjoying your solitude and your books."

It was true, and yet he couldn't imagine that solitude now. He didn't want to be in the mountains alone. He wanted to be here. With her.

He didn't think that meant anything, not really. He was essentially still who he was. A loner. A maverick. A man with too much baggage and too much danger in his life to ever drag someone like Libby into it. But that didn't mean he didn't get lonely, or that he didn't like companionship. And right now, he liked her companionship. Didn't change anything permanently. Just for now.

He could deal with that.

"If I hadn't driven up to the cabin when I did, you'd have frozen to death that night. So no, I wouldn't change anything about this week—other than to change the fact you were in trouble."

She was back to frowning. He missed her laughter, but there was a lot more for her to worry about than laugh about. "I wish I understood how I got into trouble. I don't know anything about this military suit you guys mentioned. But I guess I must know something important—or they thought I did, right? Why else would they have kidnapped me? They literally believed I knew something or had something. I guess I could have hidden whatever it was in the woods somewhere…"

"Not likely," he said. "If they kidnapped you from your home and took you to the mountain, they'd have found anything you had on you."

"That's true." She scrubbed her hands over her face and pushed a lock of hair behind her ear. "I have a feeling I'd make a terrible spy. Or maybe I'm such a damned good one that I've managed to hide my memories from myself. That's certainly a more interesting explanation than not being able to remember." She puffed up her chest. "Liberty King, international woman of mystery. Nope, just doesn't sound right."

He laughed. Damn she was cute. "I don't know why not. I have a feeling Liberty King can do anything she sets her mind to."

She smiled at him. He liked her smile. "You're awfully good for my ego, Jared—er, I've just realized I don't know your last name."

"Fraser."

"Oh, like Jamie."

"Who?"

"*Outlander?*"

"No idea what that is."

Her eyes widened. "Oh my god—it's a book, Jared!"

"Okay. I know I read a lot, but I haven't heard of that one."

She gripped his forearm. "No, I mean it's a book and I've read it! I remember reading it."

"That's good, Libby. Really good."

She seemed so happy. "It is, right? I remembered my kitchen and bedroom, and now I remember that I specifically read a book about a highlander named Jamie Fraser."

"A highlander, huh? Like Connor Macleod?"

She blinked adorably. "Who?"

He shook his head and laughed. "Never mind. It was a movie about an immortal highlander. Sci-fi stuff."

She wrinkled her nose. "I think I must not be a sci-fi fan."

"*Star Trek? Star Wars? Doctor Who?*"

"Not ringing any bells, sorry. But come to think of it, *Outlander* is also a TV show." She looked pleased. "It's not much, but at least things are coming back."

"Everything will come back. Probably sooner than you think."

"That kind of worries me, too, you know?"

He turned into his driveway. "Why?"

She fidgeted with her fingers. "What if I don't like myself very much?"

He stopped the vehicle and turned the key, then looked at her. She was utterly serious. He liked her face in those glasses, liked the smooth skin of her forehead, the slope of her nose, her full lips and narrow chin. Her eyebrows arched over the top of the glasses, and her irises were an interesting shade of golden-brown. There were flecks of black in them that made them seem darker than they were, but in full light the colors were more interesting and varied than he'd originally realized.

Libby wasn't striking at first glance, but she was beautiful when you paid attention to what you were seeing.

He started to say something flippant, but she looked so serious. Afraid. He took her hand in his, mostly because he liked the way his skin warmed whenever he touched her, and rubbed his thumb back and forth on the tender area between her thumb and forefinger.

"I know that worries you. I understand, and I'm sorry. But I don't think it's going to be a problem, Libby. You're sweet, funny, and bubbly. I barely know you and I like you. Ian, Colt, Dax, Jace, Ty, and Brett like you too."

She swallowed. "I spent an hour with them. They don't know whether they like me or not."

He put a finger over her lips—and immediately regretted it since it made him think of what it'd felt like to press his mouth to hers. Something he wanted to do again.

"I don't think you're thinking clearly, honey. You may not remember, but I promise you've met people and instantly disliked them before." He thought about that for a second. "Okay, you're so sweet that maybe you haven't—but you know what I'm talking about. You know how some people seem sketchy from the word go. You aren't one of them. They liked you, Liberty King, because you charmed them with your humor and your resilience."

He lifted her hand to his mouth and kissed the back

of it. "Promise on my honor as a former airman, a combat medic, and a knight in shining armor."

She smiled a wobbly, sweet smile that made his heart pinch for the briefest of moments. "You're sweet too, you know."

She put her palm against his jaw and the contact knocked him for a loop. The need flaring inside was strong, but he kept his gaze steady on hers and didn't act on it.

"Thank you, Jared. You always know what to say to make me feel better."

Chapter Fourteen

Ian sat at his desk, going through the intel report on Ninja Solutions, and feeling like he wanted to explode. He'd been this way for weeks now. He needed to get back into the field, go on a mission, and stop hovering at BDI like it couldn't run without him.

That was the beauty of BDI—it *could*.

He'd set it up that way on purpose. The entire organization was a cover for covert work, which was the important stuff. Their mission wasn't really about protecting executives and training security forces in foreign lands, but that's what he advertised and what they performed on the surface.

And that could be done without him being on site. Any of his team could oversee operations—and had in the past.

Lately, however, he'd stuck close to home because of *her*. He kept expecting her to contact him, to take him up on his offer of help, but so far she was silent.

She was Natasha Orlova, Jace Kaiser's little sister, the

deadly assassin Calypso. She was a mystery. A fascinating woman.

A stone-cold killer.

And she was far too young for him. He was pushing forty, and she was barely twenty-four. Not that he was interested anyway.

Ian dropped his pen and snorted. *Like hell he wasn't.*

Natasha was the only person he'd come across in recent years who had the wit and skill to hoodwink him. The last time he'd seen her, she'd been dressed as an aging and filthy flower seller on the banks of the Thames. He hadn't even known it was her until it was too late.

He tugged his desk drawer open and retrieved the scrap of paper she'd wrapped around the stems of the flowers he'd bought (out of pity, he might add).

Bang. If this had been a hit, you'd be dead. Watch yourself, Mr. Black. N

She was right. If she'd been paid to kill him, he would have been dead before he'd known what hit him.

He usually had a sixth sense about that kind of thing, but something about Natasha Orlova muddled his radar. Not a good thing considering what she was. She might be on his side for the moment—or she might not—but it wouldn't always be true. The instant someone ordered her to kill him, and paid her handsomely for it, she'd turn on him.

Or maybe she wouldn't do it for that. Maybe she'd do it for the child that someone was clearly using against her. He didn't know who that was, or even if there *was* a child, but it was the explanation that made the most sense based on the cryptic words she'd said to him once.

He couldn't help but draw parallels to another Russian spy he'd known. A spy who was now the wife of John Mendez, the general in charge of the military strike force known as the Hostile Operations Team. Kat had gone through hell to get to that point in her life, and she'd lost her child in the process. The truth about her son's death had eventually come out, but Kat had suffered for years because of it.

Ian didn't want to see Natasha suffer. She wasn't the same as Kat. She'd been born an American, but her parents were double agents and they'd been caught and sent back to Russia with their children. Children who hadn't understood or spoken a word of Russian at the time. Natasha was the younger of the two, so her memory of America was much less formed than her brother's. She'd adapted quickly, but life in Russia hadn't been charmed, especially when she and her parents were arrested for treason and thrown in a gulag. With Ian's help, her brother had escaped before he could be arrested.

It killed him that he hadn't been able to do the same for her—for all of them. Every time he saw her, however brief it typically was, he felt guilty. Maybe that was why she muddled him up inside.

It was also why he needed to pay attention to what was going on around him. Not let her get into his head so much. It was why he needed a mission. Something hard and rough and deadly. Something that challenged him and scrubbed the memory of those wounded eyes from his soul.

———

IT WAS FRUSTRATING NOT KNOWING your history. For one thing, Libby didn't know if she'd ever had a serious relationship. She was twenty-five, so maybe she had. Or maybe she hadn't.

According to Ian Black, she had not gone to college, or at least not a four-year school. She'd apparently attended a community college in Ohio, where she'd worked odd jobs while putting herself through school. She'd graduated with a certificate and a qualification to be an administrative assistant.

But why had she moved to DC two years ago? And how had she gotten hired at a company like Ninja Solutions? All her previous work seemed to be in retail shops, restaurants, and an office supply company. What had made her take such a chance? Had she moved for a man? If so, what had happened?

"Stop it," she said under her breath, pressing her hands to her temples.

It was fruitless to speculate. She simply didn't know.

She thought of the way Jared had kissed her earlier. Like he was starving for her. Hell, she'd been starving for him too. And she hadn't even cared that she didn't know him all that well, or herself, or that it was entirely possible she wasn't the kind of woman who had sex with men she wasn't in a relationship with.

All she'd cared about was feeling more of what he made her feel when he kissed her; safe, joyful, her body coiling tight in all the right places. She'd felt like a single touch from him in the right place would have made her see stars.

She wanted to see stars.

Libby sighed. *Dammit.*

Since they'd entered the house, Jared had gotten distant again. He'd retreated to his study—a small room off the foyer with a pocket door and bookshelves lining the walls—and left her to her own devices.

Libby had walked through the house, peeking into rooms, admiring the decor in the living room and kitchen, the only two rooms that seemed completely done. The house was old, with that charm that only an old house could have. Tall ceilings, rich wood accents like wainscoting, wood floors, and pocket doors.

A memory came unbidden to her mind—a white farmhouse on a small knoll, surrounded by fields and pastures. Inside the house, the furnishings were plain but welcoming. There was a kindly woman with graying blond hair who wore dresses and an apron. And there was a gruff man, plainspoken and dressed in overalls. He had ideas about women and their place in the home.

Libby blinked. She would have thought she was remembering her grandparents, but since Ian Black had told her that her parents were older when she was born—her mother had been forty-eight, her dad fifty-eight—she knew they were her mom and dad.

The funny thing was, she didn't feel like she'd ever been able to call her father *dad.* In her mind, he was firmly *sir.*

Yes, sir. No, sir. I'm sorry, sir.

And what about her sisters and brother? All older than her. Significantly so. She must not be very close to any of them since absolutely no one had reported her missing. She was supposed to be on vacation, according to Ian Black's information—but didn't someone think that her sudden request was suspicious? Wasn't *anyone* looking for her?

Libby shook her head sadly.

The memories that came to her were so random—and the ones about her parents made her unbearably sad. She was grateful to remember, but why not something more fun? Why not the past few months? How she got to DC, who her friends were, what her job was like?

Oh, and a little matter about top secret information. That would be nice to know. Did she or did she not possess it?

Libby plopped the book she'd been trying to read on the bed. She'd retreated to her room earlier, intending to take a nap, but it never happened. Not even with *War and Peace* to lull her to sleep.

"I believe I'm done with you for now, Mr. Tolstoy," she said, setting the book onto the nightstand. "You're too depressing."

What she really needed was something fun. A romance novel, perhaps. Not that she expected Jared would have a romance lying around. He was far too serious for that.

Libby shoved to her feet and plodded out the door and down the hall. There were three bedrooms upstairs, and a full bath. There were bookshelves on one side of the hall. Predictably filled with non-fiction tomes. Did Jared really read this stuff? Or was he someone who liked to collect books that he never quite got around to reading?

That didn't fit, not really. Not when she'd spent time with him in the cabin where he'd buried his nose in a large book for hours. It was incongruous that a man who looked like he did wanted solitude and a fat book to pass the time.

"Stereotype much?" Libby muttered to herself as she put a hand on the bannister and glided downstairs.

Just because the man was beautiful and kissed like he'd been born to make a woman happy didn't mean that was *all* he knew how to do. That was like saying that a beautiful woman should only be decorative. Or that a blond was dumb.

Libby examined the bookshelves in the living room. No romances, of course. She hadn't looked closely before, but now she was caught by the photos placed strategically along each shelf. Whoever this designer fiancée of his friend was, she was very good. The room looked put together, but not untouchable. It looked lived in, and welcoming. The kind of room you'd want to spend time in.

The bookshelves were on either side of the fireplace, and above the mantel hung a piece of art. Except, on closer inspection, it wasn't art at all. It was a television that displayed artwork as if it were a painting. She'd seen those advertised but had never actually seen one in person. It was very subtle.

Libby picked up a photo and studied it. Jared was

holding a certificate in his hand and standing beside a small, thin woman who looked tired. She had a tube in her nose and an oxygen canister peeked out from behind her. Her smile was genuine, as was the sparkle in her eyes as she gazed at the camera. Jared's arm was looped around her shoulders.

It didn't take a genius to realize she was his mother. They had the same bone structure, the same eyes. But there was that tube, and the oxygen…

"Which one are you looking at so intently?"

Libby squeaked and spun. She hadn't heard him come out of his study. She clutched the photo to her chest, embarrassed she'd been caught. But she was also curious. She turned the photo so he could see it as he came closer.

It took him a moment to smile. "Oh."

"I'm sorry. I shouldn't have picked it up—"

"It's fine, Libby. I wouldn't have it there if I didn't want anyone to see it, now would I?"

She shook her head.

He took the photo gently and stared at it. Then he set it on the shelf again, caressing the frame for a second. "My mother died a month after that picture was taken. I'd just gotten an award for a science project. She was so proud."

Libby's heart throbbed. "I'm sorry."

"It was a long time ago." But there was pain in his gaze as he turned it on her. "She didn't get to see me graduate, but I knew she was proud when I walked across the stage. She had lung cancer. She was never a smoker, but she worked in smoky environments over the years, and my dad smoked when he was still around. The doctors said that some people get lung cancer even when they've never smoked. She was one of the unlucky ones."

Libby felt her eyes filling with tears. Over a woman she didn't know. Or was it for the man she did? "I'm really sorry, Jared. I know that's not adequate."

He skimmed a finger over her cheek, then rubbed away the moisture he found there. "Don't cry, Libby. It's okay. It was a long time ago. I miss her, but it eases with time. She was a good mom."

She wrapped her fingers around his arm, held him there with his fingers on her cheek. "I *know* that I know what it feels like to lose your parents, but I can't remember."

"I know, honey. It'll be okay."

She sniffed as hot feelings swirled inside her. She was trembling and she needed to hang onto him to stay grounded. "I'm not trying to make this about me. Please don't comfort me when I'm the one who should be comforting you."

He dipped his lips to hers, brushed over them softly. "Maybe we should be comforting each other," he whispered.

Chapter Fifteen

Now isn't the time.

That was the refrain echoing through his head as he slipped his tongue into her mouth and felt the hot blossoming of desire in his veins and along his nerve pathways.

But it felt so good. *She* felt good.

Libby melted against him, her body fitting to his in all the right ways. She kissed him back, her arms lifting to wrap around his neck as she stretched up on tiptoe.

It would be so easy to take her up to his bedroom, strip off her clothes, and bury himself inside her. She wouldn't stop him.

But he should stop himself. It wasn't fair to her. She didn't really know who she was. How could you have sex with someone when your sense of self was so muddled? What happened when you remembered—and it turned out you'd taken a vow of celibacy until marriage?

Not that it was a typical vow to take, but what if she had? He'd be taking that away from her. Taking advantage of her lack of knowledge about herself to get some-thing he wanted.

Jared took a deep breath and broke the kiss, putting a little distance between their bodies. His throbbed with thwarted desire, but it was the right thing to do. He wasn't a romantic but what if Libby was? If they had sex, what if she ascribed too much meaning to it?

Jared nearly groaned with the thought of what he was giving up.

But it was the *right* thing to do.

Libby blinked up at him, her golden-brown eyes hazy with the same desire he felt coursing through his body.

"We shouldn't take this any farther," he rasped, his throat tight.

"Why not?"

Leave it to Libby to ask a direct question. He should have known. She wasn't the sort of person who failed to put voice to her thoughts.

He removed her arms from his neck and stepped away, raking a hand through his hair. Tugging the ends as if that little bit of pain would bring him back to his senses. His dick throbbed in protest.

"Because it's not fair to you."

She tilted her head. Folded her arms beneath her breasts, which was absolutely the wrong maneuver so far as he was concerned because it tightened her sweater and showed the outline of her nipples. Nipples that were tight little points. Nipples he wanted to suck while she moaned and begged for more.

"How is it not fair to me, Jared? I'm afraid I'm not following your logic."

He flung himself onto the couch, feeling moody. She looked down at him like a queen surveying her realm. He was beginning to feel like an idiot instead of a gentleman.

"You've lost your memory. How do you know you aren't saving yourself for marriage?"

Her mouth flattened for a second. "You're right," she finally said. "I don't know that at all. But I do know how I feel right now, and maybe it's high time I acted on the way I feel about something instead of letting outside influences dictate what I do. What if I'm saving myself for marriage for all the wrong reasons? Or what if I've had a bad experience and the me who knows who she is is afraid of having sex? What if this is an opportunity instead of a burden?"

He hadn't thought of that. Still didn't make it right, though. Not when he knew himself so well. A few times buried inside her hot little body and he'd be ready to move on. He wasn't in it for the long haul. And certainly not with a woman who talked so much he couldn't get a moment's quiet unless he went to another room and shut the door.

He liked quiet. He liked books when he wasn't fighting battles. Libby wasn't the kind of woman who would settle for those things.

And why was he thinking about what she'd settle for? He didn't care. He wasn't looking for forever. Sure, some of his friends had settled down when they hadn't intended to but that didn't mean he was going to. They were all different than him. Capable of more feeling. It was obvious when you looked at the relationships they had with their women. He wasn't wired that way. He'd grown up with the worst example of a relationship possible. He didn't know how to do normal, so he'd never tried. He wasn't starting now.

As if to prove it, he pushed back with words stripped bare. "But do you really know how you feel about meaningless sex? Because that's all it would be, Libby. Fucking for the sake of getting off. Which I'm happy to do, believe me. I don't know that you are, and pushing you in that direction when you can't remember doesn't seem like the right thing to do."

Her frown was almost frightening. She seemed... *pissed off.* Whoa.

"Are you seriously suggesting that you think if we have sex I'll fall instantly in love with you and will somehow turn into a lovesick stalker or something? Because that's just insulting."

His temples were beginning to throb. Not with a headache necessarily, but with the effort of trying to be logical and thoughtful with a woman who seemed to be getting mad because he hadn't done what he'd really wanted to do, which was fuck her until they were both hot and sweaty and so tired they couldn't drag themselves out of bed for the rest of the night.

Then he wanted to wake her up and do it all over again.

"That's not what I'm suggesting," he growled. But he really was, wasn't he? He didn't want her getting emotionally attached. He didn't want to hurt her when it ended, as it would. It always did. He wasn't a long-term kind of guy. He couldn't be because he wasn't going to be like his father. Marrying a woman, having children, abusing everyone because he felt trapped, then leaving her to fend for herself and her kids while he started the cycle over with someone new.

Jared had always intended to find his old man and kick his ass someday, but the bastard had taken that option off the table when he'd put a bullet through his own brain. The kindest thing he'd ever done for anyone, really, though it'd deprived Jared of the retribution he'd spent his childhood longing for.

"Well it sure as heck sounded like it to me." She pointed a finger at him. "If you don't want to follow through, stop kissing me, Jared. Because when you kiss me—"

Shit, she was going to cry. Her lip trembled and her eyes got big and he felt like the worst kind of asshole.

But then she didn't. She frowned harder than before, if that were possible. "When you kiss me, it feels good. I want more. I want to see what everything with you feels like, and I know that could be a mistake. But you know what? It's *my* mistake to make. If you don't want to have sex with me, fine. But don't you dare tell me you're doing it for me like I'm some kind of imbecile who can't think for herself."

Holy shit.

Jared blinked at the fire flashing in her eyes, at the way she stomped and then spun on her heel and marched away. When she reached the hallway, she stopped and spun back.

"I would like to go into your study and look for a book to read. Do you mind?"

He rose, his heart hammering a little bit and his skin tingling with the sizzle sparking off her. She'd basically told him off and dismissed him—and he wanted her even more than he had before. *Jesus.* What the hell was wrong with him?

"You're done with Tolstoy?" he asked mildly, his pulse throbbing in places he tried not to notice.

"Definitely done. He's too depressing and life's too short."

This woman did not beat around the bush. He liked that. "What are you looking for? Maybe I can help."

"Something not depressing. Something fun. A romance novel if you have it, though I'm guessing you don't."

"Actually, I do. My mom liked to read Regency romances. I kept some of her favorites."

Libby's jaw dropped open a fraction. She snapped it shut again. He felt compelled to explain.

"She had signed copies. I couldn't get rid of them."

"No. Of course not."

He walked past her—not an easy task when he wanted to push her against the wall and dominate her body with his—and into his study. He went over to one of the bookshelves and pointed at one of the lower shelves in the corner. "Here."

She trailed behind him, then stooped to read the titles. "Oh, these look fun," she breathed.

He'd asked his mom once why she read romances when she had so many classics she said she wanted to read. She'd told him, "They're fun. They take me away from everyday life for a while."

He hadn't quite understood it at the time, but having read a couple of them, he did now. You could count on a romance novel to end happily. Main characters didn't tragically die after proclaiming their love. They also didn't beat the shit out of their wives and kids. Not that he believed real life operated in perfect romance novel fashion, but if it made people happy, who was he to say otherwise?

Jared watched Libby read the backs of a couple of books. He almost felt as if he'd gotten whiplash with the way she'd been angry only moments ago and now she was happily trying to find a book.

Or maybe not happily. Maybe she was determined to pretend she wasn't still upset.

Jared closed his eyes for a second. He was bad at this because he'd never done it before. Never had a woman he was attracted to living in his house while he protected her from danger. When he spent time with women in the past, he'd known what the score was. So had they. It was about sex, not relationships—even if some of them had hoped for more.

"I'm sorry," he said.

Libby looked up at him, blinking behind her glasses. She looked like a librarian interrupted during shelving. Not that all librarians wore glasses. Hell, now he was stereotyping librarians—but he liked the fantasy of the sexy librarian. If he could get Libby into a pencil skirt before stripping it off her....

"Thank you," she said, and it took him a minute to remember what she was thanking him for.

"You're right. I shouldn't make decisions for you. But it also doesn't feel right to let things keep going when it feels like taking advantage of your memory lapse."

"Fair enough." She selected a book and straightened. "But not knowing who you are and not knowing what you want are two entirely different things. I'm still a cognizant adult and I can make decisions about what I want. Remember that the next time you're tempted to kiss me."

She sailed from the room like a queen. Jared could only stand there and try to figure out how she'd bested him when he'd been certain he was the one in the right.

Apparently not.

———

THE NEXT MORNING, Libby woke and dressed in jeans and a cream sweater. She picked up the romance novel—a delicious tale about a duke and a Regency miss—and carried it downstairs so she could exchange it for another one. Jared's mom—Patricia was her name because the author had signed the book to her—had great taste in happy books.

Despite her argument with Jared yesterday, she was in a good mood. It had taken awhile though. She'd gone up to her room, shut the door, and started reading. She'd only emerged when Jared called her to dinner, returning to finish the book—which she did around one this morning.

She'd been angry and jumpy after the encounter with Jared—and horny, damn him—but the book helped. Well, right up to the point where the duke was an amazing lover and the author described in detail what he did to the rapturous heroine. Libby had been tempted to take off her clothes and go find Jared. Surely he wouldn't refuse a naked woman asking for sex.

Except she didn't really know him, and he damned well might. Especially if he thought he was being noble. A knight in shining armor indeed.

She walked into the kitchen to find him pouring water in the coffee pot. Apparently he hadn't been up too long either. He threw her a glance.

"Morning."

"Good morning," she said, determined to be sunny. He had his back to her and she let her gaze slide down his muscular form. His shoulders tapered to a narrow waist and the finest ass she thought she'd ever seen in jeans. Not that she knew it for certain, but really, could there be a better ass than that one?

She'd seen some hot men yesterday at the Cove, and there had been some fine asses. But Jared's was finer in her estimation. He turned and she yanked her gaze to his face. What she really wanted was to peruse this side of him as thoroughly as she had the other.

But he'd notice that.

"What's on the agenda for today?" she asked. "More reading? Perhaps a trek to the mailbox? Snowman building on the lido deck at two?"

His eyebrows lifted. Then he laughed. "We can build a snowman if you want. I thought we'd head over to the Cove again. I need to talk with the guys. Maddy, Tallie, and Angie will be there too."

"Maddy, Tallie, and Angie?"

"Maddy is Jace's fiancée. Tallie is Brett's—she's the interior designer—and Angie works there. But she's also engaged to Colt."

Libby couldn't help the little bubble of excitement inside. People? Actual people she could talk to who didn't have penises and didn't think like people with penises? Oh, now that was very exciting! She literally couldn't remember the last time she'd talked to another woman. The checkout lane at Target hadn't really counted because that was polite chitchat.

"When are we going?"

"Two. Unless you'd rather build a snowman on the lido deck."

"Nope. The Cove sounds fun to me."

He nodded at the book she held. "Enjoying the story?"

"I did. Finished it last night. I thought I'd get another one."

"Sure."

Libby frowned. "I wish I could have my cellphone. Ebooks," she added. "I like changing the font size."

He grinned. "Another memory?"

"I think so. Wow." She didn't think she was a power reader like Jared, but she was pretty sure she read more than a book a year. Especially if it was a romance. And if she didn't, then she was going to

correct that ASAP. Because that duke and his moves
—whoa.

He nodded. "Good. What do you want for breakfast?"

Libby pretended to think. "Bacon with a side of bacon?"

Jared snorted. "I was thinking pancakes."

She sighed dramatically. "Fine. If we must. Can I help?"

He nodded as he pulled a bowl from a cabinet. Libby joined him at the counter and they made pancakes together like they'd been doing it every day for months. It was comfortable. And it wasn't, since she was hyperaware of him. Of his raw masculinity and the way his tongue had felt stroking against hers. Not to mention the hard ridge of his penis riding against her abdomen in those rare moments he'd held her close while kissing her.

He'd wanted her. She liked being wanted. She wondered who else had wanted her. How many lovers she'd had. Or even if she'd had any. She didn't really think she was a twenty-five year old single career woman who was still a virgin, but stranger things had probably happened.

The possibilities were endless—and frustrating.

After breakfast, they cleaned up the dishes, then Libby plucked another book off Jared's shelf and started to read. By the time they were ready to go to the Cove, she'd read half of it. She reluctantly put down the tale of an earl and his Regency miss to head for Jared's truck.

When they reached BDI's building, she was surprised to discover she was nervous to meet the three women who would be there. What if they didn't like her? What if they thought she was some kind of interloper?

But nothing could be farther from the truth. All three women hugged her and pulled her over to a table against the wall. There was a long shadow box above the table. It had a long, thin length of metal pipe in it. The plaque said *Angie with a lead pipe in the warehouse.*

Angie glanced up at it as she followed Libby's eyes. Then she grinned. "You want to know what that's all about, don't you?"

"I have to admit I'm pretty curious."

Angie shrugged as she exchanged looks with the other two women. "I, um, was being held hostage by some bad men. I knocked one out with that pipe. Then Colt and the guys were there, and I was safe."

"Wow. I'm sorry you had to go through that."

"Thanks. But it worked out in the end. I got a new job and the man of my dreams." Her gaze strayed to the tall, blond man who leaned against the bar and talked with Jared.

"Oh, and he's royalty," Tallie said, waggling her eyebrows. She had the most fascinating eyes. One was blue and one was hazel. She'd explained that it was a condition called heterochromia and it didn't affect her vision. Libby tried not to stare, but the woman was striking.

"Really?" she squeaked at that bit of news.

Angie laughed. "Well, not quite. But he has a title. In France. I guess it's the equivalent of an English earl."

Maddy rolled her eyes, but it was lovingly done. "It's definitely the equivalent of an earl and Angie knows it. She's being modest since she'll get a title too when she marries him."

Angie bumped shoulders with Maddy. It was obvious these two women were great friends. "Stop, Mads. She likes to tease me since I almost didn't give Colt the time of day," Angie explained.

Libby glanced over at the big man. "That seems like it would have been a serious mistake. Even without the title."

Maddy laughed. "Damn straight it would have been."

Angie nodded. "I had issues. Thankfully, I got over them."

Libby didn't ask what kind of issues, though she wanted to. Instead, they talked about easy things like Maddy's profession as an art appraiser, Tallie's decorating business, and Angie's genius with numbers and spreadsheets. Libby loved how friendly and inclusive the women were, but she hated that she couldn't offer up anything about herself. They seemed to know it, too, and they didn't ask awkward questions.

Until Tallie leaned in and cut her eyes toward the group of men at the bar. "So what's it been like living with Jared? Is he as serious at home as he always seems everywhere else?"

Libby glanced over at him. He was engaged in

conversation and not looking at her. She felt her skin go hot.

"He's, uh, pretty serious. He reads a lot."

"He does have a lot of books. He told me he wanted plenty of shelves when I was doing the design for his study and living room." She shrugged. "I think books look good in a space, so I had no problem getting it done."

Maddy was studying Libby more closely than the other two. "You seem a little flushed, Libby. Do you need another water?"

Libby hadn't touched the water she had yet. "No, thanks. I'm fine. Just a bit warm."

"Jared took care of me," Angie said. "When they brought me back here after I'd been held hostage. He made sure I was going to be okay. He's a good guy."

"He is," Libby said. "He found me freezing in the snow with a head wound and took care of me."

She wasn't sure how much she could say to these women, so she didn't mention that he'd killed two men who were coming after her and wounded a third. She'd been told not to talk about it, but she didn't know if it applied to them or not. Best to assume it did.

"He's handsome, too," Tallie said. "If I wasn't with Brett, well, I might be interested."

Angie scoffed. "You have eyes for no one but Brett Wheeler, girlfriend. Don't even talk like that."

A goofy grin split Tallie's face. "I know that, but I'm just saying. Jared is a *catch*. Don't you think so, Libby?"

Libby didn't know everything about herself yet, but she knew she was a talker. Knew she was a social person.

But right now she was tongue-tied. These three had surprised her with how insightful they seemed to be about her attraction to Jared. Or maybe it was just that they assumed she must be. He was gorgeous, after all, and she wasn't blind. Plus she was living in his house while he and the guys did whatever it was they had to do to figure out what kind of trouble she was in.

She started to say something non-committal, but then she decided *fuck it*. The new Libby—that was the Libby who didn't know how the old Libby acted and reacted—decided she liked these women. And she wanted to talk about those kisses and how hot they'd been.

She *needed* to talk about those kisses, or she'd explode.

So she did.

Chapter Sixteen

ONCE JARED WAS CERTAIN LIBBY WAS COMFORTABLE WITH the three women, he went over and told her he had to go upstairs to the office. Maddy was looking at him with an arched eyebrow. Angie might have been smirking. And Tallie made a noise that might have been *mmm-hmm*.

He looked at the four of them sitting there, looking like they'd been besties forever, and felt something prickling the back of his neck. It wasn't fear or discomfort or anything like that. But these women were up to no good. He'd bet his last nickel on it.

Maybe he should have told the guys to leave their women at home. Except for Angie, since she worked there. But she could have stayed upstairs and worked on her spreadsheets. That would have been infinitely safer.

Too late now.

"Take your time," Libby said, waving a hand. "I'll be fine."

Colt came over to kiss Angie, then the two of them

headed for the elevator. Once the doors closed, Colt laughed.

"Dude, you are in so much trouble."

"Don't remind me."

"Hey, you wanted the ladies to make her feel at home. Looks like they're doing it."

Yeah, they were. Damn it, he should have considered how this had been likely to go. Maddy, Angie, and Tallie were likable and friendly—and Libby was a talker. There was no chance she wasn't going to tell them about what'd happened yesterday when he'd kissed her.

The elevator took them to the fifth floor where they headed to Ian's office and the conference room attached to it. Ian was at the head of the table. Jace Kaiser, Brett Wheeler, Tyler Scott, and Dax Freed were there too. They looked up when Colt and Jared walked in.

"How's Libby?" Ian asked.

"She's fine. Enjoying the company of the ladies."

"You might regret that later," Brett murmured.

"I heard that," Jared replied.

Brett grinned. "All I'm saying is you just put your protectee in the company of three intelligent, capable, nosy women who are going to want to know everything that's happened since you found her."

"Nothing's happened," Jared said. Nothing important anyway. He'd kissed her. And they *were* probably going to talk about it, but a kiss was just a kiss.

"They'll be the judge of that," Jace replied with a laugh.

Jared yanked out a chair and flopped onto it. "I'm protecting Liberty King, not sleeping with her. This is a mission. That's all." He crossed his hands in the universal *you're out* sign used in baseball. "Nothing to see here. No romance. No love affair. Nothing."

"I can transfer her protection to someone else if you'd prefer," Ian said mildly. "Give you back your reading time."

Jared's blood was beginning to boil. Just a little bit. "She's not a pet who needs constant attention. I can read just fine with her in my house."

Ian shrugged, and Jared got the opinion the boss was enjoying this way too much. The other guys were either coughing politely or trying to hide grins behind masks of indifference.

"Just let me know if you change your mind," Ian said.

"I'll do that." He didn't clench his teeth when he said it. Barely.

"I assume she hasn't remembered anything substantial yet."

"No. But her memories are returning in bits and pieces. I expect she'll get most of it back in the next few days or weeks. That's what Dr. Puckett thinks too."

"We don't need her to remember anything to keep working on this puzzle, but it'd be nice if she did. The surveillance team watching her apartment hasn't picked up anything out of the ordinary, by the way. Whoever cased her place hasn't been back."

Jared was glad to hear it. Maybe the people looking for her had moved on to a new target. Not that he really believed that, but it was a nice thought.

Ian picked up a remote and clicked it. The overhead

projector came to life and a photo appeared on the screen. "Daniel Weir, CEO of Ninja Solutions."

Weir didn't look like a typical nerd, but he also didn't look like someone who was outdoorsy and fit. He was thin, tall, with lanky brown hair and pale skin. He probably had a boyish sort of appeal for women who liked that kind of thing. Jared found himself wondering if Libby was one of those women. Just because she'd responded to him when he'd kissed her didn't mean she didn't prefer a desk dweller with a big brain.

"Formed the company three years ago, made a big splash with a software program he designed that helped increase satellite targeting accuracy in tests. Started work on the exoskeleton afterwards, known as the RIM project, and threw all his resources behind it. Moved to the Chantilly offices last year, hired more workers, expanded operations. Wines and dines with the Washington elite frequently, which is how he managed to get research funds thrown his direction. The prototype test results are spectacular, and the Army wants to move forward with the project. Everything's coming up roses for Mr. Weir."

"Which means he'd be pretty upset if it all went sideways," Jared said, a hard knot sitting in his belly as he studied the slides.

"Ten-four," Ian said, clicking over to a new slide. "Weir just got engaged to Jessica Klein, daughter of Congressman Klein. He's building a big house in Potomac with stables for Jessica's dressage horses, he recently bought a Ferrari, and Jessica is planning a wedding with a rumored half-mil budget." Ian clicked a couple of slides. "It goes on and on. The usual for a newly rich man looking to get even richer and more connected."

"Meaning he has a lot of debt," Jared said.

"Bingo," Ian replied. "If he sells his RIM suits to the Army—which it looks like he's about to do—he's got every reason to expect earnings to continue rising."

Jared knew that Ian would have had to tap into his sources to learn that information since he wasn't officially involved in military channels—but Ian's contacts went deep. He could learn just about anything if he was determined enough.

"He'd have a lot of incentive to make sure his proprietary plans didn't get into the wrong hands. If he thought someone had stolen them with the intent to sell or share, he might hire a couple of mercenaries to shake that person down for the goods and then dispose of her," Dax said.

Jared didn't like the thought that Libby could have stolen top secret information, but he couldn't refuse to consider it. "She didn't have anything on her when I found her," Jared said. "And she didn't have it when she was abducted either. If she had, they'd have found it."

"Could be inside her head," Colt said.

"It could be," Jared replied. "It's possible she lost her memory before she could tell them what they wanted to know."

"Do you think she could have stolen the RIM plans and hid them somewhere? Or some other information to do with the project that could blow the whole thing to pieces?" Jace asked. "It would explain why her apartment was trashed."

Jared blew out a breath. "I don't know. It's possible."

"Her background doesn't indicate an obvious need for money," Ian said. "There's no relative with an incurable disease and no unusual debt. Not that others haven't stolen top secret files and sold them to the highest bidder without obvious incentives other than money. It certainly happens. Somebody gets sick of the rat race and envisions escaping to an island, or maybe they live on the edge of wealth and want it for themselves. And if it's not plans she possesses, but information related to the project, then what could be the end game there?"

"No idea," Jared said. He wanted to defend her, but he didn't. He had to look at this like he would any other operation. Coldly. Objectively. Just because he'd spent the past few days with her didn't mean he knew who she was inside, even if he felt like he did. Even if she'd been embarrassed to let him buy clothes for her and thanked him at every turn for it, that didn't mean she wasn't capable of selling information for the kind of big money that could change a life.

But everything within him told him she wasn't the kind of person to steal top secret files and sell them for personal gain. Hell, she came from a family where the kids were named for patriotic ideals and people. She would have been raised to love her country, not hate it. That didn't preclude someone from betraying their country for financial gain, though. Everyone in this room had seen it happen before.

"I'm setting up a meeting with Weir," Ian said. "As an interested buyer in his exoskeleton, of which I've heard rumors. Since the Army contract isn't final, he might be seeking other buyers in the interim."

Jared perked up at that. "When?"

"I've got Melanie arranging for sometime this week. We're inviting him to BDI."

"I want to be here when it happens."

Ian nodded. "I figured that." He turned back to the screen. "Here's Ninja Solutions' organizational hierarchy. There are a few others with access to the project. Engineers especially, but also corporate officers such as the CFO. That would be Nate Anderson, pictured here."

This guy was less of a brainy type than Daniel Weir. Forty-ish, with boyish good looks, he was the sort who would attract female attention. The sort who could manipulate it too.

"Forty-one, divorced, and pissed off about it. His wife gets a huge alimony check every month, and there's a buttload of child support too. A leading candidate for disgruntled employee looking to make a quick buck, but absolutely no evidence that points to him. In short, no plans or files we can find anywhere, but it's clear that someone thinks Libby took something important to the RIM project."

"Or somebody wanted it to look that way," Jared said.

Ian nodded. "That too." He flicked to a new slide. "Here's what the IT department found on those IDs you captured. The guns were registered to these men, so nothing wrong there."

There were three men listed, with photos. Beard Man, a.k.a. Joe Boggs, and Gaiter Man, aka Luke Byrd, had served in the infantry. Eight years enlistment each with tours in Iraq and Afghanistan. Boggs had an other than honorable discharge, and Byrd had an honorable discharge. Robert Sorrel didn't have any military history, but he sometimes worked with the other two in the company they'd started. It was called B&B Security and they advertised that no job was too small or too dirty to take on. They were based in Reston and they'd been around for a little over four years.

"Any bodies yet?" Jared asked.

"Not yet. Whoever cleaned the site did a professional job. I don't imagine anything'll turn up at any point in the next year. If ever. But the dogs are safe. They were dropped off yesterday at a no-kill shelter twenty miles from the mountain. When they were scanned for microchips, Sorrel's name came up."

"Thank goodness for that," Jared said. He didn't like the idea of innocent animals getting hurt. He'd left the dogs with Sorrel because it was clear the man cared for them. Jared had figured Ian's clean up crew would take care of the dogs along with the man. Except nobody'd been there when they'd arrived.

"Guess one of them phoned whoever'd hired them and said they'd found Libby," Brett mused. "When they didn't make contact as scheduled, somebody went looking."

Ian nodded. "And that somebody had access to a

clean-up crew that could get out there fast, in the snow, and sanitize the site."

Jared really didn't like the implications of that thought. "Whoever wants to find Libby isn't an amateur, no matter that B&B Security fucked up the job in the first place."

"Nope," Ian replied. "I expect we've got a state actor here. Or quite possibly someone in the Gemini Syndicate. They'd try to keep their distance at first, but I don't think that's possible any longer."

A chill shot down Jared's spine. They all knew the Gemini Syndicate meant trouble. Probably more trouble than Russia or China trying to buy American secrets. "I don't think Boggs and Byrd were expecting this to be a hard job. They got careless—and they underestimated Libby's will to escape."

"Plus they damned sure didn't count on you," Brett said.

"They really didn't. It probably would've worked out for them if she'd run into anybody but me." A frightening thought, but true.

"Yeah, if you hadn't been there, they'd have found her. If she'd still been alive when they did, they'd have probably gotten what they wanted out of her and whoever'd hired them would've been satisfied. But they lost her, and that put a serious kink in someone's plans."

Jace looked grim. "You realize that if it *is* Gemini behind this, we really need to watch Libby's back. Because they have the best assassin in the business and they won't let anyone fuck this up a second time."

Ian frowned. "Let's pray it's not them—because if

they've sent Calypso to capture or kill Libby King, this job just got a whole lot harder."

———

"I LIKED THEM," Libby said. "Thanks for asking them to stay with me."

Jared shot her a glance as he drove. He seemed more intense than he had last night, if that were possible. "I'm glad you had a good time."

Libby bit her lip and tried not to smile. She'd told the women about Jared kissing her last night. About him backing away, too. They'd exchanged looks, of course.

"Jared keeps to himself a lot," Maddy'd said. "But I've known him long enough to know that even though he's quiet and contemplative, there's a lot going on beneath the surface."

Tallie had nodded. "Still waters run deep. My daddy always said that."

"I've never seen him bring anyone to any of our get-togethers," Angie had added. "Not that I've been around all that long, but Jared is always alone at every function."

"Honestly, I was wondering if he was gay," Tallie'd said.

Maddy had spluttered. Angie'd laughed. Libby's jaw had dropped. Tallie had spread her hands. "I wouldn't care if he was, of course. I've puzzled over it though, believe me. He's neat, he reads a lot, he cooks, his house is nice, and I've never seen him with a woman even though he's so gorgeous he can't have *any* trouble getting a date. So I was starting to wonder. When I asked Brett once, he just laughed like I'd said the funniest thing. He told me there was no way Jared was gay, but I wondered if maybe he was just clueless."

Libby'd grinned. "Jared is very neat. And he does read a *lot*. But believe me, there was definitely something going on in his pants when he kissed me." She'd sighed. "Something I really wanted to get closer to."

Libby still couldn't believe she'd been so honest with three women she didn't know, but they'd made her feel normal for a while. Like not knowing who she really was inside didn't matter. She was a woman who wanted a man who was trying to be noble for reasons of his own, and that was enough to talk and puzzle over for better than an hour.

It was the considered opinion of all three women that if Jared kissed her again, she shouldn't let him stop until they'd both had at least two orgasms. Preferably more, for her at least.

She swallowed a laugh as heat bloomed in her cheeks. For some reason, she hadn't gotten embarrassed with those three, but thinking like this now, with Jared beside her, made the blushes come back.

"What are you thinking about?" Jared asked, startling her.

Libby dragged in a calming breath and shot him a smile. "Nothing much. Why?"

He studied her for a second before turning his gaze back to the road. They'd come to a stop light, so he had more time to look. His hands flexed on the wheel. "You're blushing again, that's why."

Libby rolled her head back against the headrest. "Can't a girl have some private thoughts without you always trying to butt in? I thought you liked quiet, not all this chattering."

His eyes were wide as he looked at her again. It was all she could do not to laugh. His gaze narrowed as her lips twitched. "I don't chatter."

"You do when you want to know what I'm thinking about. Maybe I'm thinking about that romance novel. Did you ever consider that? It was pretty racy, you know."

"Was it?"

"Yes. The duke was quite, er, thorough in his attentions."

"And you liked that."

"Who wouldn't? He focused all his passion on the heroine and it was pretty spectacular. And yes, blush-worthy."

He snorted. "I'm not sure I believe you."

"Oh really? Maybe you should read the book. Then you'll know."

"I'm sure the book is just as you described. I'm not sure I believe that's what you were thinking about."

He sounded smug. So smug that she decided it would be fun to take some of the wind from his sails. "Tallie thought you were gay."

"What?!" He drove into the parking lot of the restaurant where they were picking up takeout and turned to stare at her once they'd come to a stop.

Libby couldn't help but laugh. "She said she'd never seen you with a woman so she'd wondered.

Apparently you don't take a date to any of the parties."

He closed his eyes and shook his head. "I fucking knew it was a mistake to introduce you to those three."

"It wasn't," she said primly. "They made me forget for a while that I've got all this trouble hanging over my head. They made me feel like we were friends."

He studied her. "That's good, Libby. But I'm not gay. If I was, I wouldn't hide it."

She couldn't stop the smile that spread over her face. "I know you aren't, Jared. Though I guess you could be bi…."

He shook his head. "Not bi. Not interested in men *at all*."

"Are you quite sure?" She tried to sound innocent, but the snicker ruined it.

"I can't believe I'm having this conversation with you. But trust me when I tell you I have no desire to suck anyone's dick. The only dick I want to touch is my own." He grinned at her as fresh color flared in her cheeks. "Careful. You're going to have to start fanning yourself in a second."

"You like to make me blush."

"Hey, I didn't start it this time. That was you." He unclipped his seatbelt. "I'll be back in a minute. Just going to the window and grabbing the food."

There was a walk-up takeout window at the front of the restaurant not more than twenty feet away. She started to unclip her seatbelt. "I can get it. It's the least I can do."

He shook his head as he opened the door. "No, you stay here. I'd rather you weren't out in the open."

Libby swallowed at that reminder that no matter how much fun she'd been having, things were *not* normal for her. "Okay," she breathed.

He smiled as he opened his door. "It's okay, babe. We're going to fix this."

She watched him walk toward the restaurant, her eyes glued to his backside the whole way. Damn he was fine. And she was still hot with embarrassment at the idea of him touching his dick. Not that she didn't want to see that happen. Hell, she wanted to touch it too.

"Lordy, Libby," she said under her breath. "You are in over your head."

She pressed her hands to the cold glass of her window before laying them on her cheeks. If she was lucky, she'd be back to normal by the time he returned. If she wasn't, well, he'd probably tease her the rest of the way home.

She couldn't say that she didn't like it though. She liked it a lot. He made her feel alive and happy, in spite of everything.

A tiny current of sadness slid through her. She didn't want the feeling to end, but she knew it would. It was inevitable that she'd go back to her real life once this was over. Once he'd done his job and kept her safe. No more banter with Jared. No more conversations with Maddy, Tallie, and Angie. No more time at the Cove.

The thought of losing those things—losing him especially—made her heart ache.

Chapter Seventeen

Jared was distracted. The thought of Calypso coming for Libby wasn't a welcome one, that's for sure. The assassin had escaped BDI's operatives in the past. And she'd been released by Ian the one time they'd had her in custody. Jared hadn't agreed with that decision, but it hadn't been his to make.

Ian Black was convinced he could pull Calypso to their side if he gave her the space to operate and the promise he would protect her if she turned against her employers.

Jared knew her identity. Few of them did, but he'd been there the night she'd shot Jace and Colt. He'd helped pick up those pieces, and he knew what kind of aim she'd needed to do what she'd done. She'd shot her own brother. She'd also rescued Tallie Grant from a mountaintop monastery in Spain, though a BDI team had been on the way. Calypso had gotten there first and she'd killed the doctor who'd turned the monastery into a laboratory for his human experiments. That certainly wasn't a loss for humanity.

But Calypso was a wild card. She was unpredictable, and her motives weren't clear. If the Gemini Syndicate was somehow involved, then why not send Calypso in the first place? That was what Jared didn't understand. And if Calypso *did* come looking for Libby, was she planning to take her or kill her? It would really help if they knew just exactly what the fuck Libby was supposed to have. But since they didn't, and since she didn't remember, then they had to keep her safe and wait for the information to reveal itself.

He shoved a hand through his hair and put down the book he was reading. He couldn't concentrate on it anyway. They'd returned more than three hours ago, eaten Italian takeout at the kitchen island, and then he'd gone to his study.

Mostly to get away from Libby. Because she made him laugh, and she made him want to prove to her in the most obvious way possible that he wasn't in the least bit attracted to men.

He snorted. Tallie Grant had actually wondered about his sexual preferences. He probably shouldn't be surprised since it was true he didn't usually take a date to any of the various parties or group get-togethers they'd held. Mostly because there'd been no one he'd wanted to spend that kind of time with. His job and life, his friends, were separate from his sex life. He wasn't going to take a woman he was fucking to spend time with his friends unless he felt there was something more going on between them. It was too awkward otherwise.

He hadn't felt that way about anyone he'd been with in the past couple of years. Before that—before Tallie, Maddy, and Angie were a part of his friends' lives—he'd occasionally shown up at a bar where he'd been meeting friends with a date. It was always a hassle for one reason or another. The date didn't fit in, or she pouted because he wasn't glued to her side, or she didn't like the bar, or she turned up her nose at the food, or any of a hundred reasons that he'd grown tired of. So he'd stopped taking dates to group events long before Tallie had arrived.

Jared opened the study door and heard the television. He'd thought Libby was reading, but maybe she'd gotten bored and decided to watch TV instead. He'd told her to feel at home, and he'd shown her how to turn everything on.

When he walked into the living room, she was curled up on the couch, watching a show that featured people in historical costumes. She looked up at his approach and smiled.

"Oh, hey. I hope I didn't disturb you."

She did disturb him. She was disturbing him. Not that he'd tell her that.

"Nope. What are you watching?"

"It's *Outlander.* I thought if I watched it, since I remembered that I had before, maybe I'd remember something else. Like it might trigger a memory of where I was or what I was doing."

"And has it?"

She shook her head sadly. "Unfortunately, no. But the scenery is pretty. So are the characters."

"Did you finish reading the novel?"

"I had to stop for a while."

She didn't explain and he didn't ask.

"Me too, actually."

"Oh? What were you reading?"

"Same book I had at the cabin. About the NSA."

She rolled her eyes mockingly. "Oh, that. No wonder you had to stop. Probably putting you to sleep."

He laughed. "Actually, I find it fascinating."

"I'm sure it is."

"You're just saying that."

"Pretty much." She grinned. "Want to watch sexy Scottish men with me?"

"Uh, I think I'd better say no when you put it that way."

"Spoilsport." She looked down at the remote in her hand as if she were studying the keys. "You know I don't really think you're bisexual, right? It was a joke. I'm sorry if I offended you."

He shook his head. "You are so damned polite. I wasn't offended. A little surprised that Tallie thought I could be gay, but not shocked when I think back on it. It's true I've never taken a date to anything the group does together. The other guys bring dates sometimes, though."

"I probably shouldn't have told you she said that. Please don't tell her I did."

She seemed so worried that he couldn't do anything but agree—even if teasing her first might have been fun. "I won't. Promise."

Her smile was bright. "Thank you. I mean I know I won't be around for much longer, but if I get to talk to them again, I'd hate for her to think—any of them to think—I can't be trusted."

He knew what she meant, but he didn't like the way it sounded when she said she wasn't going to be around. "You can still be friends with them after you go back to your life."

She caressed the remote. "I know. But it's hard to say what the future's going to bring, so I'm not counting on anything staying the same."

In his experience, nothing ever stayed the same. Just when you thought you were happy and life was going your way, something happened. Your dad walked out on you and your mother. Your mother went from being there for you all the time to working all the time. Then she died before you could take care of her for a change instead of the other way around.

Jared swallowed. "You don't know what's going to happen, Libby. Take it a day at a time and don't get too twisted up about the future."

Her brown eyes were bright as she gazed up at him. "I want to remember. I want to know what my life was like—and I don't. I'm afraid of the uncertainty, and frustrated by it too."

"I know, honey. Nothing you can do about that but wait."

"If I could just have my phone back." She frowned. "I could scroll through my texts, my emails. See who I know, who I hang out with."

"It's not safe," he said in more clipped tones than he intended. She blinked at him and he softened his voice. "If you're involved in something, you can be tracked through your cell phone. If somebody were to show up here looking for you, they wouldn't be unprepared this time. I can't protect you if you compromise your safety."

She pulled in a breath, then nodded, her gaze dropping to her lap again. "I know. I'm sorry."

Shit. He'd been too harsh with her and he hated the way she seemed to fold in on herself. Because of him.

He dropped to his haunches in front of her. Without thinking about it, he reached out and brushed her hair back from where it had fallen into her face, then tipped her chin up so her gaze was even with his. His fingers skimmed her throat, her cheek, then dropped away as that persistent kernel of need started to flare deep inside.

"Do you trust me, Libby?"

"You know I do." She sounded hoarse, strained.

"I promise you that the minute it's safe to do so, I'll get your phone for you. I'm not trying to keep you in the dark on purpose, okay?"

"I know you aren't. I'm grateful, Jared. Really. If I hadn't somehow walked into your path in those woods —" He could feel her shudder as it rolled over her like a seismic wave. "I wouldn't be here. They would have found me and killed me."

He found himself studying her mouth, the way her top lip had that pretty little dip in it. The her bottom lip was full and kissable. Her eyes glittered and her cheeks glowed with health, and her cuts and bruises were healing. He wanted to kiss her. Wanted to pounce on her like a tiger and devour her.

Which was precisely why he forced himself to his

feet. She gazed up at him, puzzled. What had she just said to him? He cast backward, thinking—oh yes, that she would have been dead without him. She would have been, and that scared her. Naturally. Meanwhile, he was acting like a madman who couldn't think of anything but kissing her lush mouth and exploring her curves.

"They didn't," he croaked. "And you don't have to be grateful. It's my job."

"I know that—but doesn't anyone ever thank you for it?"

"They do. But it's not necessary." He drew in a breath. "I think I'm going to bed. Enjoy your sexy Scots."

She looked disappointed, and he hated that he'd put that expression on her face. "Okay," she said. "Good night, Jared. See you in the morning for bacon cupcakes."

He couldn't help but snort a laugh. Then he bent and kissed her cheek. " 'Night, Libby. Sleep tight."

———

LIBBY DIDN'T STAY DOWNSTAIRS MUCH LONGER. She finished the episode she'd been watching, then turned the television off with a sigh. She could still feel Jared's fingers against her skin, still see the depths of those blue eyes as he'd looked at her so seriously and asked if she trusted him.

Of course she trusted him. There was no one she trusted more. Literally, since she didn't know anyone else as well as she knew him. Libby went upstairs as quietly as she could, but the house was old and the wood creaked as she walked. She needn't have feared waking Jared, though. There was light coming from beneath his door.

She pictured him in bed, reading or scrolling through his phone. Disappointment was a bitter pill in her throat. He hadn't been tired so much as he'd wanted to escape her. Just like he had earlier after they'd eaten their dinner and he'd retreated to his office.

She'd felt guilty, like maybe she'd annoyed him by telling him what Tallie had said and then teasing him about it. She hadn't thought Jared was the sort to get bent out of shape over such a thing, but she'd had to wonder if she was wrong. Until he'd emerged and assured her he wasn't upset about it.

So why was he avoiding her? Because they'd argued last night? She didn't know, and she wasn't going to ask.

Libby got ready for bed, then climbed between the sheets and turned out the light. The house was quiet, other than creaking as it settled. She liked old houses. She'd grown up in an old farmhouse.

Libby sat bolt upright, her heart pounding. She'd grown up in an old farmhouse! She could see the white clapboard siding, the hickory stained floors, the kitchen with its white cabinets and farmer's sink beneath the big window that looked out on the yard and the fields beyond. There were chickens in a coop, and a barn with grain storage in the distance. She heard a cow lowing in the field—and a woman sat at the kitchen table, snapping beans. On the stove was a boiling pot and empty mason jars in a row on the counter.

"Canning," she said to herself. "We were canning."

Libby lay back down and tried to pull more memories from her brain. That life seemed so strange to her, so incongruous with who she felt like she was. It was like that life belonged to someone else. She wondered if she'd read it in a book, or maybe she'd watched it on television.

But no, the woman was her mother. Libby was dutifully snapping beans the way her mother showed her. She thought she was about ten. She had pigtails and she wanted to go outside to play more than she wanted to snap beans.

"You can go outside when we get these beans done, Libby."

"Yes, ma'am."

Libby sorted her memories, searching for more. But nothing else came. At one in the morning, she still hadn't fallen asleep. She threw back the covers and slipped on her socks. She'd failed to buy pajamas at Target so Jared had given her one of his T-shirts and a pair of sleep pants that she'd had to roll up several times so they didn't drag the floor. Fortunately, there was a drawstring to cinch the waist in so the pants didn't fall down.

She slipped out the door and down the stairs, trying not to hit the creakiest spots. When she reached the kitchen, she went searching for milk and a pan to heat it in, but came across an open bottle of white wine instead.

"That'll do," she muttered, finding a glass and pouring some wine in it. Warm milk was what her mother had given her when she was little and couldn't sleep, but wine was the grown-up option. She put the bottle back and closed the refrigerator door.

A shape moved in the entry. Libby bit off her scream when Jared spoke. "It's just me."

"You scared me!" she hollered.

"Sorry," he said, coming into the room. The light from a streetlamp lit his features as he moved into the open. His hair was mussed, and he wasn't wearing a shirt. *Oh dear lord....*

Sleep pants hung low on his hips, but her gaze was caught on his midsection. His ab muscles had ab muscles. And he had a happy trail of dark hair leading from his belly button before disappearing below his waistband. Everything about Jared Fraser was tight and taut and beautiful.

And Libby couldn't think of a damned word to say.

"Can't sleep?" he asked.

"Urg," she said.

He tilted his head slightly. "You okay?"

"Um... urg... um... Yes! Yes, of course," she blurted when she regained control of her voice. "Can't sleep. Sorry. Wine."

She held up the glass, then blushed because she was being a damned idiot. At least it was dark and he couldn't see her blush. Or tease her for it.

"Oh yeah, almost forgot I had that. Bought a couple of bottles when Brett and Tallie came over to celebrate that she'd finished the project. She likes white wine."

Libby took a big sip. "Me too."

Jared motioned toward the refrigerator. "I couldn't sleep either. I was coming for a beer." He walked past her and opened the fridge, pulled out a beer and twisted the cap with his bare hand. Then he came toward her again. She couldn't move. She could only stare.

The most gorgeous man of her imagination stopped in front of her and clinked his beer bottle with her glass. "Cheers," he said.

"Cheers," she croaked in the least sexy voice imaginable. Then she gulped wine to try and soothe her parched throat.

"What woke you?" he asked after he'd lowered the bottle.

"I don't think I ever slept," she said. "I remembered something that happened when I was about ten, I think. I was snapping beans with my mother because she was canning them. I remember a farmhouse, and a field. There were chickens and grain silos." She shrugged. "I kept trying to remember more, but that was it. What kept you awake?"

He lifted the bottle to his lips and drank a couple of swallows before lowering it to study her. His eyes were hot and moody and her stomach twisted as she waited for his answer.

"You did."

Chapter Eighteen

Libby's lips fell open as she stared at him. He probably shouldn't have admitted that to her, but it was the middle of the night and his guard was down. Too late now.

"Oh. I'm sorry. I didn't think I was noisy. I might have flopped around in the bed too much and—"

He put a finger over her mouth, stopping the torrent. "You didn't make any noise. It wasn't that."

"Oh, um," she said as he dropped his finger away.

She wasn't wearing a bra and her nipples were poking through the fabric of his T-shirt. *His* T-shirt. He liked the way seeing her in his clothes made him feel.

Hot. Hard. Ready to strip her out of them and make her scream.

He'd told himself all the reasons he shouldn't do it. He'd been telling himself for hours now.

Didn't matter, though. He wanted to. His needs were overriding his sense—and he'd been thinking about what she'd said to him the night before. It was *her* choice, not his. If he touched her the way he wanted to, and she said no, then he'd have his answer, wouldn't he?

But if he touched her and she responded, then it wasn't ending until they were completely spent. Until he'd explored every inch of her and made her come until she couldn't possibly come one more time.

He was still arguing with himself because the last thing he'd expected to find when he came down to the kitchen was her.

Liar.

Yeah, okay, so maybe he was a liar. He'd heard the creaking of the stairs. It could have been the house settling, but he'd known it was more than that. The sound was rhythmic, like someone moving down them.

He could see her throat move as she swallowed. "What was it then?"

Jared put a hand on her hip, inched her forward until their bodies were nearly touching. "It was the thought of everything I could be doing with you, if you'd let me."

She tipped her head back to look up at him. "I thought you didn't want to take advantage of my memory loss."

"I don't. But as you pointed out, not knowing who you are and not knowing what you want are two entirely different things."

He thought she might step away, but she lifted the hand not holding a wine glass and placed it on his chest. The contact scorched him. Lightly, she skimmed her fingers across from one pectoral muscle to the other, over his nipples—and they *were* sensitive—and then down over his upper abdomen. He didn't say a word, just let her do it. But inside he was on fire. Inside, he was molten.

"I'm having a hard time imagining why you'd want to do this with me," she said as she continued to lightly caress his skin.

He was dying here. His dick was harder than he thought it had ever been in his life, and his heart was thundering in his chest. "Why would you say that?"

She blinked up at him. "Because look at you. You're perfect."

He caught her hand and pressed it to his heart because she was touching him too lightly to feel how it beat. "You're perfect too, Libby." He slid his hand from her hip around to her ass and squeezed one cheek. "You've got the kind of ass that makes men wild, and you kiss with your whole body. I can't wait to find out what else you do when I get you naked."

He could feel the shudder ripple through her. "I thought I talked too much for you. What if I talk the whole time?"

He dipped his head and nibbled her ear lobe. She moaned, her fingers curling against his chest. He whispered into the shell of her ear, "I can think of ways to keep your mouth busy."

He dragged his tongue down her throat, then took her wine glass and set it on the island, set his beer there too, and then gripped her hips with both hands, dragging her against him. She couldn't miss how much he wanted her. His dick was stone, and his body was coiled tighter than a spring.

She gasped at the feel of him. Both her palms landed on his chest. He wondered if she might push him away, but then she slid them up and around his neck and he thanked God for it.

"If I'm dreaming, I don't want to wake up," she said as he lowered his mouth to the base of her throat.

"Me neither," he told her. He squeezed her ass again and she let out a low moan. "If you decide at any point that you aren't down for this after all, just tell me. I'll stop."

Libby laughed, but the sound was strangled. "What kind of fool would I have to be to do that?"

"Nevertheless." He ran his hands up her sides, slipping beneath the T-shirt she wore, and cupped her breasts in both hands. Rubbing his thumbs across her nipples, he fused his mouth to hers. She opened beneath him without hesitation.

Really, he shouldn't be this damned excited, but it'd been a long time and he was more than ready. His body was letting him know it, too. His pulse pounded, his skin was on fire, and his dick ached with the need to plunge into Libby's body and not stop until he'd exploded.

But that wasn't the kind of lover he was, so he put the brakes on and forced himself to slow down. Libby's tongue against his wasn't tentative, but it wasn't bold either. She kissed him as if she didn't quite know what to expect. Hell, he didn't know either. All he knew was he wanted this. He'd been wanting it for the past couple of days.

Jared broke the kiss and pushed her shirt up until he could turn his attention to her nipples. They were tight, hard little points, and he wanted to suck them until she squirmed. His mouth closed over one, his teeth barely grazing her, and then sucked hard.

"Jared... Oh hell... Oh god...."

He would have laughed if he wasn't so damned turned on. He sucked her other nipple, then slipped an arm behind her knees and lifted her. She squeaked, but she wrapped her arms around his neck.

"As much as I'd love some hot kitchen sex, I think a bed is better for the first time, don't you?"

Libby laughed, but it wasn't a nervous sound. Or not entirely anyway. There was happiness in her laugh. He liked it. "Actually, I don't remember the places I've had sex—or *if* I have, so I can't say where it's better."

"So maybe we'll test out a few locations. Find out where you like it best."

She buried her face against his neck. He suspected she was blushing, but he didn't ask. "Right now, I can't think of anything I want more," she said, her breath whispering across his skin, making him shiver with need.

He carried her through the living room and up the stairs to his bedroom. He almost took her to the guest room, thinking she might be more comfortable there, but then decided to hell with it, he wanted her in his bed. He'd never brought anyone to this house and had sex with them before. He always went to hotels, or sometimes to a woman's home, but never here. This was his space, his domain. And he didn't like anyone well enough to share it.

But Libby was different. Everything about this situation was different.

He wasn't going to analyze it. He was going to go by feel.

LIBBY WAS DIZZY. Not literally dizzy, but her head was reeling from how quickly everything had changed. One minute she was pouring a glass of wine because she couldn't sleep and the next Jared was standing there, telling her he wanted her.

Maybe she should be more careful, but the truth was she wanted him too. She was mesmerized by him, by his strength and his honor. He'd never faltered carrying her upstairs, and now he set her down and backed her toward his bed, his hands grasping the hem of her T-shirt—his, really—and tugging it upward.

Libby didn't resist as the fabric went up and over. He dropped it on the floor before his hands found her breasts, cupping them, lifting and pushing them together until her nipples were side by side.

"So pretty," he said. And then he touched his tongue to first one and then the other—and Libby couldn't stop the low moan that issued from her throat. She had no idea what she liked in bed, but this had to be one of those things. A man who played with her breasts and didn't try to rush everything so that he could get inside her and get off before she'd even gotten warmed up.

Libby clutched Jared's shoulders, her head falling back, her hair tracing a silky trail across her naked back.

"You like your nipples sucked," he murmured before

blowing on them, causing them to bud into tighter points than before.

"I think I do," she whispered. An understatement really, considering how her body tightened at every tug of his mouth.

"If you like that, I think you're really going to like the other place I want to suck you."

Libby shuddered. She couldn't say no now if her life depended on it. Her entire body ached. She *hurt*. It was a good hurt, but also not one she wanted to endure for much longer.

"Jared…"

The backs of her knees hit the bed and she crashed to a stop, her body gently colliding with his. He was so solid, so big. And definitely in control.

"I'm planning to strip off those sleep pants, Libby. Then I'm laying you back on the bed and putting my mouth on the hottest, wettest part of you. And I'm not stopping until you've screamed my name at least twice."

Libby whimpered. The only thing keeping her upright was the fact she was clinging to Jared's shoulders. But he took that away from her when he dropped to his knees and tugged her sleep pants down. The look on his face as he studied her panties made her heart skip.

"Turn around," he said hoarsely.

She stepped out of the sleep pants and did so, slowly. Jared groaned. Then he put both hands on her ass and squeezed softly.

"These fucking lacy panties. I've thought about your ass in these things since I put them in the washer that morning. I'm glad these are the ones you're wearing today."

Libby's breath caught. Her heart beat crazy hard and her pussy was so wet it hurt. Or maybe it hurt because she needed him to touch her there. Jared dragged her panties down, his mouth finding that little dip at the base of her spine before he nibbled his way down one cheek and over to the other. His fingers came around the front of her, slipping downward until he skimmed over her clit and into the wet seam between her legs.

He groaned and nipped her ass, and Libby cried out. Not from the pain of it, but from the excitement.

"Was that too hard? I'm sorry."

"No. Lord no. Please don't stop, Jared. I think I'm going to die if you stop."

"You have the prettiest ass, honey. And damn you're wet." He pressed a finger deep inside her and she jerked her hips a little bit, trying to find the pressure she wanted from him. He added another finger, fucking her slowly that way as his other hand found her clit and strummed it.

Libby could barely stand.

"So fucking pretty," he said. "I want to stay right here and make you come like this, but there are too many other things I want to do. Fuck, Libby, you're making me crazy."

She was making him crazy? She thought she would fly apart any second if he kept up that rhythmic stroking. She *wanted* to fly apart.

But Jared was too in control to let her. He stood

and pushed her onto the bed, then turned her over so he could look at her. Up until now, she'd been too caught up in what was happening to think about her body or the soft light from the lamp that spilled into the room. It was a dim light, but it was still light. Enough that he could see her imperfections, like the soft roll at her belly and the bruise on her hip—a temporary imperfection, but still—as well as the way her breasts were too small for the size of her butt. He would see it all, and she hoped he wouldn't be disappointed.

"What's going through your mind, Libby?" he asked, his eyes narrowing as he studied her.

She put an arm over her belly. "Nothing. Just waiting for you."

He put a knee on the bed, then came down on top of her, his body skimming over hers. Not really touching, but not so far away she couldn't feel his heat either. He licked a nipple, then sucked it before letting go and finding the other.

"I don't believe you," he said, popping the nipple from his mouth.

His hands skimmed her body, his gaze following. When he reached the bruise on her side and hip, his touch was tender and light.

"You should have told me it was like this." His voice was a growl as he looked closely at her injuries.

"It's not too bad."

He kissed the bruise on her hip, lightly, reverently, and she sighed, her eyes drifting closed at the sweetness of the touch.

"I'm not sorry I killed them. Though I wish I could have made them suffer more."

Libby thought she should be horrified at the violence in his voice—but she wasn't. It was for her, his fierceness, and she loved that. A deep longing pierced her then. It was a longing for acceptance and love, and it stunned her at how strong and elemental it was. She didn't know her life yet, but she knew down to her soul that she was searching for someone who accepted her. Who *chose* her and wanted her, and who would be there for her through thick and thin.

It sounded an awful lot like love was what she sought, but wasn't everyone searching for that?

Her throat was tight as she threaded her hands into his hair and whispered, "I know. Thank you for saving me."

He rolled up her body like a wave, then took her mouth in a hot kiss that seared her to the depths. Their tongues clashed and mated, and Libby arched her body against his, wanting more.

He tore his mouth from hers and dragged his sleep pants down, kicking them free before reaching into the bedside table for a box of condoms that he dropped on the bed beside her. Then he settled onto her, slowly, every inch of his hot skin touching every inch of hers.

"Where were we?" he murmured before kissing her again.

Libby wrapped her legs around him, trying to maneuver him where she wanted. Where she burned for him. He wasn't easily led, however. He kissed her with hot, deep, wet kisses that stole her breath and her sense.

His fingers slipped between them, down into the lush wetness of her, and she gasped with need.

"Jared. Please."

His blue eyes burned into her as he lifted his head and watched her. "What are you begging me for, Libby?"

"I want to come."

His smile was filled with wicked promise. "So do I." His gaze stole over her body with deliberation. "But there are so many things I want to do to you first. So many ways I want to make you say my name."

Libby closed her eyes. She had no idea if she'd ever experienced this kind of carnal sensuality before. She was positive she wasn't a virgin since nothing about the way he touched her or the way he felt pressed against her was foreign. But what kind of sex had she experienced before? Had it been this maddening, all-consuming feeling that made her feel as if her skin was on fire with every stroke of his thumb against her clitoris? Or had it been pedestrian and safe?

Jared wasn't safe. Of that she was certain.

She decided to be bold, to reach for him and wrap her hand around his hot, hard cock. He groaned when her fingers tightened. His eyes were a little unfocused, and her heart soared that she could affect him like that.

"I want you," she whispered. "Now. Please, now."

"Yes," he growled. "Fuck yes."

He reached for the condom box and tore one from the wrapper, then rolled it on swiftly. Libby watched in fascination, a part of her wanting to catalogue every moment of this experience but knowing she was going to lose the battle. The emotions and sensations were too much to remain separate, and when Jared settled between her legs and she wrapped them around his hips, Libby lost the ability to keep that part of herself to herself. With Jared, it was all or nothing.

His blue eyes searched hers. "Are you certain about this?"

"Do I strike you as uncertain?"

He let his gaze drop to her breasts, then up to her face again. "No, but I had to ask."

"Jared," she breathed. "I want this. I want you. You need to stop thinking and start feeling."

He swore softly as his cock nudged her entrance. It didn't take any effort for him to slide into her body, and she knew he had to feel a measure of relief he hadn't encountered a hymen. No matter what he'd said about it being her choice, he wouldn't have stopped thinking about the fact she might regret this once she remembered everything about herself. And she might (she doubted it) but it wouldn't be because she'd broken some crazy vow to remain a virgin until her wedding.

"You're so fucking wet," he groaned. "And you feel amazing."

She couldn't speak. She was so full of him, and her body was simply on fire with anticipation of what came next. She wanted him to move, wanted him to drive into her and make her explode. She wanted to feel like that lucky heroine had felt when her duke made love to her —completely satisfied and utterly spent.

Jared withdrew slowly and plunged forward again, and Libby gasped. It was a good gasp. A wondrous gasp.

His movements quickened, his mouth came down on hers, and they moved together in a hot, sweaty rhythm that felt perfectly right as they strained toward an explosive climax.

Libby got there first, stars exploding behind her eyes, her breath stopping in her throat, her limbs tightening and shaking with the force of the pleasure expanding inside her. Her voice wasn't her own as she gasped Jared's name over and over, as she implored him to keep moving just like *that.*

Oh god, like that.

He did as she begged—and then he found his own release with a groan and a stiffening of his body as he filled the condom.

In the aftermath, their breathing was ragged and their bodies sated. Jared started to rise, but she wrapped her arms around him and held him to her. "Please, not yet."

"I'm too heavy," he said, shifting his body so his weight wasn't crushing her into the mattress.

She lifted her fingers to his cheek. She needed to touch him, to ground herself in this reality. She felt more alive and real this very moment than she had in days. Her hip ached and he was heavy, but she didn't care. This was what it meant to be alive. This pain and pleasure were opposite sides of the same coin.

He shifted again, and her chest expanded with air. "I need to take care of the condom," he murmured. "It won't take long."

Libby closed her eyes as he lifted himself away. Her body was cold where the air rushed in, and she felt suddenly alone. "Good grief, be sensible," she muttered to herself once he was gone. "This is sex, not life."

A moment later, she sat up and started searching for her clothing. No way did she want to experience any awkward aftermath while Jared thanked her for the sex and waited for her to think about going back to her own bed. She wasn't going to be clingy, no matter how much she wanted to do it all again.

She'd just dragged her shirt on when Jared returned. "Shit," he said, and she looked up to find him studying her. He was utterly, gloriously naked, and her gaze dropped to follow that happy trail down the world's tightest abdominal muscles before landing on his half-hard dick. "Regrets already?"

"Huh?"

He nodded at her. She was standing beside the bed, sleep pants in hand. The T-shirt covered her ass, at least.

"You look like you're planning to rush back to the guest room."

"I, um—I thought you'd want me to go."

His eyes flashed. "When did I give you that impression? When my tongue was down your throat and my dick was buried deep inside you, or when I came so hard I couldn't form a coherent thought for a solid minute? Or maybe it was earlier, when I said you were making me crazy. Sure, that had to be it."

Libby didn't know what to say. When he put it that way, she felt like an idiot. "In my defense," she began, "this is pretty much my first time sleeping with a guy who saved me from people trying to kill me. I'm not sure of the protocol here."

Jared lifted an eyebrow. Then he laughed. Before she could think of a response, he closed the distance between them and tugged the T-shirt off her body. Then he took the sleep pants and panties and tossed those as well.

"Honey, the protocol is this: you're mine for the rest of the night."

Chapter Nineteen

HE DIDN'T LIKE DANIEL WEIR. JARED SAT IN THE conference room and listened silently as the man discussed the benefits of his exoskeleton with Ian. He was cocky and arrogant, the kind of person who knew he was smart and thought that meant he was better than most of those he encountered. It was interesting, considering his arrogance, that he'd come to BDI for a meeting rather than insisting that Ian visit Ninja Solutions. Jared thought it was a measure of Ian's reputation in the intelligence community that Weir had made the journey. Though Weir *had* arrived by helicopter, so it was just as likely he'd done it to impress upon them how important he was.

"Obviously, there are some proprietary modifications we've made for the US Army that we can't disclose," Weir said. "But the basic template is there to be customized by the end user. We can make modifications to your specifications, of course. The software is quite special."

"It's certainly interesting," Ian said. "But what kind of delivery date do you anticipate? This thing is still a prototype, right?"

Weir nodded. "That's right. We're moving forward very quickly and anticipate mass production to begin within a few months. We have our sources lined up for the manufacturing process, so producing the number of suits you want would be within our scope. I assume it's not the thousands the Department of Defense requires?"

"Not quite, no. I'd need to consult my team, of course, but we'd probably place an initial order between thirty and sixty. When can we preview the prototype?"

Weir looked pleased. "It will take some time to set something up since we're so busy with the Army, but I can have my secretary get back to you with some dates."

"That would be great," Ian said, offering a hand. Weir shook it, then offered his hand to Jared.

Jared squeezed. He managed to stop himself from squeezing too hard. It wasn't a contest and he didn't know that this man had anything to do with Libby's kidnapping and abuse.

After Weir had gone, Ian frowned at Jared. "Smarmy. That's my impression. You?"

"Smarmy and arrogant."

"Reminds me of a used car salesman. The kind that tries to get you to spend more than you have on a piece of shit that's gonna break down ten miles from the dealer."

"Why's he out hustling his suit if the Army is about to buy thousands of them?" Jared mused as they walked down the corridor toward the elevator that would take them to the Cove where Libby was hanging out with Angie and Maddy. Tallie'd been working on a client project today and couldn't come.

"My thoughts exactly. I need to know more about this deal with the Army. Something seems off to me."

"Agreed."

"How's she doing, Jared? Any progress at all?" Ian asked as they stepped into the elevator.

If by progress the boss meant had Jared had hot sex with Libby in the bed, the shower, on the couch, and the dining room table, then yes, there was all kinds of progress. But if he meant did she remember anything about Ninja Solutions and the exoskeleton, then no. Not that he planned to ask which definition Ian was looking for.

"She's remembering who she is. Her childhood, that kind of thing. Nothing recent. It's only been a little over a week since I found her. I expect more things will come back faster now that the memories have begun to trickle in."

"Yeah, that was Dr. Puckett's assessment too. She said there's no lasting brain damage from the trauma, but that Libby might not remember the events immediately preceding it."

Jared nodded even as his gut clenched at the idea of Libby experiencing any brain damage when Joe Boggs had thrown her into the wall. If the asshole wasn't dead already, Jared would have happily killed him again. "That's what I expect will be the case. What happened was bad enough that her brain is trying to protect her from it."

And that made him feel sick. Libby was open and warm. She was friendly, chatty as hell, and trusting. At least with him. To imagine someone hurting her, scaring her—well, it was more than he could bear. He knew that people were sick. Knew from experience that bad things happened all the time to good people, but this time he couldn't find the professional distance he needed. He was involved. Maybe too involved, but he'd crossed that line a while ago and there was no going back.

The elevator doors opened onto the Cove. The three women were sitting at the bar, drinking something fruity and laughing. They looked up when Ian and Jared appeared. Libby's smile hit Jared like a gut punch when she turned her gaze on him.

She looked happy, and it made him feel protective. He'd kill any motherfucker who tried to hurt her ever again.

Ever again?

Jared shook himself. That wasn't the kind of thought he typically entertained about a woman he was dating. Though they weren't exactly dating, were they? They'd passed dating and gone straight to getting down and dirty as often as they could. Jared didn't think Libby had a ton of experience the way she often seemed so amazed at what he did to her, but damn if she didn't catch on quickly.

Her blushes hadn't entirely disappeared, but even when she did blush, she didn't let it stop her from acting on her impulses. He loved her impulses. They were hot, sexy, dirty impulses and he encouraged them as often as she wanted to give into them.

Jared went over and kissed her. He didn't stop to think about what he was doing, he just did it. She put her hands on his face, and his skin sizzled.

"Hi," she whispered when he broke the kiss.

"Hi. You having fun?" he whispered back.

"Yes." She turned her head, and he belatedly remembered they had an audience. "Maddy was just telling me about a party she's throwing at her house Saturday night."

Maddy was looking at him with an arched eyebrow. "You should both come. We'd love to have you join us."

Jared looped an arm around Libby's shoulders. He didn't care what they thought. He liked the way she felt against him. Right as rain as his mother would say. He didn't know what this was or where it was going, but he liked it.

"Sure, sounds good," he said because he could tell that Libby wanted to go. He'd rather keep her naked and beneath him—and maybe on top of him too—but if she wanted to party, then they were partying. What-ever made her smile like that.

"Great," Maddy said. "What about you, Ian? Can you come?"

Jared looked over at Ian, who pointedly dropped his gaze to Jared's arm and then back up again with a knowing grin. "Can't make it, Dr. Cole, but thanks for asking."

Maddy frowned. "You haven't managed to make the

last two. And why are you calling me Dr. Cole all of a sudden?"

Ian laughed. "I was just remembering that time you told me only your friends got to call you Maddy, and I wasn't one of those."

Maddy rolled her eyes. "Well, you weren't. You were holding me prisoner and refusing to believe I was who I said I was. But I forgive you for it, as you're well aware. I want you to come eat yummy food and have a good time with friends."

Ian bowed his head in acknowledgement. "Thanks, Maddy. I can't, though. I've got a meeting in Rome on Saturday."

"Haven't you people heard of Zoom yet?" Maddy teased.

"Yeah, but if we teleconference everything, when do we get to see the world?"

"So it's all about the expense account then. Fine, but we'll miss you. And one of these days, you had better join us. Or I'm going to think you don't like me."

Ian laughed and went over to give Maddy a quick kiss on the cheek. "Don't tell your man, but I like you just fine, Maddy Cole. I sometimes think I should have stolen you for myself instead of letting Jace have you."

Maddy swatted him good-naturedly. "Flirt."

The elevator doors opened again and several of the guys emerged. Colt, Jace, Ty, Dax, and Rascal, who'd been gone until recently. Jared blinked. "Dude, you grew your hair out."

Rascal ran a hand over his formerly bald skull. "Yep, sure did."

The others laughed. "He's unrecognizable, right?" Ty said. "And not nearly so ugly."

Rascal snorted. "Not ugly at all, prick. Or so your momma said last night."

Dax guffawed. "Shit, he found a sense of humor when he grew his hair. Who knew?"

Rascal went behind the bar and grabbed a beer. "I love you guys, too. Missed you bastards. Beg pardon, ladies."

Angie balled up her napkin and threw it at him. "Who are you calling a lady? I work here with you people."

Rascal fist-bumped her. "Sorry, Ang. You're one of the bastards then. But my apologies to Maddy and this lovely lady," he said, turning his gaze to Libby.

She smiled and held out her hand. Jared loved how spontaneous and comfortable she was with people. Unlike him, who had to think about everything first. "I'm Libby. Pleased to meet you."

Rascal cut his gaze toward Jared. "Are you with this dweeb or can I ask for your number?"

Libby laughed. "I'm with the dweeb. But thanks for asking."

"Hey," Jared protested, tightening his grip around her shoulders. Though he also felt unaccountably proud that she'd said she was with him. "I'm not a dweeb."

"Yeah, you kinda are," Rascal said. "But you're the smartest guy I know, so it ain't all bad."

"Careful, Rascal. I can still kick your ass. Remember that time in Acamar?"

"It's a bit hard to forget. I thought you medical types were too concerned with doing no harm."

"Not this one."

"I know that *now.*" Rascal looked at Libby. "It was a friendly fight. One of the other guys bet me I couldn't take Jared down. He hadn't been with us that long, and I thought they were kidding. Found out I was wrong."

"Very wrong," Jared added.

"Definitely wrong. But I know your moves now. Might not be so hard this time."

Jared snorted. "If you want to try."

Rascal took a long pull on his beer. "Nope, not feeling suicidal today."

"Hey, who wants to play me at Frogger?" Dax asked from over near the arcade machine.

"Dude, seriously?" Ty said. "Isn't that like an eighties game or something?"

"Yep, sure is. But it's a lot harder than it looks."

The Cove filled with laughter and people talking, and Libby put her arm around Jared's waist and squeezed softly. He looked down at her. Her eyes sparkled.

"This has been a lot of fun," she said. "But if you want to leave, I wouldn't mind."

It took him a moment to realize she was asking if he wanted to leave because she knew he liked things quieter. She had no idea what he lived when he went on missions, or the absolute lack of quiet there often was. She just thought that he was an introvert who needed to be in spaces where there weren't so many people.

It touched him deeply that she thought of it. And as

much as he wanted to go so he could be alone with her, he also knew she thrived on situations filled with people and noise. Libby was as extroverted as they came. She got a charge out of people whereas he needed to be alone to recharge. They were complete opposites in that respect.

He leaned down and kissed her on the cheek. "Let's stay for a while. But when we do go, I want you naked the minute we get home."

"The very minute?"

"The very minute we walk through the door. I need you to strip for me so I can bury my face between your legs."

Libby shivered. "You've got a deal."

———

LIBBY TURNED over in bed and stretched. Light streamed through the curtains, and she could hear the shower running. She pictured water rolling down the hard muscles of Jared's body and her pussy tightened. When they'd gotten back last night, he'd made good on his promise. She'd stripped inside the door and he'd dropped to his knees and spread her apart. Then he'd rocked her world with his tongue and fingers until she'd screamed.

After that, he'd produced a condom and fucked her against the door until he exploded, his cock twitching deep inside her as he came, his breath panting in her ear with need and pleasure. Then he'd carried her up to his bed and started all over again.

She was constantly amazed at how much Jared seemed to want her. There was no doubt she wanted him like crazy, but why did he want her? That's what she couldn't quite figure out, but she wasn't going to question her good fortune. It wasn't that she didn't think she was worthy of his attention, but she could see in the mirror as well as anyone. She might not know everything about herself yet, but what she saw reflected back to her wasn't a stunning beauty.

She wasn't unattractive, but she also didn't look like the kind of woman who should be the recipient of Jared Fraser's attention. He was, quite simply, gorgeous. He was the stunning one, not her. She was just like millions of women. Pretty enough to get a man, but probably not an extraordinary one like Jared.

His body was lean and hard and strong. He moved with lethal grace—and she knew quite well how lethal he could be. His smile made her heart skip. His eyes were blue and broody, and he had a way of looking at her that made her think even if she spent a lifetime with him, she'd never know everything about him.

As if a lifetime with him was possible. She really needed to get a grip on those kinds of thoughts. There was absolutely nothing to indicate his desire for her was anything other than physical. And how could it be? You couldn't get to know someone who didn't even know herself.

What was between them was physical, and maybe it was everything to do with proximity and the fact she was so willing. What man wouldn't avail himself of the opportunity?

"Boys won't buy the cow if they can get the milk for free."

Libby was no longer shocked at the bits and pieces of her life that kept floating up to her conscious mind like flotsam after a storm. That was her mother talking, though she didn't remember the context of the conversation. Or lecture, more like. She didn't think she'd been a promiscuous teenager. She was still somewhat shy with Jared sometimes, so she didn't think she was a *been there, done all of that* kind of person.

She also hadn't been a virgin, though. Nothing about sex in general had been shocking. Dirty talk had shocked her at first, but she found that it whipped her excitement higher. Especially when Jared said things like he was going to lick her pussy or fuck her until her knees were weak. She'd even managed to start saying dirty things to him, which definitely excited her because of the way he reacted. He never made her feel silly for it. Instead, he made her feel like she had the power to make him crazy for her. It was a heady feeling, but it also worried her.

Because what was going to happen when she remembered everything and he no longer needed to protect her? They would go their separate ways. It was a thought she didn't like having, but one she had to consider. Boys didn't buy the cow when they got the milk for free. And when they were tired of milk, they'd move on.

Thanks, Mom.

Libby pushed upright in bed. The sheet fell, revealing her naked breasts. The room was chilly, but not freezing, and her nipples budded tight. She dragged the covers up again, her thoughts turning sour. What was she doing here? What was she thinking to throw her whole self into this thing with Jared?

Because she had.

She wouldn't say she was in love, but she definitely cared. The thought of going back to her life without him physically hurt. She lay back against the pillows and tried to redirect her thoughts, but she was in a spiral of negativity now. She heard the bathroom door open, heard Jared's footsteps. He kept going, past the bedroom, and down the stairs.

She should get up and go shower, but she didn't move. She lay there thinking about the future.

But how could you predict your future when you didn't know your past?

She heard Jared coming up the stairs again. A moment later, the door opened and he walked in with two cups in his hand. His hair was wet and tousled. He wore a navy henley that opened at the neck, and faded jeans that hugged his body. Dear God he was delicious. His gaze met hers, and her heart skipped at the contact. *Mercy.*

"I brought coffee."

"You're my gallant knight," she said without thinking, and immediately wanted to kick herself for it. He'd told her his call sign used to be Knight, and it was clear he had some baggage with that name, but he didn't seem phased by what she'd said. Not that she hadn't said it before, but she was determined to be careful about it.

He came over and perched on the side of the bed,

handing her the steaming mug. "I live to serve, my lady."

Libby couldn't help but smile. Her heart ached with emotion. "I believe you. Especially after last night."

He reached over and tugged the covers down until her breasts were exposed. "Ah, much better."

"You do realize it's chilly, right?"

His gaze sparkled. "Of course I do. I like the way your nipples tighten against the cold."

"So you don't mind letting me freeze for your viewing pleasure?"

He grinned as he took a sip of coffee. "Nope, not at all."

"You're a bad man, Jared Fraser."

"Only when the reward is worth it."

Libby sipped her coffee and tried to ignore the low hum of desire starting to buzz through her system. She'd had sex only a few hours ago, but she wanted more. She always wanted more. Didn't matter that she could still feel the ache from the last time, or that she was hungry and needed to shower.

Jared reached out and cupped one of her breasts. A shiver rolled through her at his touch.

"You have the prettiest nipples, Libby." His thumb ghosted over one of them, and the sizzle shot straight to her core.

"They're just nipples. I'm sure you've seen lots."

His gaze met hers. "I've seen enough to know what I like. And I like these." He pinched softly, and Libby couldn't stop the moan in her throat.

"I don't know why," she gasped. "My boobs are too

small and my nipples are too big. They aren't proportional."

Jared's hand fell away. "Are you seriously telling me I shouldn't like your breasts because they aren't proportional?"

"Um, well… maybe? I mean there are such nicer ones out there. Bigger, prettier. More to get your hands on."

She was babbling.

Jared took her coffee cup and set it on the nightstand. He set his down beside it. Then he stripped the covers off her and dragged her down until he could hover over top of her, his body big and hot above hers.

"Do I need to remind you how much you turn me on, Liberty King? How much I want to fuck you until you can't form a coherent sentence?" He dropped his mouth to her neck, trailed his tongue to a hard nipple. "I love making you so hot you can't talk. It's one of my favorite things to do."

He sucked her nipple into his mouth and her back arched. "Jared. Oh my…"

"That's right, honey. Say my name. Tell me how bad you want it."

"I do want it. I want you."

He sucked her other nipple, his fingers sliding between her legs to dip into her body. Libby squirmed, trying to get the pressure where she wanted it.

"You're so fucking hot and wet," he growled against her breast. "And all for me."

"I need you to fuck me," she moaned. "Please."

He lifted himself up and ripped his shirt off while

she fumbled with his jeans. Then he kicked them off and grabbed a condom from the nightstand. Together, they rolled it on. And then he pressed her back and entered her in a single thrust, both of them groaning with the rightness and the pleasure of it.

It felt so good. *He* felt so good inside her.

"Hang on, baby," he said. "I'm about to show you just how much I like this pretty body of yours. I don't want you wondering why ever again."

He stared to move, and Libby threaded her hands through his damp hair, dragging him down to her mouth.

It was a long time before either of them spoke again.

Chapter Twenty

MADDY AND JACE LIVED IN A CUTE HOUSE ON A QUIET street in Annapolis. It had been Maddy's grandmother's house, but now it was hers. Her grandmother was in a nursing home not too far away, and Maddy visited her often. She had dementia or she would have still been living with Maddy and Jace. Maddy talked about her grandmother, who she called Mimi, with such love and devotion as she showed Libby the house and told her about the remodeling that she and Jace had done so far.

"I miss her so much. It would have been hard to sell this house and move, but Jace never thought we should. He thought all my ideas for expanding it were great and he never balked at the cost. Not that I wanted him to pitch in any money for it, but he said if we were going to live here then he wanted to help." She turned to look dreamily at where Jace stood with Jared and Colt, talking about something they couldn't hear. "He's the best man I've ever known."

Jace must have sensed that she was looking at him

because he turned his head and their gazes met. Libby was envious of the way they looked at each other. Like they couldn't breathe without the other one in the room. Like their entire world revolved around that look. Like a million words passed between them without being spoken.

It was a private moment, and yet it was there for anyone to see. And it was beautiful.

Maddy broke the contact first, turning a bright gaze onto Libby. "Sorry, I'm supposed to be giving you the tour and all I can do is gush about Jace."

Libby laughed. "Don't worry about it. I'd gush too if I was as much in love as you two are."

Maddy gave her a sidelong glance. "So, about you and Jared…"

Libby's heart thumped with secret excitement. She hoped it didn't show on her face, but she was afraid it did. "Yes?"

Maddy took her hand and led her from the room where everyone was gathered to the master suite with its soaring cathedral ceiling and wood beams, plush bed piled with pillows, gorgeous cream rug on the floor, and closed the door behind them.

"Did he kiss you again?" Maddy asked. "Inquiring minds want to know."

There was a knock on the door before Libby could answer. It was Angie and Tallie.

"We saw you two head this way. No talking about Jared and Libby without us," Angie said.

"That's right, I need to know how wrong I was," Tallie said with a laugh.

Libby looked at the three of them watching her with eager faces. She thought she ought to be noncommittal, but that wasn't her style. Not at all. She loved talking to people, and she really loved talking to these three women. They made her feel like she belonged. She didn't know much about her life before, but she knew that was a feeling she craved.

"He did," she said.

"And?" Tallie urged.

"And yes," Libby said with a shrug. "I got the orgasms. Way more than two of them."

Angie whooped. Maddy clapped. Tallie just laughed. "Geez, when you're wrong, you're wrong. I mean I never really got the impression he was gay, but then I started overthinking it and had myself convinced it must be the case."

"No, definitely not gay," Libby said, thinking about how she'd gotten brave enough this morning to kiss her way down Jared's body and take him into her mouth. He had a thick, beautiful cock and she'd wanted to taste it—but she'd been shy about it. Not today. And not ever again with the way he'd reacted.

He made her feel sexy and confident, two things she thought she was probably lacking.

"We are not asking for details," Maddy said sternly, looking at the other two. And then she giggled. "But if you wanted to provide them, we wouldn't tell you no."

Libby laughed too. "I don't think I could do that without dying of mortification. But he's very, very talented. Not that I can remember my past yet, but I don't think I've ever felt this good with a man before."

Angie took her hand and squeezed. "Oh, honey. You'll remember. And your past doesn't really matter anyway, not when it comes to the future. Just do what needs doing with Jared and see where it leads you."

Libby felt tears threatening. "That's all I can do. What I intend to do. What happens, happens."

"Group hug!" Tallie said, wrapping her arms around everyone. The four of them hugged tight.

There was a knock at the door and then it opened to reveal Jace, who blinked at them for a second. "Uh, the oven dinged. I didn't know if I should take out whatever's in there or not."

"Oh, I'd better check. Come on, girls. Let's get some wine and keep talking about the boys before we eat." She patted Jace on the cheek. "Honey, we need more girls at these parties. You need to tell the guys to get busy finding girlfriends because you currently outnumber us and we don't like that."

Jace glanced at the women, then down at Maddy with a grin. "Yeah, I'll tell them you said that. We'll see how well it goes over."

Angie linked arms with Libby as they followed the others from the room. Being with these women felt like home. Libby never wanted the feeling to end. But she was afraid it would. She would remember her life, and she wouldn't belong here anymore. Not with them, and not with Jared. It was enough to make her want to cry.

JARED LIKED SEEING LIBBY HAPPY. She perched on a barstool at the kitchen island with the other three women. They leaned together and talked like they'd been friends their whole lives. He envied how women could do that sometimes. They could meet and then twenty minutes later you'd swear they'd been friends since they'd been in diapers. Clearly, the four of them had found common ground and seemed to enjoy talking to each other.

But there was an edge to her tonight as well. He'd noticed it earlier when she'd returned from wherever she and the others had gone when Jace went to fetch Maddy. She still smiled and laughed, but her eyes had a wary look sometimes. He wanted to go to her and make her tell him what was wrong, but then the look would go away and she'd be happy again.

It could be her past. He'd thought maybe she was remembering more and trying not to let it bother her, but then he was pretty sure if she remembered something significant she would come to him and tell him. It wasn't Libby's style to remain quiet about anything. And not to him.

Jared frowned. At least he didn't think so. She talked a lot and he'd gotten used to it. Liked her chatter, even. She didn't talk much when they were in the throes of passion, but she talked plenty before and after. It was so different from the women he'd been with before. Not that he hadn't taken a talker to bed, but he'd never listened to anything she'd said. In fact, he couldn't recall any specific incident. He had impressions of sexual partners, but no one he could recall with perfect clarity.

Oh, he remembered names and faces—and even where they'd met—but not what they talked about or what they did together other than fuck. Some dinners, some drinks. Some parties. Mostly, he didn't care.

But he remembered everything about Libby, and not only because it was so fresh. She managed to be fascinating despite not knowing much about herself. Every memory she shared interested him. She teased him and laughed at him and made him laugh at himself. He liked that. In short, she was easy to be with.

By the time the evening was over, it was nearing midnight. Jared and Libby said their goodbyes and went out to get into his truck. He opened the door for her and then kissed her before he closed it.

"That was fun," she said when he got in and started the engine. "You have such great friends."

"They are pretty great. I got lucky when I went to work for Ian."

She studied him. "Maddy said it's dangerous."

"It can be. I told you when I met you that I was a warrior."

"I know. And there were those men who tried to attack us. You didn't hesitate to kill them."

He wasn't sure he liked where this was going. "No, and I would make the same choice again. I will always protect you, Libby. With my skills if I need to. With my life if I have to."

"I'd prefer you didn't sacrifice yourself for anyone."

Her voice sounded strained. He liked that she cared. It didn't change the job, though.

"I'd prefer it too. But I'm prepared to do it if it saves an innocent life."

She was quiet for a long moment. "What do you see happening with us?"

He thought that question should make him uncomfortable, but it didn't. Strangely enough, it didn't. Was that a sign he wasn't as unsuitable for a relationship as he'd always thought? Maybe so. He knew he wasn't his father, and he knew deep down he'd never lose his shit and hit the woman he chose to be with. But he'd always thought there were other reasons he wasn't going to settle down. Like his job. It wasn't what sane people did. He watched Jace and Maddy, Colt and Angie, and Brett and Tallie, and he wondered how they were going to make it work in the long run.

"I think we should take it a day at a time. See what happens," he said carefully.

"That sounds very non-committal. Not that I'm asking for a commitment. Lord, we've only been having sex for a few days so I didn't mean I wanted you to ask me to marry you or anything. God, no. I mean that's silly, right? It's sex. Good sex, but sex—"

"Libby."

She sighed. "I'm babbling, aren't I? Sorry. I just mean that I'm not asking for anything long-term, but I like you and I like what we're doing. I hate to think I'm going to get my memory back and this will be over."

He turned into his driveway and pulled up beneath the carport. Then he shut the engine off and looked at her. She was fiddling with the seatbelt and not looking at him.

"What makes you think we're through when you remember?" he asked softly.

She gazed at him. "I don't know. It's just that I'll go home and back to work, and I won't see you as much. When we're not in the same house, maybe it'll be easy to forget me. You can go back to your quiet and your books and you'll wonder how you ever put up with me."

"I don't think you'll be easy to forget at all." He reached over and curled his hand around the back of her neck, tugged her gently toward him so he could kiss her. He kissed her until she sighed, until he could feel the current of her desire for him growing stronger. "I'm not putting up with you, Libby. I'm quite possibly taking advantage of your attraction to me, but I don't much fucking care. So long as it gets me a few hours in bed with you, I'd pretty much do whatever it takes to get you naked and hot."

She giggled suddenly. "Well, that was remarkably honest of you."

"Hell, yeah. I *like* you, Libby. I like being with you. And I like fucking you, believe me. But even without that, I'd still like you. That's the point I'm trying to make, though I'm not doing it well."

"You're kind of babbling a bit," she said with a grin. "Who knew you were capable?"

He laughed. "I'm capable. Now come on and let's get inside. I want to sleep with my body curled around yours."

"And so it begins," she intoned. "He only wants to sleep."

"You're so fucking cute," he said. "What I really

want is to make you beg me to let you come, but I wasn't going to suggest it after I basically said I only wanted to get you in bed."

She leaned forward and kissed him. "I want to beg. Please, please, take me upstairs and make me come as many times as you can."

He growled. "Is that a challenge?"

Her smile made him light up inside. "It definitely is."

His body was already responding, his dick swelling inside his jeans. But he didn't move yet. He picked up a lock of her hair and rubbed it between his fingers. "Is that what was bothering you tonight?"

Her eyes widened slightly. "What makes you think anything was bothering me?"

"I could see it. Not all the time, but sometimes. You seemed to be thinking about something. I wondered if maybe you'd gotten more memories back."

She shook her head. "No, it wasn't that. It's just…" She sighed. "I like being a part of the group, and I wondered what was going to happen when I got my memory back. Like what if I don't belong anymore? What happens when I stop being a job you're all doing?"

"I think it's pretty clear that you're more than a job, Libby. This may surprise you, but I don't usually wind up in bed with someone I protect. You're a first."

"Oh," she said softly.

"Yeah, oh." He sat back and put his hand on the door, his chest tight after that admission and her response. "Let's get inside, honey. We can talk about it some more then, if you want."

"Believe it or not, I don't want to talk. I want to feel."

Jared led her inside and up the stairs. They stripped in a rush, leaving their clothes strewn everywhere, then fell in bed together and didn't speak—except for words of passion—for the rest of the night.

Chapter Twenty-One

LIBBY DREAMED. SHE DREAMED OF HER PARENTS AND THE farm, and she dreamed about the day she left, lugging a suitcase and crying because her father had told her that if she didn't marry the man he'd picked to be her husband, then she couldn't ever come back.

Glory and Charity were there too. And her brother Lincoln, who'd told her it was a woman's duty to marry and have children. If she didn't marry Seb Wilcox, then she wasn't doing her duty to the family.

Seb was twenty years older than she was, and he'd been married twice before. He had eight children, four of whom were under the age of ten and still at home. And she was supposed to be a mother to them and have more children with him as well.

She'd only been eighteen.

When she woke with a start, the only light seeping in the cracks between the curtains was the streetlight. Her heart pounded and her throat ached. Memories crowded her mind, overflowing the edges, spilling out so fast she couldn't keep up.

She knew who she was. She knew where she came from.

"Libby?" Jared sounded more awake than he should for a man who'd been asleep only moments ago, but he sat up and put an arm around her. "What's wrong?"

Her voice wouldn't come at first. Everything was about to change.

"I remember."

He hugged her to him without hesitation, his warm body strong and comforting as he leaned them back against the headboard. "Tell me."

She put her arm across his waist, clutching him for strength.

"There's so much. So much." She swallowed. There was so much about herself she had to come to grips with, but the important stuff to him had to do with how she'd ended up on the mountain in the snow, injured and scared. "There's a software engineer—Paul Hicks— he's older, about sixty or so, sweet and quiet, and he talked to me a lot. He never talked to anyone, not really, but he would stop at my desk and talk. I don't know why."

"Of course you do. You made him comfortable."

She swallowed. "Yes. He said I was easy to talk to. Some of the other girls thought he was creepy. I just thought he was lonely. He never said or did anything wrong, I swear. But I—"

"What is it, Libby?" he asked when she didn't continue.

"He said it doesn't work," she whispered, her mind churning over the facts. "That's what it's all about!"

She shoved up and out of bed, grabbing her clothes so she could pull them on. She had to get home, and then she had to get to the office first thing in the morning. Jared was beside her in a flash, gripping her shoulders and forcing her to look at him.

"Calm down, honey. Tell me what this is about."

Libby was trembling. "RIM doesn't work the way it's supposed to. The AI can't distinguish real threats from friendlies one-hundred percent of the time. It's more like fifty-percent, but Daniel falsified the results to make it look like the suit works as advertised. I mean it *does* work —but not accurately. Paul was the chief software engineer and he had evidence. He wrote the code for the suit —though Daniel claims in all the literature that he did. Paul said it wasn't right, though. He didn't want to let it go out that way, but Daniel told him the DoD would do their own tests. They'd figure it out themselves, but the company would make millions selling the technology first. Paul disagreed and intended to take the information to the Army."

"Is there proof?"

She nodded, her heart hammering in her chest. "Yes. Paul gave me a memory card. He said it had everything on it. The software program he'd written for the AI, the real test results, recordings of the conversations he'd had with Daniel about it. He said it was a backup copy and asked me to hold onto it for him. Just in case." Her breath hitched. "And then he didn't come back to work. Oh crap, do you think they hurt him too?"

Jared swore. "I don't know, honey. But we'll find out. Can you tell me what you did with the memory card?"

"It's at work. I didn't know what to do with it, but I promised I'd keep it safe for him. It's in the plant on my desk. I wrapped it in plastic and shoved it into the dirt. That was a stupid move, wasn't it? I should have taken it home or mailed it to a reporter the minute Paul didn't return to work."

Jared gave her shoulders a squeeze. "Actually, what you did was a smart move, babe. If you'd had it on you, or in your apartment, those guys might have found it. We wouldn't be having this conversation right now. As for mailing it to a reporter, you'd have lost control of the information and had no way of knowing if it'd get to the right person or if they'd even take it seriously."

Libby shivered at the truth in his assessment. "Paul didn't come to work Wednesday, and a rumor went around the office that said he'd quit. I thought that was weird so I tried to call him, but he didn't answer. I was still trying to decide what to do when I went out for my morning run on Thursday. But then an SUV pulled up and a man got out and grabbed me. He shoved me into the car, put a hood over my head, and then we drove for what seemed like hours before they threw me into a room and left me there. When they came back, they wanted to know where the card was."

Jared palmed his phone off the side table and she knew he was sending a text to one of the men on his team. She liked those men. Every one of them was tough and professional, and while she knew they were capable of violence, she also knew they wouldn't use their strength against people who didn't deserve it. They were protectors. Unlike the men who'd grabbed her.

She remembered one of the men shoving her into the wall and threatening her with a knife—he had a beard and squinty eyes—and she remembered waking up in the dark, terrified and feeling like she was hungover. She'd climbed out the narrow second story window and onto the porch roof. She hadn't known how big the drop was because it'd been dark, but she'd seen the snow below and had thought maybe it was close enough to cushion her fall.

"Libby," Jared said softly, and she jerked at the sound of his voice.

Her limbs were shaking. "I'm okay."

He wrapped his arms around her and took them down to the bed, holding her close. "You aren't."

"I was thinking about jumping off the roof."

His arms tightened. "Better tell me about it."

"There was a window in the room where they'd put me. It was small so maybe they thought I couldn't get out of it. Or maybe they figured I wouldn't try because the room was on the second floor—plus there was nowhere to go and it was dark. B-but I did. The man with the beard—he threatened to cut out my tongue if I didn't tell him everything. I think I passed out. I remember him injecting me with something when I came to. I felt like I'd drank a fifth of whiskey and all I wanted to do was sleep. He yelled at me, but I couldn't help it. When I woke up the next time, I was alone. I could hear them downstairs though. They were laughing and shouting. There was loud music and cigarette smoke. I was scared they'd come back and hurt me again."

Libby shuddered. She'd felt sick and scared, but she remembered she'd also been determined. She'd known she had to get out of that room or things would've gotten worse.

Jared's grip on her didn't change. He held her close and she took comfort in the solid warmth of him. He was a rock. Her rock at the moment.

"It's okay, honey. You don't have to tell me about it if you're afraid."

"No." She said it firmly. "No, I want to." She sucked in a breath. "I knew I had to get away. So I went out the window. There was a roof there, and I tried to be quiet as I crawled across it. Every creak of the tin made my heart pound. I still felt kind of drunk, but it was getting better. I moved away from the music and shouting, toward the back of the cabin. The porch went all the way around, and I tried to find a place I could get down. But there wasn't anything obvious, and I started to worry they'd discover I was gone. I couldn't tell how far the drop was, but I had to make a decision. So I tried to let myself over the edge as far as I could before I let go. It was still a longer drop than I expected."

"The snow probably cushioned your fall. You're lucky you didn't break anything." His voice was gruff.

"I know. I think I hit my head or something because I don't remember how I got to where you found me. Or maybe it was whatever he injected me with that made me forget." She shrugged helplessly. "That's what I know."

"Shit, baby," Jared said, pulling her against his body as he lay back on the pillows. "That's a lot."

She liked the way he cradled her. The warmth of his naked body beside hers. She'd found something precious through this ordeal, but she didn't think it would last. That was the sad truth about her life—nothing lasted.

Her parents, her brother and sisters. Her mother died, and her father gave her an ultimatum. Marry Seb Wilcox or leave. Her siblings didn't stick up for her. She could still see Glory and Charity, their faces stern. They'd married young too, and they had twelve kids between them. They were tired women, and they had no sympathy for her since they'd done what they were told.

But neither of them had been forced to marry an older man who looked at them with ice in his expression. Maybe she could have borne it if not for that.

No, she was kidding herself. She'd have never borne it. She'd always wanted more. Always wanted to see the world and be independent. She'd wanted to go to college, but her father had told her that wasn't her path. She'd chafed at farm life, chafed at her parents strict beliefs and upbringing. She'd wanted to soar, but they'd been determined to clip her wings.

She remembered her mother getting sick, remembered the endless chores as she'd had to take over the cooking and cleaning. Remembered resenting her mother for it, and hating herself for feeling that way. After her mother died, she'd been devastated. She'd only been seventeen then, and she'd missed her mother with every fiber of her being. Still did.

Libby squeezed her eyes shut and a tear escaped to roll down her cheek. Jared's hand came up to stroke her hair, and she burrowed against him, trying to lose herself in his warmth.

"Talk to me," he said.

Libby tried to laugh, but it didn't sound very happy. Still, she was determined to brazen her way through it. "Since when do you want me to talk?"

"Since right now. You're processing a lot of memories. I want to know what you're thinking."

"So many things. Who did you text?"

He twirled a lock of her hair around his finger. "Ian."

"I thought he was in Rome or something."

"He might be, but that won't stop him from doing what needs done." He rubbed his hand up and down her arm.

"What happens now? I should probably go back to work and see if the card is still there."

He snorted. "No, honey. You aren't going back there. It's too dangerous."

"Somebody has to. And shouldn't I be at work anyway? Monday, right? I was supposed to be off for a week. Which I did not ask for, by the way."

"That right there tells you that you shouldn't walk back into Ninja Solutions like nothing happened. It's an inside job, Libby. Someone in the office knew what happened to you and filled out the vacation request. We know Weir is involved based on what Paul told you, but we don't know if he has any accomplices."

She hated to think there were others involved, but of

course it was possible. There were other people working on the RIM project besides Daniel and Paul. Any of them could have helped Daniel, especially considering the financial incentive once the Army ordered the suits. Everyone in the company had been promised big bonuses. Even her.

"What about Paul? I don't think he really quit. That isn't like him. He loved his job and believed in what he was doing. He thought they needed another couple of years to perfect the AI technology first. I think someone kidnapped him and threatened him like they did me. That's how they found out I had a copy."

"Ian will check into it, but yeah, I think you're right."

Her eyes filled with tears. "What if they killed him, Jared?" she whispered.

He hugged her tight. "We don't know that they did."

She pushed back and frowned at him. His eyes were carefully blank, and her heart fell. "Stop trying to protect me. You know it's likely."

He nodded. "Yes, it's likely. But not certain. They might have kept him alive until they had what they wanted. In case he was lying. They'd want to make sure he hadn't stashed other copies with other people."

She hadn't thought of that, but it gave her hope. Paul was a nice man. Nerdy, goofy, and shy, he didn't exude confidence with women. But somehow he'd found the strength to talk to her. She didn't think it had been easy at first, but she'd never been rude or short with him. She'd listened to his stories, asked questions, and laughed at his jokes. Kristin said he was flirting with her, but Libby didn't believe it. She thought he just wanted someone to talk to, and she was an easy person to talk to because she liked people. He was lonely and brilliant, and even if she didn't understand brilliant, she definitely understood lonely. She definitely understood that sense of not belonging, and being desperate to belong for a change.

She thought of her friends, the men and women she often hung out with, and she knew those relationships were mostly superficial. It was her fault, because she had trouble letting anyone in. They were people she hung out with at clubs, coworkers who went for drinks together, but there were only a couple she'd call friends. Kristin, who'd gotten her the job at Ninja Solutions. And her cousin, Merry, who'd called her up and told her to move to DC two years ago. Merry had needed a roommate, and Libby had needed a change from the office supply company so she'd thought *why not?*

She didn't regret it, either, even if Merry had moved out a couple of months ago to live with her boyfriend. Making the rent on her salary from Ninja Solutions wasn't difficult, but now she faced the prospect of having to find another job when this was over. The company wasn't going to survive the scandal when the truth came out. Not that she wanted to keep working there anyway. Not after this.

"I don't think I can go back to sleep," she said as her mind continued whirling.

"No, of course not. Get dressed. We'll fix some coffee and wait to hear from Ian."

"What do you think will happen now?"

"We need to get the memory card and find out what's on it. If it's as bad as Paul told you, we'll have to find out how deep it goes."

"And you'll find Paul, right?"

He hesitated for an instant. "We'll find him, honey. But I can't guarantee it'll be good when we do."

Her heart thumped. "I know." She reached for his hand. Squeezed. It felt odd to do that now that she knew who she was—her fears and foibles, her insecurities—and yet it felt right too. "Thank you."

He lifted her hand to his mouth and kissed it. "You're welcome, babe."

Warmth flooded her. And fear too. This wasn't going to last. She knew it in her bones.

Nothing good ever did. Not for her.

Chapter Twenty-Two

"THE QUICKEST WAY TO GET THE CARD IS TO SEND HER back there," Colt said. "She's got a badge and she can get past security. It'll take us too long to fake the credentials needed."

Jared wanted to growl. And yet he knew Colt wasn't wrong. "I don't like it. Besides, we don't know that her badge hasn't been inactivated."

"We'll know quickly enough. If it doesn't work, we'll extract her."

"We'll be watching all the exits," Brett said. "And she'll be wearing a wire, so we'll know everything that happens and everyone she talks to. We can breach if we have to get her out."

"We still don't know if someone in the Gemini Syndicate is involved," Jared said. "And we have no fucking clue what happened to Paul Hicks. I don't like the risk."

They'd been looking for information on Hicks, but so far they'd come up with nothing. He'd last been seen getting into his car at his home in Manassas on Tuesday evening by a neighbor. He hadn't returned, and the next day the HR department at Ninja Solutions said he'd quit.

"If Gemini is involved, they haven't sent Calypso to deal with the situation," Ian said from the screen hanging at one end of the conference room.

"You know that for certain?" Jace asked, his eyes narrowing on the projection. Ian was transmitting from a secure area of BDI's Rome operations. There was a backdrop of the Roman skyline behind him, but it was a static background. He wasn't really sitting on a rooftop terrace, discussing classified information.

"Yes."

"How?"

"She made contact. She doesn't know who Paul Hicks or Libby King are, and she's not involved in any mission pertaining to Ninja Solutions."

Jared frowned. Jace frowned harder.

"She told you that?" Jace asked. "And you trust her?"

"I don't trust her, but I believe she's telling the truth on this one. Besides, if she'd been sent to bring Libby in —or kill her—why is she in Rome?"

Jace seemed flabbergasted. "She's in Rome?"

"She was as of three hours ago. She's probably gone now."

Jared had sympathy for Jace, who was Calypso's brother but seemed not to have any contact with her, yet that wasn't his primary concern at the moment. "Can we turn this back to the matter at hand?" he said. "Like who the hell cleaned up the bodies on the mountain and left no trace? I don't think that's Daniel Weir's doing."

"No," Ian said. "I don't either. Gemini could still be involved somehow, but I don't think they're operating on the micro level. They'd be buyers so long as they don't know the suit doesn't work, but I doubt they'd have incentive to keep Paul Hicks or Libby from exposing the truth the way someone closer to the project would."

"We need to find out who the investors are," Jared said. "That's who'd have the most incentive to keep the test results secret. Someone who'd put in a lot of money and expected a lot in return. It isn't just Daniel Weir who stands to make millions from the RIM sale. Anyone who's worried about their big payday would have motive to eliminate Hicks and anyone he shared the information with."

"I'm working on it," Ian said. "But we're going to need that memory card. Sooner rather than later. It's the only way we can end the threat to Libby. We have to expose the truth and stop the deal with the Army from going through. Sending her in to retrieve the card is the best way to do it."

Dull anger flared in Jared's gut, but he wasn't going to argue. They needed that card, and Libby knew where it was. She'd have the least trouble getting it. It would be risky, but not overtly dangerous. No one was going to hurt her in front of witnesses. Besides, they'd learn a lot from the reactions of those around her when she walked back in like nothing had ever happened. Most people expected her to return. Someone—maybe more than one—didn't, and they were likely to be shocked when she did.

They'd probably also be pretty desperate, which didn't make any of this sit well with Jared. But he'd be outside with his team, and they'd be listening to everything that happened inside. They'd know if Libby was in trouble, and they'd breach the place if they had to, security be damned. They knew how to breach a building with speed and stealth when necessary, and they could do it so that no one got hurt.

But it wouldn't go unnoticed and Ian would have a lot of explaining to do afterwards.

"She's due back at work tomorrow morning," Dax said. "According to what I was told when I called and asked for her."

"Tomorrow morning it is then. Make sure she's ready, Jared," Ian said.

"She'll be ready."

"Good. You kids figure it out and I'll see you tomorrow."

The projection of Ian went blank and Jared looked at his teammates. They were watching him with varying expressions of sympathy and understanding. The single guys didn't look much fazed by the whole thing. The attached ones, however...

"She'll be fine," Jace said. "We won't let anything happen to her."

Colt nodded. "Angie, Maddy, and Tallie like her a lot. The three of them are made of steel, so I expect Libby is too. Our women aren't fainting flowers, man."

Our women.

Jared blinked as the words rolled around in his head. They felt… right. Libby *was* his woman. He'd known her for less than two weeks, but he knew he wanted to know more of her. He wanted her mornings and her nights, and he wanted her curled around him in sleep and clinging to him in passion. He didn't know where it was leading, but he was learning that he didn't mind the journey.

"Libby is tough," he said. "I know she is, but she's already been through a lot. I don't want her hurt again."

"We aren't going to let that happen."

Jared shoved a hand over his head, raking it through his hair. "We need the card. And she's the one who can get it. So let's make a plan, and I'll go and tell her what she needs to do."

Dax called up a schematic projection of Ninja Solutions' office building. "Here are all the entry and exit points to the building. We can station a team in front and one in back. Since Libby will be miked up and wearing a tracking device, we'll know where she is at all times. If she moves toward any of the exits other than the front door, we'll be there waiting."

Jared didn't want her moving toward any exits. He wanted her to go in, get the card, and bring it back out again without talking to anyone. But he knew that's not how it was going to go. It'd be too suspicious for one thing. And it wouldn't give them the first clue about who the traitors in the company were.

They spent the next hour going over the plan from top to bottom, refining and tweaking, before everyone was satisfied. Then Jared went downstairs to the Cove with Colt and Jace. Angie and Maddy were there with Libby. They were laughing about something when Jared and the other two entered. Libby's eyes met his, her gaze sparkling with heat and humor, and his heart did a slow thump in his chest.

He really liked this woman. A lot. She made him laugh, and she made him hard, and even though she talked way more than he would have ever thought he could deal with, he liked the things she said. Silly things. Sexy things. Profound things.

Libby shared her emotions easily, and yet she hid herself away too. It was the damndest thing, really. She was open and eager, but he sensed there was a heart of glass beneath her easy manner. Like she thought maybe she wasn't worth it somehow. Like she expected people to abandon her.

He needed to find out what that was all about. They hadn't talked about her past yet. They'd been too busy talking about everything that'd happened recently. She hadn't mentioned her family since her memory had returned. Before that, she'd told him about random memories such as fields planted with corn and gathering eggs in a basket. Nothing deep, and nothing painful.

Now, he wondered. He went over to her and squeezed her shoulder. She smiled up at him with all the trust in the world. Like he was her knight in shining armor. His gut tightened. He damn well intended to be.

"Is it settled now?" she asked.

"We have a plan," he told her. "But we need your help."

She bit her lip. "Okay. I guess it was too much to

241

hope you'd come in here and tell me you had the card already."

She'd been eager to go get the card when she'd first remembered, but he thought the danger of that choice had probably sunk in during the interim.

"Yeah, sorry."

She glanced at Angie and Maddy. They looked fierce, and he was glad that fierceness was for her. Tough women, those two.

Angie reached over and patted her arm. "You can do this, Libby. Whatever it is. These guys won't let you down. None of us will."

"I know. I just hope I don't let all of you down," she finished softly.

Jared dropped to a knee beside her, forced her to look at him. Her eyes were filled with the kind of fear that came from not believing you were good enough. He knew that fear because he'd had it too. Once upon a time, with an abusive asshole for a father, he'd believed he wasn't worthy. He knew differently now.

"You aren't going to let anyone down," he told her. "You're smart and brave, and you got away from those men before they could hurt you further. You jumped off a damned roof, Liberty King. And you trudged through the snow for almost a mile until you found me. I'd say you're pretty amazing."

She smiled. The corners of her mouth trembled, but he knew the smile was genuine. She was trying not to cry.

"Thanks. You're amazing too. If not for you, I wouldn't be here, would I?" She put a finger over his lips before he could speak. "Don't answer that because we both know the truth."

He kissed her finger and didn't say a word.

She sucked in a breath and lifted her chin, her gaze taking in everyone there. "All right. Tell me what I have to do. I'm ready and willing."

Chapter Twenty-Three

Nerves punched Libby's belly as Jared drove her to work the next morning. She'd wanted to go to her apartment and get ready there but Jared had told her it was best if she didn't. If someone was watching for her, they'd lose the element of surprise when she walked into Ninja Solutions after nine days away.

She smoothed the navy pencil skirt over her thighs and stared out the window. Dax and Colt had gone to her apartment and picked up some of her clothes and shoes, her coat, her makeup bag from the bathroom, her curling iron, and her purse, which contained her company badge and her driver's license.

It was weird to think of them entering her home without her and going through her things, but at least she liked Dax and Colt. It wasn't quite the same as random strangers going through her stuff. They'd already been there once, which she'd realized when she got her memory back and knew the glasses they'd given her weren't actually new. They were hers. She always had an extra pair because she was afraid of misplacing one.

Jared had told her then that someone had broken into her apartment and turned it upside down looking for the memory card. She'd been anguished over that, but he still wouldn't relent and allow her to return. After this morning, after she retrieved the card, maybe life could get back to normal again.

Libby's throat tightened. What was normal anyway? Her life wasn't quite what she'd expected it to be, but then whose was? Jared had said she was friendly and bubbly and that she surely had a lot of friends when she couldn't remember her life, but now that she had, it was shocking to realize that she really didn't have close friends.

It was her fault. Her personality. She liked to talk, liked to listen, but she didn't like to let people in. Letting people in meant they would see the real you.

And when they saw the real you, they'd know you weren't as together as you pretended. They'd know you were insecure and faking it to get by. When they knew that, they wouldn't stick around. As a result, she had a handful of superficial relationships with people she had fun with. Even Kristin and Merry weren't allowed much deeper than the surface for fear of getting hurt if they rejected her. Maddy, Angie, and Tallie had made it past her defenses because she didn't know who she was at the time. Now she did, and she knew she had to be careful with them as well.

Not that she expected to be around much longer. Once she'd gotten the card back, the reason for her and

Jared to be together would be over. Even if she'd believed last night, when he'd been deep inside her and making her scream his name, that maybe there was more to what was happening between them than just sex.

But he'd never said so, and neither had she. They hadn't talked of anything important yesterday. They hadn't talked much at all, preferring to spend their time naked and wrapped up in each other. Words weren't necessary then.

"You're quiet," Jared said.

She pasted on a smile and looked at him, her heart flipping as always. He made butterflies swirl in her belly, and hot, sweet need flare in her core. He thrilled her and scared her in equal measure. She wanted him more than ever, and she was afraid too. What happened when he got tired of the sex between them? She'd be back to square one, lonely and unwilling to risk her heart again.

She'd had boyfriends before, but never one she'd been serious about. Never one who made her feel the way Jared made her feel. She had to wonder if she would have let it happen if she hadn't forgotten who she was. That thought made her frown.

No, it wouldn't have happened at all because Jared wouldn't have been interested in her in the first place. *You don't know that.*

Do too.

"Libby?"

"Sorry. Just thinking about getting that card. I doubt anyone threw my plant away in a week, but I guess it's possible."

His hands tightened on the wheel. "God, I hope not. Though even if someone didn't expect you to return, I'd think they wouldn't have gotten rid of your stuff so quickly if they wanted people to believe you were on vacation."

"True." She frowned. "It has to be Daniel, don't you think?"

"I think he's the most likely suspect, yes. But there are others who stand to lose a lot of money if this project doesn't go through."

"Anyone else I should watch out for?"

Daniel wasn't in the office this morning according to Jared's information. He was at a meeting at the Pentagon. One less person for her to worry about running into. But who else could be involved?

Jared shot her a look. "*Everyone* is suspect, Libby. There's not a person at Ninja Solutions who isn't invested in the company's success, though I'd think the top-level officers have more to lose than anyone else. Just go in and act as normal as you can. The guys are covering all the exits, and we can see and hear everything. If there's a problem, we'll come get you."

She felt slightly better knowing that. She also felt like she was in a James Bond movie. She was wearing a blush-colored silk blouse, one of her favorites, with a navy blazer and her favorite cream coat. Jared had given her a jeweled pin to affix to the lapel of the blazer. Inside the pin was a camera and microphone. She could hardly believe it until he'd shown her the feed. It was on a small computer that Dax carried. Dax would be watching her, but everyone else could also hear her through the tiny earpieces they wore.

"I sure hope I don't have to pee," she muttered. "I don't want you guys listening to that."

He laughed. "Babe, we've listened to worse. Think of it like this. Right now, you're one of us. You're on a mission, and we're your support. You need us to hear it all. You need Dax to see it all."

She liked the idea of being one of them, even if only for a little while. She'd worry about tomorrow, tomorrow. "Aye aye, captain," she said with a smart salute.

Jared shook his head as he laughed. "You're seriously cute, you know that?"

She couldn't help the warmth inside. "I'm glad you think so. It's been my lifelong goal for a sexy man to think I'm merely cute."

"If this wasn't important," he growled in that sexy growl of his, "I'd turn around and head straight back home, throw you over my shoulder, then take you up to my bed and keep you in it all day long just so you'd know exactly how hot I think you are."

"Promises, promises," she said, the warmth inside her turning into something more. She knew what it was like to spend the day in bed with Jared Fraser, and she wanted more days like that. Yesterday, after his meeting at BDI, he'd returned to the Cove where he'd left her with Angie and Maddy and then told her what she needed to do. She'd listened carefully, her stomach knotting. But she *wanted* to do it. She wanted to get that damned card and find out what had happened to Paul. Mostly, she wanted to live without the fear someone was going to snatch her off a street and threaten her again.

After he'd explained everything, he'd taken her back to his place—and they'd ended up naked on the couch, then the floor, and then they'd made their way upstairs where he'd made her come so many times she'd been limp and exhausted. He'd ordered food from a delivery service late that day, and they'd eaten a Mexican meal in the kitchen, talking about nothing more important than the weather and the fact she couldn't wait for spring.

At eight that evening, Colt, Jace, and Dax arrived with her belongings and the equipment she was going to need. They'd gone over the plan with her, and then they'd left. She and Jared fell into bed, unable to stop from touching and tasting, and then they'd gone to sleep tangled together.

She was happy with him, and that terrified her. Happy never lasted.

Jared reached over and squeezed her hand. "It *is* a promise, babe."

She squeezed back. "I'm glad. I just hope today goes according to plan."

"You've got this, Libby. Those assholes grabbed you off the street, but they didn't break you. You didn't tell them about the card, and you didn't give up. You got away. They're dead and you aren't, and you're going to rock this, honey. Go in and get that card, then text me. I'll be waiting at the door for you."

She had a new phone in her purse. Not her phone, which was apparently gone, and not a new phone with her number ported over. A new phone with a new number. For now, Jared had said. Until this was over, she couldn't have her old number back in case someone wanted to track her movements. This phone wasn't registered to her, so nobody knew it was hers.

"Okie dokie."

Jared turned into the parking lot for Ninja Solutions. It was a red brick building with darkened windows. Inside were the offices and testing facility where the RIM project prototype resided. She'd never seen it in person, as she wasn't cleared to that level, but she'd seen the promotional videos for it. They all had. It was a spectacular piece of modern engineering. Except that it was flawed and not safe.

Libby put her controlled access card around her neck and drew in a breath. Her fingers trembled as she clutched her purse in her lap. Jared stopped the truck and leaned over to kiss her. "You look hot in that skirt, by the way. I really want to strip you out of it and fuck you in those heels. Think about that while you're sashaying that gorgeous ass of yours into the building."

Her core liquified. "I will," she said in a whisper. "Wait, can the guys hear us?"

He grinned. "Yeah, afraid so. But who cares?"

Color heated her cheeks as she shook her head. "You're rotten, you know that?"

"Yup."

She kissed him back and opened the door. It was now or never. Get the card. Get out alive. Worry about tomorrow, tomorrow.

"I'm with you every step of the way. Don't forget that."

"I know. Thanks, Jared."

Those words seemed inadequate, but the ones she really wanted to say were inappropriate. She knew, looking at him as she clutched the door handle in her fingers, at his serious expression and melty eyes, that she'd fallen to a pretty deep place she'd never been before. No matter how often she told herself this wasn't going to last, that it was temporary, that men like him—handsome, serious, exciting, wicked smart—didn't fall for women like her—basic, boring, too talkative—her heart hadn't listened. Her heart had fallen hard, and it held out eternal hope his would do the same.

Stupid heart.

Libby opened the door with trembling fingers.

"Libby."

She turned back to him, hope a living thing inside her. "Yes?"

"I believe in you."

It wasn't what she'd wanted to hear, but it was more than she'd expected. She couldn't help but smile. "I believe in you too, Knight."

Then she stood on the pavement and shut the door before marching toward the entrance like she owned the place.

———

"KNIGHT, HUH?" It was Dax's voice in his ear. "Been wondering what your codename was. You never told us."

"It wasn't important." But he didn't have that tight

feeling inside that he usually did whenever he thought of the name. Maybe because Libby believed he was her knight, or maybe he'd finally made his peace with it. Whatever the case, he felt perfectly fine hearing it from his teammate's lips.

"If you say so," Dax replied.

Jared parked across the street from the unmarked van where Dax was currently monitoring the camera feed. Colt and Rascal were there with him. Tyler, Jace, and Brett were in another location at the back of the building. Jared got out of the vehicle and sauntered over to the van, surveying his surroundings before opening the door and jumping inside. Three pairs of eyes looked at him.

"I'm glad you're here," Rascal said. "It was getting hot in this little space listening to you talk to Libby."

Jared sat on one of the benches lining the van's interior. "Fuck you," he said mildly.

Rascal laughed.

"Is she through security?" Jared asked.

"Yep," Dax said. "Her badge worked without a hitch."

They'd worried that maybe her access had been revoked since someone clearly didn't expect her to return, but it hadn't been. With the touch of a button on his comm link, Jared could hear her as she made her way through the building, but without a visual he wasn't entirely sure where she was. Unfortunately, Libby couldn't hear him. They'd decided it was better if she wasn't wearing an earpiece of her own. She had a tracker, and she had the microphone and camera that recorded everything. She also had a cell phone as a backup way to track her and communicate if necessary. That had to be enough.

Besides, she wasn't accustomed to wearing a comm link and she might give it away with her movements when she pushed the button or if she stopped when there was a voice in her ear. They'd decided she didn't need it with everything else, so she was in there without any encouragement from him.

He hated that, but he understood it. Still, the worry sitting like a stone in his belly hadn't eased in the least. From the moment she'd walked toward the building, he'd been dealing with this low-level anxiety that twisted his guts and made him want to shove his way into Ninja Solutions and sweep Libby out of there before anything could happen. Not that he expected anything to happen, but since they didn't know precisely who was behind Paul Hicks's disappearance and Libby's abduction, they didn't know what that person would do when they saw Libby sashaying into the office like nothing had happened.

They had intel that Daniel Weir was at the Pentagon, but that didn't mean Libby was in the clear. Somebody was going to be surprised when she walked in. If they were lucky, that person wouldn't figure out what to do until Libby'd exited the building.

"Have you heard from Ian?" Jared asked no one in particular.

"He's touching down in an hour," Colt said.

"Do you think he went to Rome to meet with Calypso, or did it just happen?" Rascal asked.

"Knowing him, he went to Rome because he guessed she'd be there," Colt said. He rubbed a spot over his ribs almost absently. It was where Calypso had shot him when she'd abducted Maddy from the safe house where Colt had been guarding her for Jace.

"What does Jace think about Ian trying to turn his sister?" Dax said.

"I don't know. He doesn't talk about it," Colt replied.

"She shot Jace, too," Jared said, in case anyone had forgotten.

"She's cold-blooded," Dax added. "Seeing her on that mountain when we were rescuing Tallie was a surprise. Even more surprising was her handing Tallie over and going after the doctor."

"She killed him. Killed the pilot too."

"Then she flew the damned helicopter." Colt shook his head. "Didn't see that one coming. I think Jace was stunned when Ian told him what'd happened."

"Whatever happened to her in the years after Jace escaped is a mystery. But she's a survivor. You have to give her that."

"Yeah, she really is. I think that's why the boss is fascinated with her."

Jared cocked his head. "You think he's interested in Calypso?"

Dax shrugged. "I think it's possible. She's a master of disguise, an assassin, and a pilot—that we know of. I don't think the boss can help but be interested. Hell, I'd be interested too if I thought she had a soul."

Jared frowned. "I hope you're wrong. A woman like that could do a lot of damage before she's through."

"If she doesn't kill him first," Rascal muttered.

"Heads up. Libby's walking into her work area," Dax said, eyes fixed on the screen.

Jared hit the button to listen. She greeted her coworkers, who seemed genuinely happy to see her. They asked about her vacation and if everything was all right since it'd happened so suddenly. No one had known she was leaving so they figured it must have been a family emergency or something.

Libby played her part well. She improvised on the fly, telling them her sister had needed emergency surgery and she'd had to fly home to be at her side. It was a good lie, and everyone offered their best wishes for her sister's recovery. She accepted them gratefully, but Jared knew it had to hurt to pretend like she had a relationship with her family. She hadn't talked about them since she'd recovered her memory, which told him more than she thought it did. Knowing that her parents were gone, and that her brother and sisters were old enough to be her parents, he guessed that she didn't have a close relationship with any of them.

That would be the kind of thing that bothered someone as sunny and sweet as Libby King. He vowed to ask her about it the moment this was over and he had her safely in his arms again. Then he vowed to tell her how he felt about her. He didn't know what this was, precisely, but he knew it was more than he'd ever felt for anyone before. That scared the hell out of him, but he was in it now. He wasn't turning back, and he wasn't bailing.

He realized Colt was watching him. Jared met the other man's gaze evenly. "Welcome to the club, brother," Colt said.

Before Jared could say a word in response, he heard Libby's voice in his ear.

"Where in heck is my plant?"

Chapter Twenty-Four

ONCE LIBBY BADGED INTO THE BUILDING AND SECURITY didn't come running, she was able to let out the breath she'd been holding. Jared and the others were listening for any signs of trouble, which was a comfort. She just had to continue up to her cubicle like normal.

She headed for the elevator, greeting a coworker who held the door for her as she scooted inside. Once she reached the third floor where the administrative offices were, she sucked in a deep breath and strode from the elevator like she had every day before someone had tried to kill her.

Lisa Norton, her cubicle mate, was coming out of the copier room when she saw Libby. "Hey, girl! I missed you last week."

"I missed you too," Libby said as they walked back to their cubicle together. She liked Lisa. The other woman was her age, but she already had a husband and toddler at home and never had time outside of work to herself. She chatted amiably about things that had happened last week and didn't seem surprised by Libby's return. Not that Libby had suspected Lisa for a moment. The girl would need a clone to have enough time to get into trouble.

Some of Libby's other coworkers stopped her progress through the building to express their happiness at her return.

"Is everything okay?" Susie Jenkins asked. Susie was an older lady, severely dressed in all black, and nosy as the day was long. But sweet. Susie would give someone the shirt off her back if they needed it. "You took leave so suddenly, we wondered if you'd had a family emergency. Kristin didn't seem to know either."

Libby smiled. She hadn't seen Kristin yet, but she couldn't wait to talk to her friend. Not about Jared, of course, because that was still a secret. But maybe Kristin would know if anything weird had happened last week. Not that Libby could ask about that either. But if it had, Kristin would spill. She wasn't a secret keeper.

"My sister had to have emergency surgery. I went out there to help with the kids and everything. She's going to be fine, though. It was just so unexpected I didn't have time to tell anyone. And I lost my phone," she added. "On the plane. The airline is *still* searching for it, though I have a temporary one a friend loaned me. You know how that goes."

"Oh, honey, yes," Susie said. "My niece lost her iPad on a trip to Florida and never did get it back. I think one of them flight attendants took it."

Libby very much doubted that, but she didn't argue. It wasn't worth the breath when it came to Susie. The woman believed what she believed. Finally, Libby got herself away from everyone and headed for her cubicle. Lisa was already there. Libby rounded the barrier and stopped. Her desk looked the same as she'd left it. With one exception.

"Where in heck is my plant?"

Lisa glanced up, her eyes widening. "Oh no! Crap. It's my fault. It was getting some brown leaves so I took it to the kitchen and pruned them off Friday morning. I was going to bring it back but I got a call from the daycare and forgot about it. I think it's still there." She jumped up. "I'll go get it."

Libby held up a hand to stop her. Inside, she was shaking. Outside, she tried to project calm. "It's fine, I'll go. Thanks for looking after it for me."

Lisa looked contrite. "I'm so sorry. I should have brought it straight back, but I forgot everything then."

"Is your son okay?"

"Oh yes. He'd gotten into an ant mound and got stung, but he was fine. I had to go get him and take him to the doctor, of course. He cried a lot, but he's not allergic or anything."

"I'm glad he's well." Libby hooked her thumb over her shoulder. "I'll just go get my plant."

She turned to go, then reached into her purse and grabbed her new phone to slip it into her jacket. She'd been without one for more than a week and though this one didn't contain anything to do with her life yet, she felt naked without it. She knew the guys were watching and listening, but what if something happened to the feed and they couldn't see or hear her? At least she'd have a phone.

When she reached the kitchen, her plant was sitting on the counter. Libby hurried over and grabbed it. The plant wasn't big, a spider plant because those were hard to kill (though she was convinced if anyone could kill it, she could), and it did look a bit better now that Lisa had removed the brown leaves. No matter how much Libby watered it, or didn't, she couldn't seem to prevent the dang thing from getting brown on the edges. For a farmer's daughter, she definitely didn't have a green thumb.

"I heard you were back."

Libby spun around. Kristin stood in the doorway, looking a little bit angry. She felt guilty for making her friend worry, because of course Kristin would have. But Libby couldn't explain why she hadn't texted or called.

"Yes, I'm back. I had to go to Ohio for a family emergency." It had sounded so good when she'd told the others, but saying it to Kristin, she could taste the lie. If anyone would see through the story, Kristin would.

Kristin walked into the room, arms crossed. "You don't talk to your family. Why would you go to Ohio for any of them? And why didn't you *tell* me? I've been so worried!"

Kristin threw her arms around Libby and squeezed. Libby clutched the plant as she squeezed back. Then Kristin took a step back and dabbed at her eye with a tissue she pulled from her sweater.

"I'm sorry, Kris. It was very last minute. I was

rattled, and then I lost my phone. I've been out of touch with everyone."

"Still, didn't *anyone* have a phone where you were?"

"Yes, of course. But I don't *know* your number. It's in my phone. I couldn't recite it if you paid me."

Kristin blew out a breath. "Well, fine. Still." Her dark brows drew down as she focused on Libby's face. Libby knew it couldn't be the scrape on her head because she'd covered it with makeup and styled her hair over it. But then Kristin's gaze dropped a fraction before she grinned. "Did you meet a man in Ohio?"

"Why do you ask that?"

"Your neck. Looks like a love bite—or a beard burn."

Libby felt herself coloring. The guys were listening. Not that they hadn't heard an earful already this morning. Jared was listening, too. And Kristin was still waiting for a reply.

Libby put her hand up to her neck where she could still feel the slight tingle of Jared's mouth as he'd nipped and sucked. "One night stand. I, um, was feeling sort of blue and the kind of man you don't want to turn down showed interest. So yeah, that's what happened."

Oh god, her face was on *fire*.

Kristin waggled her brows. "Oh my. I want to hear *all* about it. Every juicy detail. We can go to lunch and you can tell me everything."

"Sure. Anything fun happen around here when I was gone?"

Kristin shook her head. "Nah. Same old, same old. Daniel's running around like a chicken with his head cut off, and Nate's growling at everybody. I think his ex-wife petitioned for more child support." She seemed to hesitate, but then she came closer and glanced behind her. "There's a rumor that Paul Hicks had something damaging about the company, but nobody knows what it is."

"Really? Wow. I thought he quit, though."

"He did. But he used to talk to you a lot, didn't he? Did he ever mention anything?"

Libby's belly twisted. Her friend was staring at her expectantly, but she wasn't about to drag Kristin into this. "Paul mentioned a *lot* of things. I didn't listen to half of them. I was just being nice. He was a lonely guy and nobody around here ever really talked to him."

"The rumor is he had proof. But nobody's heard from him since he quit."

"I haven't either. I wonder what he knew? Maybe it's not about the company at all. It could be about Daniel, which is almost the same thing. What if he's having an affair or something? He might not want anyone to know that, especially now that he's engaged. The congressman could pull his support for RIM. No more appropriations. No inside track with the Army."

Kristin frowned. "That would definitely be bad for the company. But I got the impression it was more to do with something technical."

"Well I definitely wouldn't know anything about *that*. I'm the least technical person on the planet. Don't even try to explain how computers work to me. I just know that they do."

Kristin laughed and looped an arm inside Libby's.

"Girl, I hear you. Oh well, I just thought he might have said something to you. Or gave you something since he was so sweet on you."

Libby stiffened, then covered the lapse by pulling away and coughing. "Sorry. Think I might be coming down with something. Plane air."

"Oh, I hope not. That's the worst!"

"I've been drinking orange juice and popping vitamin C. I think it'll be okay."

"Good. Because I want to hear about this man you got busy with at lunch! I don't want you to cough through it."

Libby hugged her plant. "I can't wait to tell you all about him. Not that I expect to hear from him again." She waved her hand around. "One night stand and all that."

"Must have been a good one considering how red your face is right now."

Libby winced inside. The guys were listening. Not that Maddy, Tallie, and Angie hadn't told their men the gist of what Libby had said to them, but it was somehow worse when she knew they could hear her talking.

Kristin went over to the refrigerator and grabbed a bottle of water. "Well, better get back to work for now. Only two more hours of drudgery until lunch."

Libby laughed and they left the kitchen together. When she got back to her desk, she smiled reassuringly at Lisa, who was on the phone. Libby gave her a thumbs up, then put the plant down and sat in her chair. Her nerves were on edge as she logged into her computer. She kept glancing up and looking around, waiting for someone to swoop in and ask her what she was doing there, but nobody did. When she felt like no one was watching her, she stuck a finger into the dirt and pushed downward until she felt a hard ridge. Relief rolled over her.

"It's still here," she said softly for the benefit of the BDI guys. She pulled the plant closer as she dipped a second finger in. Then she slowly pulled the media card upward, keeping an eye on her surroundings as she did so. Once she had it free, she dropped it to the floor beneath her desk and put her foot over it. Then she raked the dirt back into place around the plant and set it into its usual spot.

Libby shook the dirt off her fingers over the trash can. She wanted to pick up the card and unwrap it, but first she took out the cell phone and sent a text to Jared using the code word he'd told her.

Got your order. What do you want me to do?

His reply was swift. *Leave now. Make up an excuse if you have to, or just walk out. I'll meet you in front.*

She typed back. *Okay.*

She hated to bail when she'd just gotten back, but she couldn't keep the media card with her now that she knew what was on it. She couldn't pretend to work all day and then waltz out of there later like nothing was wrong, carrying information that would probably ruin Ninja Solutions and take everyone's jobs with it. She hated to be the one who ruined it for everyone, but it wasn't really her fault in the end. It was Daniel's for lying about RIM and trying to push the development forward when it wasn't ready.

Libby put the phone in her pocket, then reached down and picked up the media card after making sure no one was watching. Lisa's back was to her and nobody else could see the floor of their cubicle unless they stopped in the opening. Still, she was afraid of someone seeing so she slipped it from the plastic and tucked it into her shoe, beneath her toes, while pretending to scratch her foot. Then she gathered her purse and stood.

"Heading to the restroom if anyone asks," she said to Lisa, who nodded.

She waved at a few people as she walked between the cubicles, then kept going once she reached the hallway that led to the elevator. All she had to do was step into the elevator, take it down to the first floor, and then walk out the doors like she had so many times before. Easy peasy.

She punched the down button, then glanced at the door to the stairs. She could run down them quicker than waiting for the elevator. She started for the stairwell door when the elevator dinged. The doors slid open. Nate Anderson stood inside.

"Libby," he said cheerfully. "Welcome back."

Kristin stood behind him, holding her iPad dutifully as she accompanied him to some meeting or other. She rolled her eyes and made a face behind Nate's back. Libby tried not to laugh. He was handsome, but definitely stuffy. Kristin had often said that if it wasn't for his ex-wife troubles, he'd be husband material. Older, rich, and easy on the eyes. But he couldn't take care of a new wife when the old one was giving him such hell— and threatening his wealth on a regular basis. Besides, he was boring—and that was unforgivable in Kristin's eyes.

Libby tore her eyes from Kristin, who was making even more comical faces now. "Thank you, Mr. Anderson. It's nice to be back."

"Can we give you a lift?" he asked with a pleasant smile.

She hesitated. There was no reason not to get into the elevator. No reason to take three flights of stairs when she could ride down. Kristin put her hands on either side of her iPad like she was praying and mouthed the word, "Please."

Libby bit the inside of her lip. Then she stepped onto the elevator. The doors closed with a swoosh. Nate let out a long sigh. "Well, that was certainly easier than I'd hoped," he said as he punched a code into the elevator panel once it started to move. It glided to a stop, then reversed and began to go up instead of down.

Libby blinked. "Um, I was going down."

Nate didn't look at her as he spoke. "Not anymore. Kristin was just coming to get you, but you saved her the trouble. And you've caused a *lot* of trouble, Miss King. But that ends today."

Libby stumbled backward, hitting the wall. Her eyes darted to Kristin, who looked at her sadly. "You should have cooperated, Libby."

Shock reverberated through her, followed by anger. "You're a part of this? How could you be a part of it? How could you let *things* mean more to you than the truth—than human *lives?* My God, Kris."

Nate glanced at Kristin. A look passed between

them then, and Libby knew. Stupid, stupid Kristin. She'd gone and fallen for this asshole. She'd disparaged him—made fun of him—to throw Libby off the scent. To throw *everyone* off the scent.

Libby felt sick. This woman was her friend. Someone she'd trusted—at least as much as she trusted anyone. But she'd been wrong, like always. She *believed* in people and they betrayed her. Would she never learn?

"No lives are in danger, Libby. The suit works," Nate said. "And the Army will make their own adjustments once they take delivery."

"It works, but it can't distinguish friend from foe at least fifty percent of the time when the AI component is in control," she grated.

One of Nate's eyebrows went up. "I guess he told you a lot, didn't he? What else did he say?"

Libby frowned. "Where's Paul?" she asked with a coolness she didn't feel.

Her heart was in her throat and her palms were wet with sweat, but she told herself Jared was listening. He could hear her, and Dax could see where she was, and they would come. They *would*. So she'd get Nate Anderson to talk and she'd let him incriminate himself. He would take her to his office and try to get her to tell him where the copy was, but he wouldn't get a chance to find out. Jared and the guys would be there. Soon.

"How would I know?" Nate said just as coolly. "He quit. For all I know, he left town." He took his phone out and looked at it. "Ah, yes. Daniel is arriving now."

The elevator kept going, past the fifth floor, then the sixth. There were only eight floors in the building. When they passed the eighth, she knew they were going to the roof. The elevator glided to a stop and the doors opened. A helicopter touched down on the pad, rotors spinning as a swift breeze picked up her hair and tossed it.

Libby tried to shrink backward into the elevator, but Nate took a firm grip of her arm and tugged her toward the waiting craft. Kristin followed, eyes hard and mouth set in a firm line.

"Where are you taking me?" Libby demanded.

"Somewhere we can talk," Nate said. "Without interruption."

The door to the helicopter opened and Daniel sat there, looking vaguely anxious. Nate shoved her inside despite her struggles. She screamed, but it wasn't going to do any damned good on the roof with no one to help her. Nate backhanded her before he picked her up and tossed her onto the seat opposite Daniel. He climbed in and sat beside her while Kristin joined Daniel. The helicopter lifted off at Daniel's signal.

Fear clogged Libby's throat. Jared was down there. The guys were all down there, and none of them had anticipated this. They couldn't follow her now. They couldn't burst in and save her.

She was on her own.

Chapter Twenty-Five

Jared's blood was ice. He'd listened to the exchange between Libby, Nate Anderson, and Kristin Martin, and he'd hated that he wasn't in the elevator with her—but he'd known he was going to be by her side in the next few minutes when his team breached the building and went to her rescue.

Until a new sound came over the comm.

"That's a helicopter," he said as the silence of the elevator was broken by noise. "Didn't anybody fucking know that Daniel Weir took a helicopter to the Pentagon? Shit!"

"They've gone to the roof," Dax replied. "Weir just landed."

He heard Libby ask where they were going as the helicopter noise grew louder.

"Somewhere we can talk. Without interruption."

They heard the sounds of a struggle and then Libby screamed. There was a solid sound and a gasp from

Libby. Someone had hit her. The rotor noise became slightly muted as if someone had shut a door. Jared recognized the whine of the engine as the speed increased. Anderson and Weir were abducting Libby by air, a possibility nobody had considered when they'd made their plans.

Jared had been waiting in his truck for Libby to exit the building and join him, but now he sped around to where he'd left the others in the surveillance van. He shoved his truck into park halfway on the sidewalk, not caring that it wasn't a proper parking spot, and jerked the door of the van open to jump inside with his team-mates. Dax's gaze was fixed on the screen. Colt was in the driver's seat. The instant Jared joined them, he shoved the van in gear and began to drive.

"Where are they going?" Jared asked.

"Looks like they're headed north at the moment."

Jared clenched his jaw. "They could take her anywhere. We won't be able to keep up." He punched the side of the van, swearing. Rascal and Dax looked at him. Colt glanced into the rearview. "I shouldn't have let her go in. She's got the card, but now they've got her— and that card is her only insurance. If they get it, they'll kill her."

"Libby's not stupid. She'll keep them guessing as long as she can."

"And how long is that going to be if they search her? Jesus!"

"We just need them to touch down," Dax said. "Soon as we know that, we can hone in on their location."

Jared swore again. None of it was good enough for him. Just a few short minutes ago, this whole thing was nearly over. Libby had the card and she was on her way downstairs. He'd been waiting for her. And then everything changed, and she was gone.

His head pounded with guilt. His throat was tight. He'd been in this situation before, but he'd never been as emotionally invested as he was now. He'd parachuted in to save injured combatants hundreds of times. He'd extracted hurt soldiers from combat zones, wounded civilians from disaster areas, and he'd done it without letting his emotions get involved. Even that last brutal mission in the Hindu Kush where he'd nearly lost his own life, he'd never felt the way he did now.

Like his heart had been ripped from his chest. Like his soul had been torn in two. The woman he'd sworn to protect—*promised* to protect—was in danger because he'd failed to keep her safe. And that was killing him inside.

He didn't know what was happening anymore because the range of the comm unit had been exceeded. Dax couldn't see anything on the camera feed any longer. They couldn't hear Libby. But they still had the cell phone, and the tracking device he'd placed on her skin, and Dax had a lock on both. Colt drove according to Dax's general instructions, but they had no way of knowing where Anderson and Weir were taking Libby. Tyler, Jace, and Brett were also in pursuit as Dax's instructions were fed to them through the comm link.

"The helicopter isn't tracking north anymore," Dax said a few minutes later.

Jared's heart throbbed with hope. If they were touching down, they hadn't gone too far. Which meant Jared and his team had a chance to get to Libby.

"Where are they?" he asked when Dax didn't say anything.

"Bringing it up on GPS... Just a sec..." Dax wore a look of concentration as he tried to pinpoint the location. When he suddenly grinned, Jared let out the breath he'd been holding. He was still pissed, still scared shitless, but his teammate smiling was a good sign. "They're near Harper's Ferry. I'll have the location in a few seconds. Tyler, can you find out if Anderson or Weir— or hell, Kristin Martin—has property in Harper's Ferry?"

"Copy. I'm on it," Ty said through the earpiece.

"I've got the coordinates," Dax said. "And an address."

"Kristin Martin has a house on the Potomac River in West Virginia, bought a month ago. That's the address."

Dax did a little finger wave thing like he'd dropped a bomb. "Boom. We've got them." His fingers moved fast across the keyboard. "It'll take us an hour to get there from here."

"Shit," Jared swore. "Anything could happen in an hour."

"We'll make it," Colt said as he pressed the pedal down. "She just needs to stall."

"I'll call Ian. Maybe he can make some magic happen," Dax said.

"If they search her, it's over," Jared said, the knot in his chest tightening. If those guys found the media card and verified the contents, they'd have no more need for Libby. This time, she wouldn't escape.

And he'd lose her forever.

———

LIBBY STARED at the terrain below. They flew north, until the packed buildings and clogged roads of Virginia gave way to long stretches of forest and hills that were still blanketed in white. There were roads here, but not as packed with traffic. There was a river, which had to be the Potomac, and then a smaller river which branched off it. She didn't know which river that was, but the helicopter banked and started to descend, flying low as they skirted along the water. When it stopped moving and began to descend onto a snowy bank, she didn't know which river she was looking at. There was a brick house in a clearing nearby. It was a big house with a spectacular view of trees and water.

Nate slid the door of the craft open. Daniel went first, then Nate hopped down behind him. "Let's go," he said to Libby, jerking his head at her.

Libby's belly twisted. Her eyes stung as her gaze met Kristin's. "You were my friend," she said, betrayal a hard knot in her throat.

Kristin's expression seemed stricken, but then it hardened. "And you were mine until you threatened to ruin everything."

"Me? I didn't do anything," Libby cried.

"You listened to Paul's lies. You helped him smuggle information off classified servers. Don't you care about all the people who will lose their jobs if his lies get out?"

"I didn't steal anything. I had nothing to do with Paul except to be nice to him. You know I'm nice to everyone!"

Kristin jerked her head toward Nate, who was waiting. Daniel was walking toward the house, talking on a cell phone. "Get out and let's go."

"And if I don't?"

Kristin laughed. "If you don't, then Tom up there is going to have to get out of the pilot's seat and make you. He won't be happy about that either."

As if to punctuate the sentence, Tom turned around and leveled her with a menacing look. Libby unclipped the seatbelt and clutched her purse to her as she jumped down. She was very aware of the media card in her shoe, and trying to figure out how she could possibly keep it concealed. If they made her take her shoes off, it was over. They'd know it was exactly what they wanted.

She looked at the river beyond, but there was no escape that way. Not unless she could swim to the other side, and she wasn't dumb enough to think that was a possibility. Not in the clothes she was wearing, and not at all considering she was a terrible swimmer in the best of circumstances. Not to mention the water was frigid right now. The woods were a possibility, even though the trees were bare. There were a lot of trees, and her coat was almost white. She eyed the woods as they walked toward the house.

"Don't bother trying to run into the woods," Kristin said from behind her. "You won't get far. Tom is an expert marksman, and he's carrying a rifle. And even if you did get away, he'd find you and bring you back. He's a former special forces soldier, and he won't let you escape the way those others did."

Libby whirled to face Kristin, fury burning her up inside. Kristin stopped abruptly. Behind her, Tom was exiting the helicopter. The rotors spun slower, and the engine was no longer running. Tom had a rifle slung over one shoulder, like Kristin had said.

"You knew about that? You knew those men snatched me off the street? That they scared me and hurt me and were planning to *kill me?* How could you care so little about me? We were friends!"

Kristin shook her head. "I'm sorry, Libby, but I told you. When you threatened the company like that—our livelihoods, our futures—I couldn't make excuses for you. I couldn't take your side. I recommended you for the job, and that's how you repaid me. Repaid all of us. You and Paul were going to take it all down, and for what? So you could feel important somehow? So you could finally say you'd accomplished something big? You'd be in the news, wouldn't you? A hero who could sell her story about the big bad company she'd helped to destroy."

Libby's heart hurt. She'd spent many evenings talking with Kristin about her life, about her upbringing and the way her family had always marginalized her. She'd wanted to accomplish big things in her life, but her parents had told her the only thing she was meant to do was be a wife and mother. Not that there was anything wrong with being a wife and mother, and not that she didn't want to do those things too, but it wasn't *all* she wanted to do. She wanted to find love and she wanted to see the world. She wanted to feel needed and important to *someone*, yes. But she wouldn't lie or hurt others to make it happen.

"If you think I want to destroy Ninja Solutions to feed my own ego or my need for approval, then you never really knew me at all, did you? Because it's apparent I never knew you. I thought you cared about the truth, Kristin. About right and wrong. But instead you only care about getting ahead—about snagging yourself a rich husband and living the life you think you deserve—"

Kristin slapped her so hard her head snapped to the side. Her cheek stung and she could taste blood where a tooth had sliced into the tender flesh inside her mouth.

"You shut up. You don't know a damned thing. I've worked hard all my life, and I won't let you ruin it. I won't let you ruin this company, not when we're so close to making all our dreams come true. You'd have gotten a lot of money when the deal went through—we all would. But that's not enough for you, is it? You want to be *important*."

There was nothing Libby could say that would change Kristin's mind. The friend she thought she'd known, the woman she'd spent hours laughing and talking with, wasn't real. It had all been a lie. She'd known Kristin was a bit more interested in fashion and luxury than Libby had thought reasonable, but if the girl wanted to spend a month's paycheck buying a Louis Vuitton bag, then who was Libby to tell her she couldn't do it? After all, she'd met Kristin, and gotten this job, because the woman had a shopping addiction and kept coming to Libby when she'd worked in a retail store. But how could those things mean more to Kristin than people did?

Libby turned and started toward the house, her eyes blurring with tears. Not tears of pain from being slapped, but tears of betrayal. How did she always choose the wrong people to care about? Why did she put her heart on the line when she knew how it was going to turn out?

Nate stood on the wide front porch, waiting. Libby shot a longing look at the woods. But running would give her less time than staying would. If she ran, Tom would shoot her. If she did what Nate asked, then maybe she could buy enough time for Jared and his teammates to arrive.

Despair filled her. They were back in Chantilly and they were driving, not flying. Even if they knew where she was, it would take them too long to get here. She could stall for a little bit of time, but not enough.

Still, she had to try. She thought of Jared, of his soulful blue eyes and serious expression. Of the way he touched her and made her body come alive with sensation. She'd never felt like she did with Jared. It didn't take a genius to figure out why.

Love. She was in love with him. She could deny it, but why? Now wasn't the time to lie to herself. Not when she was so close to dying. She might not mean anything to him other than a good time, but she couldn't regret a moment of their time together.

Libby trudged up the steps and took one last look around before walking inside the house behind Nate. Whatever happened now, she wasn't going to give up hope that Jared would find her.

Chapter Twenty-Six

THERE WERE TWO OTHER MEN INSIDE THE HOUSE BESIDES Daniel and Nate. Libby's pulse pounded in her throat as Nate shoved her into a chair and one of the men looped a pair of zip ties around her wrists and tugged them tight. Then he did the same to her ankles, tying them to the chair legs instead of each other.

Daniel was still on the phone, talking about delivery dates and meeting times as if he were in a boardroom instead of present at an abduction. Nate stood with arms crossed over his chest, glaring at her. He was a handsome man, but all she could see was the ugliness in his expression. Kristin entered the room and took a seat on the couch opposite Libby, picking up her iPad and tapping something on it.

"Now, Libby," Nate began. "I need you to tell me where you put the media card Paul Hicks gave you"

"Um," she said, her eyes darting between the two men and Nate. "I-I don't have a media card."

Nate nodded and one of the men stepped between

her and Nate and punched her in the stomach. The blow whooshed the air from her lungs and made tears spring to her eyes, though she thought it could have been a lot worse. They must not want her incapacitated just yet.

Nate turned to Kristin. "Search her purse and pockets."

Libby was still gasping for air when Kristin took her handbag and dumped the contents on the floor. She stooped and dug through everything—Libby's lipstick pouch, her wallet, the pockets of her bag—and unfolded every piece of paper. When she didn't find anything, she stood and shoved her hands into Libby's pockets. Thankfully, there was nothing but the phone. She handed that over to Nate.

"Unlock it," he said, handing it back to Kristin to give to Libby. She typed in the numbers, though she considered refusing. He wasn't going to find much, however, and that might buy her a little time.

"Who is Knight?" Nate asked. Daniel ended his call and walked over to stand behind Nate. He didn't look as angry as Nate, but she didn't kid herself that he was innocent. He was there, after all.

"A man I met. We've, uh, been having sex."

"What do you mean you have his order?"

Her face flamed and her belly hurt. Thank God Jared had told her to be vague and never mention what she really had. She'd thought he'd read too many tomes about the National Security Agency and spies when in fact he was right. "It's kinky stuff. I was answering his command."

Nate scrolled upward. There were no other texts. "Where is this command?"

"It was in email. I deleted it."

He handed the phone to Daniel. "I see."

Daniel's gaze flicked over the texts. "Who helped you escape, Libby?" he asked in a mild voice.

A chill washed over her. If she'd thought Daniel was somehow oblivious, she'd just gotten proof that he wasn't. In fact, he was less emotional about the entire thing than Nate. Which probably made him more dangerous.

"No one. I climbed out the window when they thought I was too groggy to do anything. Then I walked until a man found me. He took me in and helped me until I felt better."

"But where have you been all this time? Who were you staying with?"

She lifted her chin. "The same man. I fell for him, and I do what he tells me. It's a master-slave thing."

God, could she sound any more ridiculous? She knew people did that kind of thing, and more power to them if that was their kink, but it wasn't hers. She really didn't like being told what to do. If she did, maybe she'd have married Seb Wilcox and never left rural Ohio.

"And how did this man make the men on the mountain disappear? Because that was one hell of a trick. Men, guns, snowmobiles, dogs. All gone."

Libby blinked. "I-I have no idea. What do you mean disappear?"

"As in gone. As in they haven't made contact since they said they'd found you staying with a man in another cabin. What happened? Did you give this man the media card? Did he pay them off or promise them something? Who is he?"

Fear crawled down her throat at his questions. Not because she didn't know the answers, but because she was beginning to feel like time was running out. Where was Jared? How much longer could she do this?

As long as you have to, Libby.

Yes, as long as she had to. Because she was strong enough, and she had enough faith. And he *was* coming. He'd promised. It was her job to stay alive until he did.

"He said he was former special forces. I didn't give him anything because I didn't have anything."

"He was meeting you outside the building this morning. Why?"

"I told you. It was about sex. He wanted me to walk out of the building and go have sex in his car. He's kinky that way."

Daniel studied her. Nate was glaring. Kristin looked intrigued. Then she shook her head. "It's a lie. Libby is too goody two-shoes for that kind of thing. In all the time I've known her, I've never known her to have a one-night stand. She wants the ring and the church, not kinky sex in a public parking lot with a mystery man."

Daniel leaned against the arm of the sofa and crossed his legs. He was wearing a gray business suit made of expensive fabric and tailored to fit, and a crisp white shirt with cufflinks and a red tie. Someone had probably told him it was a power tie. Maybe his fiancée. He scratched absently behind one ear. Then he held out a hand to one of the men. The man placed a gun in his fingers.

Libby's pulse skyrocketed. Was he about to shoot her? But Daniel walked out of the room, carrying her phone with him. A few more seconds and an ear-shattering bang made her jump and squeak. Daniel returned moments later without the phone and gave the gun back to the thug who'd given it to him.

"Phone's dead," he told her. "Nobody can track you here. So I suggest you get busy telling us where that card is, or this is going to be a very painful day for you."

Her stomach fell. What if he was right and Jared couldn't find her now? He'd put something on the skin of her back this morning and told her it was a tracker, but what if it wasn't working right?

Have faith.

"I don't have a card. Paul told me that RIM doesn't work the way it's supposed to, and he told me all he needed was a couple more years to fix it—but you wouldn't let him. That's all I know. That's all he ever said."

Daniel's eyes narrowed. "That's not what Paul said to us. He said he made a copy and gave it to you. So I need to know what you did with it, and if you gave it to anyone else."

Her heart thumped. This was it. She was dead. But she'd be damned if she'd let these assholes win.

Daniel sighed. "Tell you what—we can do this easy or hard. Tell me where the card is and you can die quickly, without pain. Lie to me, and I'll make sure every bone in your body is broken first. It won't be pleasant.

These two men are experts in torture. They can make you wish you were dead while keeping you alive to suffer every unpleasant moment of pain. Your choice."

Libby's heart thumped but she didn't speak. At a nod from Daniel, one of the men stalked over and hauled back a fist to hit her. The blow landed hard on her jaw and her head snapped to the side. The momentum kept carrying her until the chair tipped and crashed to the floor. Pain rolled over her in waves as she tried to catch her breath.

"What's that?" Kristin said as Libby's head reeled.

Libby tried to focus on where her former friend was pointing. It wasn't until Kristin picked the item up and straightened that Libby realized what had happened. Her shoe had come off when the chair fell. Kristin was holding the media card.

Libby moaned as she stared at the dark piece of plastic.

Now they really would kill her.

———

JARED PRAYED he could reach Libby in time. He knew what it was like to fail at the mission, but this was one mission he couldn't fail. If he did, it would break him. He knew it deep in his bones. If he didn't get to Libby in time, if he didn't protect her from harm and keep her safe, he didn't know how he'd survive the pain.

He sat against one wall in the military-grade helicopter Ian had managed to produce, as it winged its way toward Harper's Ferry and Kristin Martin's house, and stared at the blue sky beyond. If he didn't get there in time, if he lost Libby…

If he lost the woman he didn't want to live without…

Dax's hand closed over his shoulder, squeezing. "We'll get her, man. We're only fifteen minutes behind them at this point."

A lot could happen in fifteen minutes and they all knew it. But nobody said that. Brett Wheeler fixed him with a knowing look. "Your girl's a fighter, Jared. She'll do what she has to do to survive."

His girl.

She was his girl, and he wanted her to know it. More than anything, he needed to get to her before it was too late and let her know how he felt. What she'd done to him. How she'd taken what he'd thought was broken and showed him that it wasn't. That he was better with her in his life than without.

Fucking hell.

"Shit," Dax said. He was studying the computer screen.

"What?" Jared asked.

"We've lost the phone. It went dead. But the tracker you put on her is still there."

"That's why we did it," Jared said, thanking God they had. Praying it was enough.

"ETA in five," Colt called back to them from his seat beside the pilot.

They'd gone back and forth over the plan, but had finally settled on a direct assault. The more time they wasted trying to infiltrate quietly, the more danger there was for Libby. She had the media card on her. If Weir or Anderson got it and accessed the information, they'd have no more use for her. There wasn't a moment to spare. It was still a risk to storm the property, but they hoped the element of surprise would be on their side long enough to get to Libby.

"She's still on the ground floor," Dax said. "In the same room she entered a few minutes ago." He pulled up a schematic of the house. "It's the living room, to the left of the entry, and it runs the width of the house. There are eight windows—two in front, six along the side. The rear wall has a set of french doors. The front of the house faces the river while the rear faces woods and a long drive to the main road."

If there were fewer woods, they could have set down somewhere close by and infiltrated more stealthily, but the only spot to land was the long stretch of property that sloped down to the river. The helicopter was equipped with stealth technologies to reduce rotor noise and the pilot was combat-trained. He would set them down as close to the house as he could manage. From there, they'd storm the building and rescue Libby.

Dax held up a hand as he seemed to be staring at the computer. Then he whooped. "I've got audio. The transmitter's still working. Should have visual here in a second."

Jared pressed the button so he could hear Libby talk. He needed to know she was still alive.

"You need an access code," she was saying. She dragged in heavy breaths like she was hurting, and that made his blood boil. What had they done to her? "The card won't work without it. And I'm not telling you the code unless you tell me where Paul is."

"We'll see about that," a male voice said.

"Is that Weir?"

"Yeah," Dax replied. "They're putting the card into a reader. I can see Anderson now. She's facing him and he's got the computer. There's another man standing by. Dark hair, mustache, mid-thirties maybe. Ah, and there's Weir. He just walked into view."

"Jesus, we only need a couple more minutes," Jared growled.

"Almost there," Jace said. "Hang on."

The sound of typing came over the comm. Then Weir swore.

"She's not lying," Anderson said. "There's an access code required, same as on Paul's card. But the code isn't the same. Canny bastard." He paused for a moment. "We don't really need it. We know this is the right card. Let's just destroy it and get rid of her. We've got this, Dan."

"No. We have to verify the information. If we don't, we'll always be watching our backs and wondering if Hicks left a ticking time bomb somewhere. If this card isn't it, or if there's something different on it, we need to know."

"Then we need a code."

Weir strode toward Libby. A moment later, the sound of a hand connecting to flesh echoed in their ears. Libby cried out in pain, and anger clawed at Jared's insides. If he got his hands on Daniel Weir, he was going

to kill him. Smarmy fucking used car salesman. Trai-
torous bastard.

"What's the access code?" he demanded.

"Where's Paul?" she asked again.

"He's dead," Weir told her. "As dead as you're about
to be if you don't give me the code."

"Go ahead," she said with a sneer. "But you won't
get the information on that card—and you won't find
out who else has a copy. If I don't return, they know
what to do with it."

Jared had to admire her balls, but he was terrified for
her too. She was making shit up as she went and she was
probably scared to death. She'd probably also given up
on the idea of him rescuing her like he'd promised.

"Hang in there, Libby," he said. "We're coming."

"Damn," Dax said with a whistle. "She's brave. Weir
looks ready to pop a blood vessel—but he's not moving."

"He's still trying to decide if she's bullshitting him or
not," Tyler said. "She's doing a fucking great job of it.
I'd hesitate too if I were him."

"We're about to drop onto the landing zone. Get
ready for the go order," Colt said.

Thank fuck.

The helicopter dropped swiftly. They were out the
doors before the craft touched the ground, weapons
drawn. A shot came from the house, but Jared kept
running toward it. There was another shot, and a man
dropped onto the porch as one of Jared's teammates
took him out. The door whipped open and a second
man stood there with a gun, aiming it directly at Jared.

The man fired. The bullet whizzed past Jared's ear

as he returned fire. The man dropped as Jared's bullet found its target. Jared leapt onto the porch and burst through the door, guns at the ready as his teammates shattered windows and doors with their entry into the room.

Nate Anderson started to run for the back but Ty tackled him and took him to the ground. Another man stood beside Libby, hands up as if he knew it was best to embrace the inevitable. Daniel Weir was gone. So was Kristin Martin.

"Get Libby," Brett said through the comm. "We've got these two. Sweeping for the others. They can't have gone far."

Jared rushed to Libby's side and gripped her chin gently, forcing her to look at him. "Baby, it's me. I'm here."

Tears leaked from her eyes. One lid was swollen shut and her face was purpling where she'd been hit. Blood dripped from the corner of her mouth and her lip was split. Her glasses lay smashed on the floor and one shoe was off. She had a knot forming on her skull when he carefully probed. His heart dropped to his toes.

"Jared?" she whispered, her breathing strangled. She'd been hit more times than they'd heard and not just in the face. Black anger swirled inside him at the thought of her enduring that kind of pain. Any pain. Libby didn't deserve that.

"Yes, baby. I'm here. You're safe."

"I knew you'd come. I stalled them. I did my best, but I was ready to give up. It hurt so much. My face, my stomach… Couldn't breathe…."

He kissed her forehead. "You didn't give up. You were perfect." He pulled out a knife and cut her wrists free, then dropped and freed her ankles.

"Oh god, that hurts," she said. "So bad."

"It's the blood rushing back into your extremities," he told her, though he didn't know it wasn't something worse. Not until he examined her.

Jared turned. Brett and Ty had Nate and the other man subdued. They knelt on the ground, hands clasped behind their necks. As much as Jared wanted to beat the shit out of both of them, he bent to pick up Libby instead. "I'm taking you to the helicopter. We're getting out of here."

She clung to him. "Thank you for coming."

He wanted to laugh at the way she said it. If the whole damned thing wasn't so heartbreaking, he would. That was his Libby. So polite. She lifted her hand, fingers trembling, and pressed them to his jaw, touching him sweetly.

"I'll always find you, Libby. I told you that."

"You're my knight in shining armor."

He was, and he was damned glad of it. He carried her outside and stepped down to the yard, striding toward the waiting helicopter. A shape darted toward him from the side of the house. At first he thought it was one of his guys, but when the stride didn't slacken, he threw a glance in that direction.

Kristin Martin ran at him. "Liar!" she screamed.

Too late, Jared realized she had a gun. And she was aiming it at Libby, who lay in his arms with nothing between her and the bullet that Kristin was intent on firing.

Nothing but him. As Kristin kept running, Jared turned away, putting his body between her and Libby. He didn't have time to get to the helicopter. He didn't have time to do anything but protect his woman with his life.

The gun roared a moment later. When the bullet hit, he felt the fire of it all the way to his toes. Then he dropped to his knees as Libby screamed.

Chapter Twenty-Seven

"JARED!"

He'd collapsed on top of her, pressing her into the snow. Libby's ears were ringing with the sound of gunfire and everything seemed like it was coming at her in a dream. In fact, she prayed she'd wake up and find out this whole thing had been a nightmare. She'd be beside Jared, naked in his bed, her body replete from his lovemaking. Nothing bad would be happening. She could shiver and cling to him and it would all go away. She'd wake in the morning to the scent of bacon and coffee, and Jared would smile at her over the breakfast table and make her world seem so damned full of hope and possibilities.

But the man whose body was so heavy on hers groaned, and she sobbed his name again. "Jared! Please, please, Jared. Please be okay."

He didn't move and panic started to claw at her insides. If he was dead…

Libby blinked up at the pale sky, her good eye aching as light stabbed into her retina. The other eye was swollen shut. A shape appeared above them. Kristin stood with long hair streaming over her shoulders, face looking wild and angry. She had both her hands clasped together, holding the gun she'd shot Jared with. She was shaking so hard she couldn't quite aim the gun properly, though.

Anger flooded Libby's body like a hot wave. She had to do *something*.

She moved her free hand, hoping to push Jared off her, and brushed something hard and metallic. Jared's gun. It was in a holster at his waist. She prayed it was ready to fire since she couldn't do that thing he'd shown her with the top of the gun right now. He'd told her before that if there was a bullet in the chamber, the gun would fire. It was getting the first bullet in there that required her to pull the top. But if he'd fired the gun, it was already there.

He groaned again and Libby made a decision. She dragged the gun out and up, intending to blast Kristin into eternity. But Kristin cried out suddenly.

"Don't shoot, Libby. I've got her." It was Rascal.

"Jared," Libby said again, more weakly this time. Everything hurt. And he was so heavy.

He rolled to the side, taking her with him, and she could breathe again. Hope flared to life like a tiny candle flame. "Jared?"

"I'm okay, honey," he said. He sat up and tugged her into his lap, and she sobbed in relief. He wasn't dead.

He hadn't sacrificed himself for her. In the background, the soft whirring of a helicopter sounded and a frigid breeze blew over her skin, freezing the tears on her cheeks.

She pressed her fingers to his face, caressing that beautiful jaw of his. His mouth. Then she pressed her mouth to his, crying out at the pain where her teeth had cut the inside of her lip. One of them was loose.

Jared grasped her hand and pulled it up to his face, kissing her fingers. "Shh. Don't try to kiss me. Not until we get you taken care of."

"She shot you," Libby said. "I felt it hit, and then you fell to the ground."

"I'm wearing body armor, baby. It still hurts like a motherfucker to get hit, knocks the breath out of you, but I'm okay. She didn't do any damage."

He held her and rocked her against him. She clung to him, shaking. "Thank God for that."

She looked up to where Rascal had Kristin subdued. Her hands were cuffed behind her back and she yelled obscenities at the big man. "I want up," she said, suddenly determined.

Jared got to his feet slowly, dragging her with him. "Are you sure you can stand?"

"Yes," she gritted. It hurt, but she had something to do. She started hobbling toward Kristin.

"Baby," Jared said.

"No. I have to do this."

"Lean on me," he told her, putting his arm around her waist like he had the night he'd found her. Together, they made it to where Kristin sat in the snow with Nate

Anderson and one of the thugs. Colt shoved Daniel Weir out the door and toward the little group as Libby swayed against Jared.

"Get up," Libby said to the woman who glared at her with such hatred.

Kristin made no move to do so. Rascal put a big hand under her elbow and dragged her upright. She tottered in the snow for a second before straightening.

"We could have been rich," she said to Libby. "You. Me. All of us. But you had to believe that toad Hicks. You had to give him someone to talk to. He wasn't going to say anything if not for you. But you told him you were sure he would do the right thing."

Libby blinked. She remembered that moment. Paul had been telling her his worries about the RIM software and how Daniel wanted the project to go ahead anyway. He had ideas for how to put the brakes on but he wasn't sure which one was best. She'd told him she was sure he would do the right thing. She hadn't spurred him to expose the truth. She'd merely told him he would choose the right way for everyone involved.

"You're wrong, Kris. Paul had a conscience and he couldn't let the project move forward until it was perfect. He was always going to tell the truth. I had nothing to do with it."

"He wanted to impress you. You strung him along and gave him hope he had a chance with you."

Libby sucked in a breath. Everything hurt and she was losing her resolve. "You're going to believe what you want, no matter what I say. But before you spend time in prison for being an accessory to murder, I just wanted to give you something to remember me by."

She'd intended to use her fist but in the end she hit Kristin open-handed, putting her whole body into it and slapping her former friend as hard as she could. The shock of it reverberated down her arm, making her already injured body hurt even worse. But it was fucking worth it, especially when Kristin cried out and stumbled sideways. It felt so good she tried to do it again—but Jared was there, pulling her back into the warmth of his body, holding her firmly.

"That's good, baby. You don't want to make yourself hurt worse, do you?"

She turned into him, burying her face in his chest. "I feel like it might be worth it."

He chuckled softly. "Bloodthirsty girl. Come on, we need to get you to the hospital and get you checked out."

She leaned into him as they started toward the heli-copter. "This isn't how I thought today would go when I walked into work this morning. This morning—" Libby swallowed, her throat tightening. "This morning she was still my friend. I had no idea she was this person. A person who could betray everything and everyone they pretended to care about."

"It's not your fault, Libby. She made her own choice. It has nothing to do with you and everything to do with her."

He made sense, and yet she couldn't help but think there was something wrong with *her.* Why did people who claimed they cared about her become suddenly able to discard her like yesterday's trash?

Libby stumbled to a stop as pain flared in her belly. She dragged in a lungful of air and moaned. Jared swung her into his arms and strode toward the helicopter. She clung to him, her head buried in his neck, fighting the pain but failing. Once they were onboard, he probed her with careful fingers.

"What did they do to you? I need to know so I know what to look for."

"Th-they hit me in the stomach. That's where it hurts the most. Someone kicked me when the chair fell. They punched my face. I cried, Jared. I couldn't help it."

"Of course you couldn't." He sounded gruff, and she sniffled.

"Anything else?"

"No. Daniel told me they were going to break every bone in my body, but they found the card in my shoe so it didn't happen. I told them there was an access code so they wouldn't kill me right then. I didn't know if there really was. But it was true."

"Thank God for that."

"They were going to torture it out of me, but the joke would have been on them." Not that she thought it was funny in the least, but she'd just been trying to get through each moment in the hopes that Jared would come for her.

And he had. Her knight.

There was a sting in her arm. "What's that?"

"Painkillers," Jared said as the sting eased. He rubbed her arm and put a bandage on the place where he'd stuck the needle in. "You're going to go to sleep soon, Libby. I'll be there when you wake up."

She was already starting to feel groggy. "Promise?"

His lips ghosted over her forehead. "I promise. We'll talk then."

"Okay," she whispered before the world faded to nothing.

―――――

JARED SAT by the hospital bed in a private room in Riverstone and watched Libby sleep. The beating she'd suffered had ruptured blood vessels in her abdomen, causing internal bleeding severe enough that she'd needed surgery to stop it. Fortunately, she would make a full recovery. Her ribs were also bruised and her face looked like she'd gone ten rounds with a prizefighter.

Jared wanted to maim every person who'd been in that house with her in the most painful way possible, but he couldn't. The law would deal with them and that would have to be enough.

His concern was Libby. Physically, she would be fine. But mentally?

That's what worried him most. He simply didn't know how she was going to react as time passed and the gravity of what'd happened sank in. Libby'd had her trust broken by someone she cared about. Kristin Martin had been her friend—the woman who'd helped her get the job at Ninja Solutions, someone she'd texted with on a regular basis and shared the kinds of personal things that women shared with each other—and Kristin had tried to kill her. Libby's faith in others had to be pretty shaky right now.

He hated that for her. So much. Which meant he wasn't going to be anywhere but here when she woke up. He sat beside her and held her hand for what seemed like days though it was probably only an hour or two. At one point, the door opened silently and he looked up.

Ian was standing there, looking tired and angry.

"How's she doing?" he asked softly.

Jared sat up and scrubbed a hand over his face. "She's going to be okay. But she'll be in pain for a few days."

"Rascal told me she hit Kristin Martin."

Jared couldn't help but grin just a little. "Slapped that bitch silly."

"Good for her. She's a thinker, too. Heard how she kept them guessing about an access code."

"She's quick on her feet."

"Good qualities to have."

Jared stood and stretched, shaking his limbs to ease the kinks of sitting for so long. "I assume you've got news for me."

Ian nodded. "I do. Anderson and Martin are in custody."

"What about Weir?"

"Sprung for the moment. Don't forget he's engaged to a congressman's daughter. They've brought out the big guns, and they're arguing that Weir didn't know anything. It was all Anderson and Martin's doing. They were having an affair, of course. Nate bought the house on the river. He put it in Kristin's name in order to avoid having another asset for the courts to consider in his ongoing alimony and child support suits with his ex. Weir's lawyers plan to argue that Nate and Kristin had financial motives to stop Paul Hicks from telling the truth while Weir could have afforded to wait two years or better while the AI stayed in development."

"Bullshit. We heard him. He's the one who said Hicks was dead. He's the one who threatened Libby."

"I know. We've got the recordings, but we're not dealing with overworked public defenders here. There's a lot of money going into Weir's defense. We've got to make sure we do this absolutely right or the whole thing will fall apart and what we have will be inadmissible. We've got Hicks's information, and it's very damning for RIM, but a good lawyer can make the case Hicks was a disgruntled employee and that Weir didn't know the details. Hell, they might even say Hicks was trying to sabotage Weir's business because he didn't feel appreciated enough or some such bullshit."

Jared knew what the boss was saying was true. Someone like Weir, with money and connections, had incredible luck at avoiding consequences. It was what was wrong with the world, in Jared's view. The richer you were, the more connected you were, the worse you could behave. And nobody would hold your feet to the fire for it.

"I hope you're digging into Weir's finances. There's got to be something to incriminate him."

"I am. He's leveraged to the max, but with backers like his future father-in-law and other high-powered

Washington elites, his financial situation doesn't look as dire on the surface as Anderson's does. Still, Ninja Solutions needed the influx of cash. They weren't going to survive for two years—or more—while Paul Hicks tinkered with the AI software. They needed that suit to work, and they needed the Army contract to happen before someone else built a better product and got there first."

"That's a motive. Are you seriously telling me he has lawyers who plan to argue otherwise?"

"Yep. The good news is that the Army was already suspicious. Hicks had arranged a meeting with General Comstock where he planned to share his information, but apparently Weir didn't trust him and he'd had his office bugged. He knew about the upcoming meeting and used B&B Security to put a stop to it."

"So there's a link between Weir and B&B?"

Ian shook his head. "No. Anderson used them in the past and he made the calls. He's saying he did it at Weir's direction, but of course it's his word against Weir's, especially since he had a past relationship with Byrd and Boggs. He also said Weir ordered the bugging of Hicks's office, but Anderson's the one who placed the equipment."

Jared blew out a breath. Weir was smart. The only time he'd gotten directly involved was when they'd taken Libby from the office building. And that must have been because they'd had to scramble to do it once she returned unexpectedly. Time hadn't been on their side when she'd walked back into the building. Must have given the three of them a heart attack. Weir'd been at the Pentagon, but he'd clearly cut that short and returned as soon as he'd been informed. If he'd arrived any other way besides a helicopter, they wouldn't have gotten Libby out of the building.

"What about the bodies on the mountain? Who did that?"

Ian frowned. "I don't know. Besides the helo pilot, there were two hired thugs with Anderson, Weir, and Martin. You shot one. The other surrendered when you guys infiltrated the house."

Jared nodded. He remembered that guy. He'd been calmly standing there with his hands over his head when Jared breached the room. Anderson had tried to run, but not that guy.

"He's Army CID. But, so far, no one in CID is admitting to cleaning the site. They thought we did it."

"Army CID was there and let Libby get beat like that?" Jared growled.

"He couldn't compromise his cover. You know that."

He did know it. But he didn't have to like it.

"He didn't participate in beating her," Ian said. "He swears he pulled the only punch he delivered and made it look worse than it was. He was trying to mitigate what was happening to her without blowing his cover."

"And what the fuck would he have done if they'd killed her?" Rage was a bitter stew inside him.

Ian put a hand on his shoulder. "They didn't, Jared. She's alive and she's going to need you to be her rock when she wakes up. You have to get past it. Like every other job we do, you have to let it go. The Army agent is a witness to what happened in the house before we got there, and his testimony will be useful."

It was all true, and yet Libby's swollen face made him feel helpless and impotently angry. He'd wanted to beat the shit out of his dad all the times the man had done the same to Jared's mother, but he never had. And now he couldn't punish any of the people who'd done this to sweet Libby either. He'd shot one of the hired thugs when he was racing toward the house to rescue her. It wasn't enough to satisfy his thirst for justice, but it was something.

"Weir needs to go down," he growled.

"I know. I intend to make it happen, but it's going to take time. Anderson has already turned on him, and Kristin Martin's done nothing but cry and swear they forced her to go along with it. I don't think she knows anything beyond what Anderson told her, but if she does, CID will get it out of her. They have as much incentive to nail Weir as we do. More, since the Army nearly spent millions on something that could have caused troop casualties."

"Jared?"

His head snapped around at the weak sound from the bed.

"I'm here, Libby," he said, dropping into the chair and taking her hand gently in his.

"Where am I?"

"You're at Riverstone, honey. The private hospital where I brought you before."

He heard the door snick quietly as Ian left. There

was still so much he wanted to know, but he'd worry about it later.

"Oh yes," she whispered. "They were nice." A frown crossed her features. "I feel like hell. But I still know who I am."

He kissed her fingers, stomping down the hot emotion swirling in his belly. "That's good, baby. You're going to be fine. We got there in time."

Not in time to prevent her from being injured, but he wasn't going to split hairs. They'd prevented her death, and that was what mattered most. If he told himself that often enough, maybe he'd stop feeling so fucking guilty that she'd been hurt at all.

"You shouldn't be upset at yourself anymore, you know. You save people. You deserve your nickname."

His throat was tight. "Thank you, honey. I appreciate that."

"I hear the doubt in your voice," she said, frowning. She turned her good eye toward him. The other was still swollen nearly shut. "You aren't allowed to doubt. I'm still alive because of you. Twice now, and that's not nothing."

"No, it's definitely not nothing."

She squeezed his hand where he held hers. He was encouraged by the strength in her grip.

"We're going to talk about this when I feel better, okay? I want to know what's making you doubt yourself."

How could she tell? That's what he wanted to know. It's not what he said though. "Do I have a choice?" he teased.

"Not really. I'll talk your ear off until you tell me what I want to know."

He snorted. "Yeah, I guess you will." He kissed her hand again. "Go back to sleep, Libby. You need to heal, and sleep will help."

"You'll be here when I wake up?"

"I'll be here."

Chapter Twenty-Eight

EACH TIME SHE WOKE, JARED WAS THERE. LIBBY DIDN'T know how he managed it, but he'd promised he would be there and he was. She barely had to open her mouth to say his name, and he was whispering softly to her. Comforting her.

She had so many thoughts racing around in her head, many of them to do with him and what was going to happen once she recovered. She wanted to tell him how she felt about him, wanted to tell him everything about her life, but how did she begin? And what if he didn't want to hear it?

He'd saved her life but that didn't mean he loved her or anything. It was what he did. What he'd do for anyone.

When she woke again, soft light streamed into her room. She blinked up at the ceiling, hearing the beeps of the medical equipment, but there was no touch on her hand. No voice to say her name. She shifted, her heart squeezing—and he was there, his head thrown back on the recliner they'd brought into the room for him. His hand hung over the side, as if he'd dropped it in sleep and hadn't yet noticed.

He had ridiculously pretty eyelashes, she decided. And he had that scruffy beard she'd come to love. When those eyes opened, they'd be as blue as sapphires. His lips were full and kissable, and she wished she could lean over and press her mouth to his.

A nurse entered the room then, and Jared jerked awake at the sound. His gaze landed on the nurse first and then immediately darted to her. Libby smiled. Or at least she hoped it looked like a smile and not a grimace. She still hurt all over, but she thought it was getting better. Hoped it was.

Jared was at her side immediately, looking down at her with those fathomless eyes. "Hey, sunshine. How are you?"

Sunshine. She liked that.

"Feels like I fell off a horse again. But it's getting better."

"Good. Excellent."

The nurse busied herself taking Libby's vitals and writing it on a chart. "The doctor will be by this morning," she said. "I think she's going to let you go home so long as you promise not to do any dancing."

"Thank heavens," Libby replied. "Not that the hospitality isn't great around here, but it'll be nice to sleep through the night without someone waking me every few hours to check my temperature or poke me with a needle."

The nurse smiled. "That's the down side of hanging

out with us, I'm afraid. Breakfast will be here in a few minutes. After that, you can shower if you like."

She would definitely like that. Once the nurse was gone, she pressed the button to bring the bed upright—and thought for the first time since she'd entered River-stone that she must look like hell. She dropped her gaze, suddenly embarrassed that Jared was looking at her.

She picked the covers nervously. "Thanks, um, for being here."

"I told you I would be."

"I know. But surely you had to eat sometime. Sleep? Shower?" She waved her hand around. "You know, all the normal stuff."

"I did all the normal stuff. I did it when I knew you were medicated and unlikely to wake."

"Oh, of course. That combat medic training of yours."

"Yes." He didn't say anything for a moment and she kept staring at the blanket, picking at it. "What's wrong, Libby?"

"I don't want you to see me like this," she blurted.

"I've seen people in the hospital before. It's nothing new for me."

Heat flared in her cheeks. "My hair has to be a mess, and I haven't showered since yesterday at your house—" Her eyes widened. "It *was* yesterday, right? Please don't tell me it's been a week or anything."

"It was three days ago, honey. The pain meds knocked you out for a lot of it. You had to have surgery to stop some internal bleeding, and they wanted to keep you for observation."

"Oh shit," she groaned. She remembered being told about the internal bleeding before, but she'd been so tired and groggy that she didn't remember a whole lot about the past few days. "Now I know I look like hell. And no wonder my abdomen feels like I got kicked by that horse after he dumped me."

"You look gorgeous to me."

Her heart thumped despite everything. "Flattery will get you everywhere, Jared Fraser. But a girl might like a little time to make herself presentable, you know."

He stood. "Do you want me to go?"

"I…" She closed her eyes. "I don't what you to *go*. But I want you to disappear for about half an hour or so."

She thought he'd be angry with her, but instead he grinned. "Fine. I'll go. In fact, when your breakfast arrives, I'll go until you text me and tell me to come back."

"Text you? Oh wow, I can do that, can't I?"

"Your phone is on the bedside table, plugged into the charger. A brand new phone with your old number ported over, so all your contacts are there."

Relief washed over her, as well as a little current of sadness at the idea of one contact in particular. "Thank you."

He picked up the phone and handed it to her. "I think you might want to have a look at your messages. Some new friends have your number, and they won't stop texting."

She must have looked confused because he continued.

"Maddy, Tallie, and Angie have been texting you. They were worried."

"Oh," she said, her heart throbbing.

"You have friends, Libby. Kristin Martin may not have been a real friend, but that doesn't mean there aren't others who care about you. Women who'd *cut a bitch for you*, as Angie told me last night. She said you were one of them, no matter what."

Libby couldn't help but smile. She loved those women. She'd spent a lot of time worrying that she was going to lose them when this was over, but maybe she wasn't. Her poor heart wanted to believe, but her head kept telling her not to get her hopes up. Everyone always left her, one way or another.

"What else did she say?"

"She said if you need anything, to call her. Maddy and Tallie said the same thing."

"That's so nice." She held the phone tight. "Thank you for telling me."

The door opened and the nurse came in with a breakfast tray, which she place on the table over the bed. Then she rolled it up to where Libby could reach everything.

Jared walked to the door and stopped. "We've got a lot to talk about Liberty King. But there's time. Call or text me when you're ready."

————

IT WAS CLOSER to two hours before Libby texted Jared, but between breakfast, showering, and the doctor coming to examine and release her, it took more time than she expected. There'd been a fresh outfit waiting for her in the closet. She'd teared up at the sight. It was the pair of jeans and pink sweater Jared had bought for her when he'd been taking her to his place after they'd left the mountain cabin.

There was fresh underwear, a bra, socks, and her boots. He'd thought of everything. Or maybe it hadn't been him. Maybe one of the women had told him what he should bring. Still, didn't matter, the clothes were there and she was touched more than she could say.

They didn't say much once they were in his truck and moving down the road. She didn't know if he was taking her back to her place or his, but it soon became apparent the destination was his house. She teared up again, but turned her head to keep him from seeing. Stupid emotions.

Jared helped her inside with a hand firmly on her elbow and the other wrapped around her waist. Gently, of course.

"Do you want to sit on the couch or would you prefer the bed?"

"I want to be where you are," she said somewhat shyly.

"You tell me where you'd be more comfortable, and that's where I'll be."

She smiled a watery smile. Darn him for being so perfect. "I want to sit on the couch then. Maybe read some Tolstoy."

He snorted. "Liar."

She couldn't help but laugh. "Okay, maybe not

Tolstoy. In fact, I don't really want to read. I want to talk."

"Tell me something I don't know," he teased.

He got her settled on the couch with a pillow behind her back and a blanket over her lap, even though she'd said she wasn't cold. He unzipped her boots and took them off for her, placing them neatly on the floor under the coffee table. Jared was nothing if not neat and tidy.

He fixed her some hot tea, even though she didn't ask for it, then sat in the chair opposite and waited.

Libby sipped the tea. Though she'd said she wanted to talk, she didn't know how to begin. "Thanks for everything, Jared. I don't think I'd like being alone right now. I could probably call my cousin, but she's busy with her boyfriend and, well, I'd hate to bother her. But I hate to bother you too…"

Her stomach twisted with nerves. He got up and sat next to her. Not too close, but close enough he could take her hand. "You aren't bothering me. This is where you belong."

Her heart thumped. "Is it?"

He ran his fingers across her cheek. Lightly so he didn't hurt her bruises, but just enough she could feel the heat of him. "I need to tell you some things," he said.

"Okay." Her stomach twisted with nerves, but she wanted to hear it. If this was the *I like you, but* speech, it was best to get it over with now. Before her heart built more castles in the sky.

"You're right that I felt guilty for what happened. I shouldn't have let you go into Ninja Solutions. I felt like it was my fault for not insisting we do the job another way."

"Jared," she whispered.

He put a finger over her lips before she could continue. "My father was abusive, Libby. He beat my mother, and he sometimes beat me. And there wasn't a damned thing I could do about it, no matter how much I wanted to. I was too young, too small, too scared maybe. He left us before I got big enough to give him the ass beating he deserved. Best thing he ever did was leave. But I carried a lot of guilt that I didn't do a better job of protecting my mother, and I swore I wouldn't stand by and let that shit happen to anyone else."

Her heart ached for the little boy he'd been. For the honorable man he was. "It wasn't your fault."

"I know. But that didn't mean I wasn't tortured by the thought I could have changed something. When I was a kid, and then three days ago when they took you away in a helicopter. I should have done something different. I should have stopped it from happening."

"It wasn't your fault," she repeated. "Not when you were a child, and definitely not now. Nobody forced me to go to work. I had to do it. If I hadn't, Paul would have died for nothing. He really is dead, right?"

Jared nodded. "The police found his remains in a cave on the mountain, close to where you were held. I'm sorry."

A knot of tears lodged in her throat. "He was awkward and sweet. But he had a moral code, and that code wasn't going to let him sit idly by while the company profited off something he knew wasn't right. I wish he'd seen the danger to himself, though."

"And to you," Jared said. "He put you in danger, whether he meant to or not. And you'd still be in danger if you hadn't gotten the media card. Logically, I know it's true, even if I wish I'd found another way to retrieve it." He caressed her cheek again. "You were brave, Libby. You handled yourself well."

"I just did what made sense at the time. But I thought they were going to kill me before you could get there. I didn't stop believing you'd come. Not even when Daniel took my phone outside and shot it."

His eyes flashed. "I'm sorry for everything that happened, and I'm sorry you were scared. But thank you for believing in me."

"I can never repay you for what you did for me. You took a bullet for me, Jared. Even if you were wearing body armor, it was much braver than anything I did."

He was shaking his head. "No, it wasn't. And you don't owe me anything, Libby. It's what I do. I protect the innocent."

"Like a knight in shining armor," she said with a smile.

He nodded. "Like that." He sucked in a breath, his eyes closing for a second. When he opened them again, blue eyes bored into hers. "I thought I'd lost you when you were forced onto that helicopter, and that nearly gutted me."

The moment stretched between them while she processed what he'd said. Heat flared in her cheeks, flooded her skin, made her hot everywhere. Her heart hammered a staccato beat and she wasn't sure what he was saying. Was it guilt? Something more? She desperately wanted to know what he meant by that, but she didn't know how to ask. So she did a typically Libby thing and blurted "I think I love you."

He blinked like a startled owl. Inside, the scared little girl who expected rejection, who expected to never be good enough to keep, was cringing. But then a smile lit his face. The best smile in the world in her not so unbiased opinion.

"Liberty King, you just can't stand not stealing the show, can you?"

"Oh god," she said, closing her eyes as humiliation cascaded through her. "I'm an idiot. Please don't say anything. Let's pretend it never happened—"

"Shut up, Libby." He tipped her chin up and placed the most delicate of kisses on her lips. She wanted him to deepen the kiss, but it would hurt and he knew it. He took such care not to hurt her. She adored him, even if she wanted to disappear.

"I love you, too, baby. Even though you only *think* you love me."

Libby wanted to sink into the cushions. "I love you, Jared. I was just nervous. And hedging my bets in case you were about to tell me it was a sense of duty that made you feel guilty." She shook her head. "I'm babbling. Why do I do that?"

He laughed. "Hell if I know, but it's one of the things I love about you."

"Oh please. You wanted me to shut up when you first met me."

"Yeah, I guess so. But then I got used to the chatter and now I can't live without it. Besides, you say the funniest things when your mouth is running ahead of your brain. You make me laugh."

She rolled her eyes, but it was a teasing gesture. Inside, her belly was doing somersaults and her heart was shaking some serious-assed pompoms. "Just what I always wanted. To make the man of my dreams laugh."

"Nothing wrong with that. But just in case you were wondering, there are other things you make happen for me." He settled her against him, cradling her gently.

"Such as?"

"Well, you make me hard. No doubt about that. In fact, it's going to be torture for the next few days wanting to make love to you but having to refrain because I don't want to hurt you."

"Maybe we can get creative."

He kissed her on top of the head. "Maybe. We'll see. Let me think... you also make me realize what I've been missing in life. I've always been a loner, and I thought I liked it that way. Hell, I'm pretty sure I do still like it that way. But now I want to be a loner *with* you. You and me, baby. Except I know you need people and interaction, so I'll have to venture out of the cave to hang out some-times too."

"I like being alone with you, Jared. And I'm learning that the only people I need to give my time to are people who care about me. I've spent too many years wanting approval, craving it. But none of those people were worth my time. None of them loved me for me." She sucked in a pained breath. "Not even my family."

"Do you want to talk about it?"

Did she? Yes, with him, she did. She told him everything. About her childhood, her dad's strict beliefs, the arranged marriage she'd refused, and the way her family had cast her out when she did.

"I'm sorry, Libby." His voice was gruff as he spoke. "You deserved so much more."

"I think that's why I don't trust that people will stick around. If a parent can turn their own child away, if they can care more about what they believe than about their own flesh and blood, then how can you ever trust anyone to really love you? Aren't your parents supposed to want the best for you and love you no matter what?"

Jared frowned. "You'd think so, but it doesn't always work out that way. My dad was an asshole, but I try to remember he was once an innocent kid too. Doesn't make me hate him any less. It's okay to be angry about what your dad tried to do, and it's okay to be angry with your brother and sisters for not taking your side. But those things are their burden to bear, not yours. There's nothing wrong with you, Libby. You just got a raw deal when God was handing out family."

"So did you."

"Half a raw deal. I had my mom, and she was terrific."

"My mom loved me. I know she did. But I don't think she'd have gone against what my father wanted if she'd been alive. She'd have watched me drag my suitcase up that dusty drive too. She'd have cried, probably, but she wouldn't have said a word."

"You don't have to worry about that anymore,

honey. I've got your back. Always. And not just me. BDI has your back too. You're one of us now. Even if I wasn't crazy about you, even if I didn't plan to spend my life with you, you'd be one of us. You went to the mat for us, and you didn't break. You're tough and honorable, Liberty King. We all know it, too."

Happiness swirled inside her. "I love you, Jared. I love all of you, really."

"Oh great, now I'm just one of the gang."

She could hear the humor in his voice. "Hardly. I love everyone at BDI, but it's not the same as the way I love *you* particularly."

"And how's that, sunshine?"

"I plan to show you in detail. Soon as I'm able."

He chuckled. "I look forward to it. But for right now I'm content just holding you."

"I'm not. I want more."

He stroked her hair as he held her. "We've got all the time in the world, Libby. In fact, I think you should move in with me."

"Oh," she breathed.

"Good *oh* or bad *oh?*"

"Good *oh*. Definitely good… But I don't have a job anymore. I can't pay my share until I find one."

"First, this house is paid for. Second, I'm pretty sure you won't be unemployed long. If Ian doesn't have anything for you at BDI, he'll know someone who does. Third, I'm not asking you to split costs with me."

She huffed. "I don't see why not. I'm not a free-loader, and I've had a roommate before. I'm fine with splitting costs—"

He put a finger over her mouth. "I'm not doing this right, I can tell. I'm not asking you to be my roommate, Libby. I'm asking you to move in and be mine in every way. And then, when the time is right and *not* when you're recovering from injuries, I plan to ask you something else. Something involving rings and churches and forever. But not right now, because we can't celebrate properly—and I don't have a ring to give you. But soon. So think about that, and think about your answer so you can say it right away when I get up the courage to do the deed."

Libby couldn't help but laugh. He was so serious, and so perfect. He was exactly what her heart needed. This man was constant. Unwavering. Her bright and shiny knight.

"There's nothing I would rather do than say yes to your, er, proposition. When the time is right, of course. When you actually ask me. Consider this a preview of my answer."

He snorted. "Damn, I love you. You're always going to make me laugh."

"Probably. And not always on purpose. But I hope you never get tired of it. Or me."

"Not a chance, sunshine. Not a frigging chance in hell."

He pressed his lips to hers. It wasn't the kind of kiss she wanted, but it was the kind of kiss she needed right now.

Finally, she'd found where she belonged.

And that was the best feeling in the world.

Epilogue

THE ROOM WAS SMALL AND BARE EXCEPT FOR A METAL table and four metal chairs. There was two-way glass lining one side of the room. Behind the glass, Ian Black watched the interrogation. Daniel Weir sat across the desk from the interviewing detective, impatient and annoyed. His attorney sat beside him, making notes and advising his client when to answer and when to stay silent.

General Comstock stood beside Ian, grunting as the interview went on. "Pompous little ass," he said. "I never liked the prick, but damn if that exoskeleton wasn't a thing of beauty. Too bad it doesn't work."

"It could work," Ian said mildly. "It just needs more time in development."

He'd seen the plans. Paul Hicks had been the engineer behind RIM, not Weir. Weir had more in common with a conman than he did with the genius he'd pretended to be. He'd graduated MIT, and he'd developed a satellite targeting program that'd made his reputation. But Ian would bet his last nickel that Weir hadn't developed it at all. He'd stolen it, same as he had the AI software for RIM. It was a legal theft, though. He'd made his engineers sign development agreements that stated anything they developed while working for the company belonged to the company.

It was a common enough practice in companies with research and development departments. And it made sense in some ways. Companies didn't want to pay people to develop patents that they could then take elsewhere. It was the company's time and money that made it possible for the developer to work, after all.

"That's what DARPA thinks, too," Comstock said. "I wouldn't be surprised if they start working on something similar."

DARPA was the Defense Advanced Research Projects Agency, and they were responsible for much of the cutting edge tech that benefited society these days. If they were going to take over work on the exoskeleton, then it wasn't a hopeless project. That was both good and bad since other nations would also be eager to get their hands on the technology.

"It's a brave new world," Ian said.

"Indeed. I prefer the old one in some ways," the general replied. "The battles of the future will be fought with the kinds of things we only thought existed in sci-fi movies, though. We either develop these things ourselves or get left behind."

"Very true, sir."

"I don't know that we're going to pin anything on

him," he said after a moment. "I'm getting pressure from higher up to make a case or stop pursuing it."

Higher up for a general in Comstock's position very likely meant Congress. Which meant Congressman Klein.

"We caught him in the middle of a crime scene, he admitted Hicks was dead on a recording from that scene, and The Washington Post published a story about Ninja Solutions trying to defraud the Department of Defense. If nothing else, Weir is the very public CEO of the company. And none of that's good enough," Ian murmured.

"You know as well as I do that Weir could print a confession on page one of the Post and those lawyers of his would claim it never happened and didn't exist. And the shame of it is that people would believe them, too."

Ian didn't disagree. You could tell people the sky was blue, show them a blue sky, explain the science behind why the sky was blue, and they'd still claim that something they'd read on social media, written by someone with less education than a kindergartner, was correct about why the sky wasn't blue, had never been blue, and how the effort to convince people it was blue was nothing but a hoax.

Sometimes, Ian despaired for humanity.

The interviewer turned off the recorder and stood. Weir and his lawyer stood too. The door opened and the two of them waltzed out, Weir looking smug and his lawyer looking as serious as a heart attack.

Ian thanked the general and walked outside. Weir and his lawyer were getting into a black SUV that idled beside the curb. Ian watched as the doors closed and the SUV moved toward him. It was only when the SUV was even with him that the driver turned and met his gaze.

Shock jolted him as their eyes clashed. Then the driver winked and pressed the accelerator. Ian cursed and sprinted for his Porsche. He'd never catch up now. And even if he did, it was definitely too late for Daniel Weir.

Maybe that wasn't a bad thing.

———

WASHINGTON, DC at night was an awe-inspiring sight. Ian loved the city during the day, but he loved it even more at night. Especially the Jefferson Memorial. There was something about the rotunda with its bronze statue of Thomas Jefferson, with those beautiful words from the Declaration of Independence carved in its circular walls, that filled him with pride and awe every time.

No, it wasn't perfect considering the words hadn't applied to slaves or women when they were written, but it was still something that stood the test of time.

We hold these truths to be self-evident…

He sat on the steps and waited, certain she would come. He wasn't wrong. At precisely ten p.m., a woman in a white coat and fur hat came striding around the Tidal Basin. She approached without fear or hesitation. He watched her, wondering at her confidence. How did she know he wasn't planning to take her prisoner this time? To take her and keep her. It would certainly deal a blow to her bosses if he did. If they knew she was talking to him, her days were numbered. If he captured her, perhaps he could keep her safe.

"Hello, Mr. Black." Her hands were thrust in her pockets. Her hair was tucked inside the hat so that he couldn't tell if it was long or short. Black or blond. But at least she looked like herself—or as much like herself as he imagined her. There was no telling with Calypso, but he could see her brother in her face this time, which made him think it was truly her own without heavy makeup or disguise.

"Hello, Cally."

She made a noise. "Don't call me that."

"Fine." He walked down the stairs until he was standing in front of her. She wasn't very tall, though he'd seen her be taller. Lifts. This time he suspected it was her true height since she was only about five-four. Small, but not too small. "You lied to me, Natasha."

She shrugged. "I told you before. I do what I have to. I don't owe you anything."

"No, you don't, I suppose. Though I let you go once before."

"So you could use me. Don't pretend like you did it for noble reasons."

"Okay, I won't."

She snorted. "This is why I like you, Ian Black. You don't lie unless you have to. Same as me."

She sounded American, because she had been born here, and yet she sometimes had the speech patterns of someone whose native language was Russian. But not a hint of a Russian accent.

"You were sent to eliminate Weir. Why?"

"Because he was an embarrassment. Because he was threatening people who didn't like being threatened."

"I see. Care to tell me who?"

She laughed. "Oh, yes, of course. Shall we dig our graves first? It'll be easier for them to hide our bodies."

He knew she wouldn't talk, but he'd had to ask. "You said in Rome that you didn't know anything about Ninja Solutions."

"I did, didn't I?"

She was exasperating, and intriguing. Damn her for both. "Was Weir in the Syndicate?"

Her lips flattened into a line. Then she nodded. "In a manner of speaking. He was being brought in. He was not a good fit, it turned out."

"Where is he?"

"I believe he will be found floating in the Potomac tomorrow with a bullet through his head."

"Rather obvious, isn't it?"

"A warning, I imagine. For others."

"I see." He shoved his hands in his pockets and gazed at the lights across the basin. "Do you ever get tired of it, Natasha?"

"All the time," she said softly. "I don't like who I am made to be."

He turned and grabbed her by the shoulders, forced her to look at him. Her eyes were green like a forest and fathomless. Filled with pain. "Stay with me. You don't have to go back. I'll help you."

"I… I can't."

Ian groaned. And then he did the one thing he'd

sworn he was never going to do. He tugged her into his arms and kissed her. She melted into him, kissing him back with a passion that stunned him. Their tongues met and melded, and desire streaked through his body, making him instantly hard. If they were anywhere else, he'd turn up the heat between them. But they were outside, in public, and neither of them were free to pursue this thing. It wasn't safe.

And then she made a choking sound before she shoved at his shoulders. He stepped back, letting her go.

Her eyes sparked. He thought she was angry, but then a tear slid down her cheek. "You shouldn't have done that," she whispered. "I-I have to go."

She turned and hurried away, disappearing into the darkness. He didn't follow her.

There would be other times. Other meetings.

It was enough.

Bonus Epilogue

GERMANY IN MAY WAS BEAUTIFUL. JARED LOVED THE long days, the fresh spring blooms, the festivals and the food—but most of all he loved the woman he was with. Libby walked in front of him along the ramparts of an old city. Rothenburg ob der Tauber still had a medieval wall encircling most of the city, and you could walk along it for two miles. They passed other tourists doing the same, and Libby greeted them all with a cheery hello or *guten tag*.

She turned to him now, her face flushed with exercise, her smile the brightest and best thing in his life at that very moment. "This is so much fun," she breathed. She'd traded her glasses for contacts today. Her hair was caught in a ponytail that swung across her back and she wore black leggings with a white stretchy T-shirt and walking shoes. He couldn't wait to get her back to the hotel and get her naked again.

"I'm glad you think so," he said. "Rothenburg is one of my favorite cities in Germany."

She gazed out at the half-timbered medieval city arrayed below. "I can see why. It's so picturesque. I don't think I would have believed how beautiful it was if I weren't here to see it myself."

"I promised you Germany, and Germany you're getting."

She slipped into his arms and stood with him, watching the people walking below. "You're so good to me," she said.

He kissed the top of her head. "No, you're good to me."

"You mean like last night when I made you take that night watchman tour and talked to all those people so much that they invited us to join them for drinks? And then we didn't leave until midnight?"

He laughed. "I didn't mind."

"You'd have rather been in bed reading some boring tome about the CIA."

"No, I'd have rather been in bed making love to you."

She still blushed when he said things like that, though this time it was partly the exercise coloring her cheeks too. She smacked him playfully. "You got to do that after we returned to our room. And again this morning."

"And I'm planning to do it again tonight. Twice."

"Only twice? Are you slowing down, old man?"

"Twice so you can still walk tomorrow," he said with a growl.

She shivered in his arms. "Well, there is *that.*"

He took her hand and led her toward the steps that

would take them to the city street. They walked hand in hand into the Burggarten, admiring the statuary and the flowers, until they reached the edge of the city wall where the views gave way to the Tauber Valley below and the old city in the distance with the medieval wall as support. It was, in a word, breathtaking.

Jared led her beneath the pergola with its profusion of greenery and listened while she sighed happily. They'd come here yesterday too, but he hadn't been brave enough to do what he'd planned. Hell, maybe he wasn't brave enough now. She wasn't wearing a dress—not that he cared but maybe she did—and he was in jeans and hiking boots.

He started to doubt himself. Maybe he should do this in the Alps. Or maybe he should do it when they got to Venice. Shit. They'd planned a month in Europe and he had plenty of time. Plenty of perfect places. Since Libby had moved in with him, she'd started working as a virtual assistant for online business owners, which meant she could do her work from anywhere she had an internet connection. It gave them the freedom to make trips like this one.

"Jared?"

He looked up to find her watching him with a wry smile on her lips. She'd leaned back against one of the wood supports for the pergola, and she alternately gazed at the view and at him.

"Yes, baby?"

"Is something wrong?"

He loved how she knew when he was brooding on something. In the past few months, they'd grown closer than he would have ever thought possible. He hadn't known this kind of thing was real, not even when he'd watched his friends fall in love. But it was real. So real it scared him sometimes when he thought about how close he'd come to losing her. How narrow the window to save her had been when he and his teammates had found her in that house on the Potomac, bloody and beaten—but not defeated. Never that.

"Nothing's wrong, Libby."

"I heard Brett call you Knight last week. It's not that, is it?"

He wasn't surprised she'd noticed, but he should have reassured her then. "No, it doesn't bother me anymore. I told them it was okay." And it was. He liked hearing that name again.

She smiled. "Good. You deserve it and it suits you."

"You're biased."

"For sure. But it still suits you."

She arched her back and he tried not to be distracted by her breasts. He was doing a bad job of it though. He was busy thinking about how they looked when she was naked and arching her back like that. About how much he wanted them in his mouth and hands. Soon.

"I heard from Lincoln again," she said.

He focused in an instant. He knew she'd been talking to her brother from time to time, but she usually wanted to tell him about it right away. Not this time, apparently. "You didn't tell me. When?"

"The night before we left. He called me."

"Damn, baby. Why didn't you say so."

She shrugged. "I was thinking. It's not all bad, but I didn't want to detract from our trip."

He went over and pulled her into his arms, holding her loosely. "If you want to tell me, I'm listening."

She sighed. "He said Glory and Charity aren't ready to talk to me yet. But he is. He's sorry he didn't stand up for me before. He has a thirteen year old daughter now. He said he just can't imagine doing anything to make her unhappy."

"Libby," he said, his mouth against her hair. His heart ached with love for her. And sorrow that she hadn't had a dad like that.

"I know, right? But it's a good thing."

"It is."

"He's coming to DC next month for a conference. He wants to meet you."

"That sounds good."

She squeezed him and then stepped away. "Okay, I told you what was on my mind. Now tell me what's on yours."

He laughed in surprise. "I should have known."

"You know I won't let it go."

"No, I know that. I don't know if this is the right time though. Maybe when we get to the Alps."

She squeezed his upper arms and shook him as much as a woman of her size could possibly shake a man of his. "Jared! Teeeeellll meeeeeee."

He looked at her face, that face he loved so much, that was looking up at him with exasperation and determination—and he suddenly knew the time was right. He didn't need the perfect fairytale setting or moment. He just needed her. And he didn't want another minute to pass without her knowing it.

He reached into his jeans pocket and pulled out the small ring box he'd been carrying around for days. Then he dropped to one knee while Libby gasped. Her hands flew to her mouth. "Oh my god."

He held the box up in both hands like a knight supplicant. "My lady, I could think of nowhere better to ask you to be my wife than in a medieval city. Will you marry me, Liberty Grace King?"

She reached for the box with trembling fingers. He popped it open to reveal the perfect oval diamond set in a band of platinum and smaller diamonds that he'd painstakingly picked out. Not too big, not too small. Perfectly Libby, or so he hoped.

Maddy, Tallie, and Angie had assured him it was the right one. So had Libby's cousin, Merry. He liked Merry, and she'd proved she could keep secrets if the way Libby was looking at him was any indication.

"Jared," she whispered. "Yes. Of course, yes. A million times yes!"

Someone whooped in the garden behind them, and Jared realized they had an audience. Ah well, why not?

He stood and slipped the ring on her finger, and then he crushed her to him and kissed her with his entire heart and soul. She kissed him back with everything she had, and he knew this was right. So very right.

Jared Fraser was getting married. And he couldn't be happier about it.

Books by Lynn Raye Harris

———

The HOT SEAL Team Books

Book 4: HOT SEAL BRIDE - Cash & Ella

Book 5: HOT SEAL REDEMPTION - Alex & Bailey

Book 6: HOT SEAL TARGET - Blade & Quinn

Book 7: HOT SEAL HERO - Ryan & Chloe

Book 8: HOT SEAL DEVOTION - Zach & Kayla

The HOT Novella in Liliana Hart's MacKenzie Family Series

HOT WITNESS - Jake & Eva

———

7 Brides for 7 Brothers

MAX (Book 5) - Max & Ellie

7 Brides for 7 Soldiers

WYATT (Book 4) - Max & Ellie

7 Brides for 7 Blackthornes

ROSS (Book 3) - Ross & Holly

———

Who's HOT?

Alpha Squad
Matt "Richie Rich" Girard (Book 0 & 1)
Sam "Knight Rider" McKnight (Book 2)
Kev "Big Mac" MacDonald (Book 3)
Billy "the Kid" Blake (Book 4)
Jack "Hawk" Hunter (Book 5)
Nick "Brandy" Brandon (Book 6)
Garrett "Iceman" Spencer (Book 7)
Ryan "Flash" Gordon (Book 8)
Chase "Fiddler" Daniels (Book 9)
Dex "Double Dee" Davidson (Book 10)

Commander
John "Viper" Mendez (Book 11)

Deputy Commander
Alex "Ghost" Bishop

Echo Squad

Cade "Saint" Rodgers (Book 12)
Sky "Hacker" Kelley (Book 13)
Dean "Wolf" Garner (Book 14)
Malcom "Mal" McCoy (Book 15)
Jake "Harley" Ryan (HOT WITNESS)
Jax "Gem" Stone
Noah "Easy" Cross
Ryder "Muffin" Hanson

SEAL Team
Dane "Viking" Erikson (Book 1)
Remy "Cage" Marchand (Book 2)
Cody "Cowboy" McCormick (Book 3)
Cash "Money" McQuaid (Book 4)
Alexei "Camel" Kamarov (Book 5)
Adam "Blade" Garrison (Book 6)
Ryan "Dirty Harry" Callahan (Book 7)
Zach "Neo" Anderson (Book 8)
Corey "Shade" Vance

Black's Bandits
Jace Kaiser (Book 1)
Brett Wheeler (Book 2)
Colton Duchaine (Book 3)
Jared Fraser (Book 4)
Ian Black (Book 5)
Tyler Scott
Thomas "Rascal" Bradley
Dax Freed
Jamie Hayes
Mandy Parker (Airborne Ops)

Melanie (Reception)
? Unnamed Team Members

Freelance Contractors
Lucinda "Lucky" San Ramos, now MacDonald (Book 3)
Victoria "Vee" Royal, now Brandon (Book 6)
Emily Royal, now Gordon (Book 8)
Miranda Lockwood, now McCormick (SEAL Team
Book 3)
Bliss Bennett, (Book 13)

About the Author

Lynn Raye Harris is a Southern girl, military wife, wannabe cat lady, and horse lover. She's also the New York Times and USA Today bestselling author of the HOSTILE OPERATIONS TEAM ® SERIES of military romances, and 20 books about sexy billionaires for Harlequin.

A former finalist for the Romance Writers of America's Golden Heart Award and the National Readers Choice Award, Lynn lives in Alabama with her handsome former-military husband, one fluffy princess of a cat, and a very spoiled American Saddlebred horse who enjoys bucking at random in order to keep Lynn on her toes.

Lynn's books have been called "exceptional and emotional," "intense," and "sizzling" -- and have sold in excess of 4.5 million copies worldwide.

To connect with Lynn online:
www.LynnRayeHarris.com
Lynn@LynnRayeHarris.com